Isabella Fyvie Mayo

Gold and Dross

Isabella Fyvie Mayo

Gold and Dross

ISBN/EAN: 9783337078843

Printed in Europe, USA, Canada, Australia, Japan

Cover: Foto ©Andreas Hilbeck / pixelio.de

More available books at **www.hansebooks.com**

BY

EDWARD GARRETT,

AUTHOR OF "CROOKED PLACES," "OCCUPATIONS OF A RE-
TIRED LIFE," ETC., ETC.

NEW YORK:
DODD & MEAD, PUBLISHERS,
762 BROADWAY.

1874.

CONTENTS.

CHAPTER I.
PAGE

A Family Circle in Bloomsbury 7

CHAPTER II.

Out of Tune 18

CHAPTER III.

The Salt of the Earth 32

CHAPTER IV.

A Portrait and a Puzzle 50

CHAPTER V.

"Fair and Honorable." 60

CHAPTER VI.

Poor Dora 69

CHAPTER VII.

Sweet Sibyl 80

CHAPTER VIII.

PAGE

The Nail on the Floor. . . . 85

CHAPTER IX.

What Next? 101

CHAPTER X.

A Gentleman at Large. . . . 111

CHAPTER XI.

Three Love Stories. . . . 127

CHAPTER XII.

Down Stairs. 143

CHAPTER XIII.

Mr. Capel's Walk. 158

CHAPTER XIV.

Ends and Beginnings. . . . 169

CHAPTER XV.

Diverging Paths. 179

CHAPTER XVI.

Knight-Errantry in 1800. . . . 191

CHAPTER XVII.

"In all Time of our Tribulation." . 203

CHAPTER XVIII.

PAGE

SPILT SALT. 222

CHAPTER XIX.

TOO LATE. 232

CHAPTER XX.

LEFT LETTERS. 240

CHAPTER XXI.

DARKNESS. 256

CHAPTER XXII.

DREAMS AND AWAKENINGS. 267

CHAPTER XXIII.

A PATENT AND A FLUTE. . . . - 277

CHAPTER XXIV.

THE DAY OF THANKSGIVING. 291

CHAPTER XXV.

CONCLUSION. 301

CHAPTER VIII.

PAGE

THE NAIL ON THE FLOOR. 85

CHAPTER IX.

WHAT NEXT? 101

CHAPTER X.

A GENTLEMAN AT LARGE. . . . 111

CHAPTER XI.

THREE LOVE STORIES. 127

CHAPTER XII.

DOWN STAIRS. 143

CHAPTER XIII.

MR. CAPEL'S WALK. 158

CHAPTER XIV.

ENDS AND BEGINNINGS. 169

CHAPTER XV.

DIVERGING PATHS. 179

CHAPTER XVI.

KNIGHT-ERRANTRY IN 1800. . . . 191

CHAPTER XVII.

"IN ALL TIME OF OUR TRIBULATION." . . 203

CONTENTS. V

CHAPTER XVIII.

PAGE

Spilt Salt. 222

CHAPTER XIX.

Too Late. 232

CHAPTER XX.

Left Letters. 240

CHAPTER XXI.

Darkness. 256

CHAPTER XXII.

Dreams and Awakenings. 267

CHAPTER XXIII.

A Patent and a Flute. . . . - 277

CHAPTER XXIV.

The Day of Thanksgiving. 291

CHAPTER XXV.

Conclusion. 301

Gold and Dross.

CHAPTER I.

A FAMILY CIRCLE IN BLOOMSBURY.

T was four o'clock on an autumn afternoon at the Great Northern Terminus. A train had just come in from the Midlands, and crowds of bewildered people were exchanging hurried kisses and greetings, and then suspending civilities to hover excitedly over confused heaps of luggage.

But in the crowd there was one (doubtless there were many!) for whom nobody was waiting. There was nobody to distract his attention, as he disentangled a trunk and a portmanteau from the mass, and secured a cab for their removal. He had never been in London before, and he looked curiously to the right and to the left, as he drove from the station. His first glimpse was of a very draggled skirt of the mighty Queen city. Streams of meager people poured down interminable shabby streets that opened into still shabbier alleys, and about all hung a dreadful sense of struggle—of life forced to live on, after all beauty and hope were beaten out of it. How can any body who does not believe in a just and merciful God bear to live in London! Yet in the engine-shriek through those sordid suburbs, our young traveller could hear a modern version of the old promise which "Bow Bells" sang to Dick Whittington in the twilight on the pleasant old Highgate coach-road. There is vitality in the ancient legend yet. Dick is immortal. He comes up from the country in every train!

Our traveller, Philip Lewis, was no mere boy. He was more than four and twenty—a well-doing energetic young man, who had his own way to make, and was not afraid of the task. He was "the only son of his mother, and she was a widow," with an income so narrow that she had nothing to spare for ornament, even in her boy's education. Philip had not learned Latin or German till he paid the fees of an evening class from his first earnings in an architect's office. And now he had come to try his fortune in London, a well-educated well-appointed young man, owing little to any one but himself, and with a bright belief that few enjoyed better chances or greater blessings than he—a pleasant faith whence he derived that air of prosperous activity which promises so much, though it has its own bitter lessons to learn, and its own peculiar trials to undergo.

The cab suddenly stopped between a row of high

gloomy houses, and a dead wall overhung by skeleton trees. One hall door stood open, and a glow of cheerful light came over the black greasy pavement. There was a girl on the steps with her left hand raised to secure a jaunty cap that was very much inclined to fly away in the bleak east wind.

"Is it here you're wanting?" she asked, rather vaguely, as the cab drew up.

"Yes, Mr. Capel's;" said Philip, already tugging at his boxes. The girl was by his side in a moment, offering her assistance. "There's been cabs for next door a-drivin up every half hour this evening, sir," she said, in apparent apology for her question. "I've been in and out ten times if I've been once. 'Cause strangers as don't know the window-curtains, is often ever so long in finding out the numbers hereabouts. Don't you carry in nothin' yourself, sir. Me and the cabby will do it all, sir."

It was a well-lit hall which Philip entered,—handsome too, though the oil-cloth had nearly lost its pattern, and the slab and chairs were very old-fashioned. A lady stepped forward to welcome him.

"My father has been unexpectedly called from home this evening," she said, "but the maid will take your trunks to your room, and we have tea quite ready. You must be tired after your journey."

The lady was at least thirty years of age. But her voice was so timidly sweet and her blue eyes so softly kind that Philip was quite nonplused. He was not used to women, except his own mother, who stood

1*

five feet nine inches and spoke bass. So he mut-
tered assenting thanks and was led to his chamber,
whence he presently returned to the parlor.

It was a plain square apartment, lit by one small
lamp, with a green shade, which gave out a mysterious
twilight, so that, at first, Philip could scarcely discern
how many people were in the room. One stood mani-
fold, in the flush of the glorious fire. This was a girl
of about twenty-two, with a broad forehead and an
apple-blossom complexion, cheerily contrasting with
her dark blue dress. She was measuring tea out of
the caddy, but she looked up with a ready smile and
was introduced by Miss Capel, as " my youngest sister,
Hester."

In the shadows over the sofa, Philip made out
another figure. It only half rose to greet him, while
the face shone out of the gloom with almost spectral
whiteness. It was a face with great dark blue eyes,
set deep beneath delicately-marked brows, and was all
too weird and grave for the almost childish form ;
so that it made a discord with the sunny tone in
which the hostess named " Our cousin, Dora Cunning-
ham."

" And you have never been in London before, Mr.
Lewis," observed Miss Capel, kindly anxious to make
conversation for the stranger.

" Never," answered Philip.

" What shall you go to see, first ? " asked Hester.

" The new Houses of Parliament," Philip answered
promptly, for he had his mind quite made up on that

point, and added, " as the old Abbey is down that way, I shall be able to take it in at the same time."

" The Abbey is worth a visit to itself," said Dora, with an emphasis which Hester Capel seemed to understand, for she looked up, and smiled, half slily.

" I suppose so," Philip assented, innocently. " But still abbeys are abbeys, and when you've seen one, you've seen nearly all. I've seen York Minster, and Beverley Minster, and I went over St. Mungo's, Glasgow, when I was there about the Water Company's new offices."

" But Westminster Abbey has such association—for anybody who cares for such things," said Dora.

" I suppose so," Philip responded ; " but, really, not being a native, I scarcely know who is buried there—except all the old royalties."

" Nearly all the kings and queens—but not Oliver Cromwell," said Hetty, drily. " Some very genteel poets,—but not Shakespeare nor Milton."

" Fine monuments ? " asked Philip, who could scarcely be expected to recognize satire, never having met it before.

" Very," returned Hester, demurely ; " elaborate sepulchers in every shade of whiteness."

" The Abbey itself is a monument of Britain's glory and greatness," said Dora, impatiently.

" You would like to be buried there yourself, wouldn't you Dora ? " asked Hester, laughing.

" You have no veneration in you, cousin," said the girl, with an irritable movement.

"Not for Congreve, nor yet for Cowley," she retorted, "nor very much for any honors which they share. I'd count it a better thing to be buried near Bunyan in Bunhill fields."

"You see, I am interested in the new houses of Parliament in a professional light—as an architect, observed Philip.

"Of course you are," responded Hester.

"Yet I should think that in yours, as in every profession, the present is so barren, that it is scarcely a profitable study," said Dora.

"Mr. Lewis has a bit of the present for himself to make fruitful," hinted Hetty.

"Modern buildings are not like the grand old classic models," Philip admitted ; but then those are not all that are wanted now. They don't fulfil every modern requirement."

"Only it is a pity we don't have something as good in its way, which does," sighed Hetty, in an undertone.

"Taste is dead in England at the present date," said Dora, dogmatically, " being chiefly patriotic towards ruins and dead dust."

"I don't know that," Philip answered, quite briskly. "I wouldn't say so. It has been said too often already, till it has bullied our people out of their common sense, which is the best part of taste after all. It bullies them into all sorts of copies, unsuited to English habits or atmosphere. For my own part, I'm a great believer in the Elizabethan style. That was an era when most things were done well."

" I suppose commonplace must be commonplace," said Dora, who had been following her own thoughts rather than Philip's: " One can't give a new villa the interest and romance that hang around an old feudal castle. But the utilitarian spirit seems determined to tread out even the old traces. If people would only pause somewhere in their changes!" and she broke off with a sigh.

" Set the example yourself, said Hetty, mischievously, " Have your next dress made after the cut of the old one. I'm sure the last fashion was the prettiest."

Dora's face flushed a little, but otherwise she ignored the utterance of such frivolity.

" Modern life is petty," she said. " All bricks and mortar, and engines and money. No space or time for tragedy or romance."

" Do you think so?" Hetty asked, quietly. " I think that wherever a human being can live at all, there is room for both, if we only have eyes to see, and hearts to understand ! "

" Shall I bring in the supper, ma'am ?" asked a subdued voice from outside.

" If you please, Mrs. Edwards," said Miss Capel, folding away her work. " Popps will be late at chapel to-night, because there is a special prayer-meeting after the service."

Philip turned to look at the new arrival on the domestic scene. Only a charwoman, he concluded right-ly.   A tall thin woman, who somehow looked as if she ought to have been stout and comely.   Very shabby, with a downcast broken-hearted face, and eyes that kept to the table-cloth as she set the plates and dishes.

Then a loud double knock called her away to open the hall door.   There was no sound of voices in the passage—the new comer swept straight on to the parlor, and as the door opened, Miss Capel said :

" This is my sister Sibyl."

Not a bit like the others, thought Philip.   In quite a different style.   The manner of her dress might have something to do with the difference, though it was simple enough.   Just a black silk robe, sweeping long on the floor, a soft white burnous folded round the slender arrow-like figure, and a spray of scarlet geranium set against the heavy coils of black hair which crowned the small high head.   Not a broad wise-like head, like Hetty's.   But what young man criticizes a head which has a face like Sibyl Capel's? " She's a downright beauty," said Philip to himself. And so she was, as far as perfect Greek features can make one.   You could not see the soul that looked through those quick dark eyes.   The lashes might be longer than Hetty's, and the brow more clearly arched, but the eyes were like those windows where those within can watch unseen.   She crossed the room to the fireplace, and stood on the rug, drawing off dainty lilac gloves.   She had very white hands, and wore two or three rings, adornments which neither of her sisters boasted.   Then she let the burnous gradually fall about her, and out peeped a pair of snowy shoulders, set off by a pelerine, which, had Philip been a judge, he would have known to be both old and costly.

"Where's papa?" asked the eldest sister.

"Just as our cab stopped, Mr. Drew and Mr. Drake came up and they were off to supper at some hotel, and he joined them. So I should say, you need not expect him just yet."

She said these last words with a meaning, and laughed shortly and lightly. Neither of her sisters responded. It seemed almost as if they caught in their breath, perhaps lest it should be a sigh.

"So ho!" thought Philip, "I begin to understand how it is, that I have my present appointment and my prospective partnership on such favorable terms. It is no steady professional fogy who leaves his daughter on the door-step and goes off unexpectedly to an impromptu conviviality at a public house!"

And now Sibyl was by the sofa, bending over her cousin, stroking her soft brown hair and cooing, "Darling, have they utterly neglected and ill-used you? Have you had any tea? Have you had any supper? Dear me, has my place been so well supplied that you have never missed me? Well, at least I know they have not played to you. That's one office they can't take away from poor Sibyl. Come into the drawing-room, my darling, and I'll play you such a beautiful bit out of our concert to-night."

And the wayward invalid girl (she had only recent-

ly recovered from a severe illness,) draped her preco·
cious gravity and smiled up in the beauty's face like a
spoiled child.

"It's too cold in the drawing-room," warned Miss
Capel; "there has been no fire there to-day, and it
is a damp miserable night, and Dora has been sitting
in the glow of this hearth all the evening.

"Oh, come away, my treasure!" said Sibyl, drawing the thin little hand through her arm, and accom-
modating her swift, stately pace to the slow movement
of Dora's weakness. "It won't hurt her, Elizabeth.
The music is ringing in my head, and will be all gone
to-morrow if I don't get it out of my fingers to-night."
And she led Dora away—a very willing captive.

Philip presently made his excuses and retired to
his own room. He met the downcast charwoman in
the passage, ready dressed for her homeward walk;
and as he climbed the stairs he heard sweet sounds
issuing from the front room on the first floor. The
Capels evidently possessed a good piano, and Sibyl
a voice something more than to match. He paused
to listen for a moment and then went on, thinking to
himself that he would have a rare treat some evening.

Tired as he was, Philip Lewis kneeled down and
prayed God to bless and keep his mother and all
friends at home, and to watch over and prosper him
in London, so that he might rejoice his parent's heart
in her old age, and do credit to all the sacrifices she
had made for him in his youth.

He was asleep as soon as his head touched the

pillow. What did it matter to him that Elizabeth and Hester Capel looked into the drawing-room on their way to their own chamber, and that Sibyl whirled round on her music stool, and said:

"Isn't he a country bumpkin!"

" I think there is something in him that has never come yet," said the little sentimental Dora, "perhaps he has had no chance."

" I believe he thinks he can roll the world before him!" laughed Hester, " and forgets that somebody else may be rolling it the other way."

" How all you children talk!" said Elizabeth. " I'm sure he seems a very pleasant young gentleman."

And they each went their ways. In a little closet Dora read the Litany to herself with many an intonation. She herself heard more of her prayer than God did, since he only hears what comes from the heart. And Sibyl went to her room—she had one to herself —and when she had locked the door she drew from her pocket a note not sealed, but intricately folded ; a note penciled on a page torn from a gilt-leaved diary. And she read it, and laughed triumphantly in the face of the glorious reflection that smiled back from her mirror—and then read it again—and then went to bed, and never noticed that she absolutely forgot even to kneel for a form of prayer. And Elizabeth and Hester went to their room and read a chapter, verse about, and kneeled down, one at each side of the little white bed, where half an hour after they were asleep in each other's arms.

CHAPTER II.

OUT OF TUNE.

PHILIP LEWIS woke early the next morning, and feared to compose himself to sleep again, lest he should sleep too long, being one of those really estimable people who think it a brand of shame to saunter down late upon a breakfast party. He heard one or two steps upon the stairs—one particularly energetic which he instantly connected with tawny-locked, chapel-going Popps, but beyond these, the house continued so quiet, that Philip thought there must be some mistake, and ventured down unsummoned. A smell of toast and tea met him from the dining-room, and entering that apartment he found Miss Capel seated behind the urn, and Hester arranging breakfast paraphernalia on two small trays.

"We were going to send up your breakfast. We thought you might not care to rise early this morning," explained the hostess.

"You are very kind, ma'am," Philip answered, primly. "I was only fearful lest I was late. It is nearly nine o'clock."

"Good morning, sir," said Popps, bouncing into the room. "Is this the master's tray?" and she seized one bearing a huge cup of black coffee, flanked by a tiny fragment of delicate brown toast, unbuttered. And Popps disappeared.

To Philip it seemed an oddly free and easy household. Fancy his mother's decorous serving-damsel saluting a guest in the middle of a meal! It rather perplexed him. He had always moved by rule, and he felt like a child with its leading-string suddenly taken away. And where was Sibyl? And Dora? And did "the master" always breakfast in bed?

"What is your servant's name?" he asked; "you call her something which sounds very droll."

"Popps," answered Hester, laughing. "It is her surname."

"I suppose the other is Julia Maria, or Evelina, or some other incongruous mouthful," said Philip.

"No, indeed!" replied Miss Capel. "It is just my own simple name—Elizabeth."

"The best name in all the world!" said Hetty: "but we just keep to Popps to save any confusion."

"You might call her Bessie or Betty; it makes quite a different name," remarked Philip.

"But then my sister is Elizabeth to most people, Lizzie to us, and Bessie to her father," returned Hester. "Dear me, Lizzie, wouldn't it be funny if you were only Elizabeth to everybody. I never call you Elizabeth, except when we are quarreling, do I, Lizzie ?   And then you call me Hester, and that is the extent of our hostilities.   When you call me Hester I begin to take notice what I am about, and grow particularly civil.   I wonder what you'd do next, if I didn't, Lizzie.   I'm half a mind I'll try next time."

Then, in came Sibyl, arrayed in a bright-hued loose breakfast-gown, with enticing little ruffs at the throat and wrists.   She gave quite an air of distinction to the whole table, and made her sisters look positively shabby in their carefully-preserved brown alpacas.   There was considerable graciousness in her " Good-morning" to Philip, for there was no unread note in her pocket now, and there could be no excitement of any sort for hours, unless she extracted some from " the country bumpkin."

Dora appeared just as everybody else had finished their meal, and as soon as she had poured out her tea, Miss Capel left the table and Hester presently followed her.   The other three lingered long, having found a mutually agreeable topic in music.   Philip had attended a singing-class, and had heard a great deal of fine melody murdered at provincial concerts, but also he had never lost an opportunity to improve his taste during his brief professional visits to great towns. Towards music he had a yearning that could not be content only to admire.   He possessed a flute and a concertina, which no mortal eyes but their makers' and his own ever beheld, since he had never " tried " them anywhere but in his empty office, before and after business hours.   He was but a plain-minded practical young man, who never felt any particular inclination to open a novel or read a poem, but this only made it the more touching to think how longingly and blindly and fruitlessly he strove to utter the song that lay muffled in him : how he would linger to listen to a barrel-organ in the village, and how he strove to pick up hints from the one or two piano-playing families with whom his own exchanged visits. It was his one glimpse of the ideal : the only spot in his soul unguarded by armor of matter-of-fact. There, he felt a pleasant pain that never troubled the rest of his unintrospective nature. He himself half shame-facedly called it his " weak point," but it is through such weak points that the arrows enter, which prick our souls away from their fetters of the earth, earthy.

Sibyl was acknowledged to be " musical." She had made her first teacher's life burdensome by cry-ing and storming, till books were put away and the piano opened. She had enjoyed the best instruction and every opportunity and advantage for the cultivation of her decided talent. Her whole education, such as it was, had converged around that point. Then she had heard almost every musical celebrity in almost every musical masterpiece, and Philip listened with respect-ful awe to her glib criticisms which came second-hand from her pretty mouth as smartly as if they were ori-ginal. And an hour's conversation between the three (during which Popps peeped in several times to re-move the tray, but found Miss Sibyl still toying with a half-empty cup), ended in their adjournment to the drawing-room to hear a " Reverie " which the young lady announced to be " near perfection."

She was in the midst of her performance, Philip standing in dumb admiration, losing the place in her rapid manipulation, and so not daring to turn the page, and Dora, lying back in the great easy chair, with her earnest blue eyes gazing as if she saw the very soul of the sweet, sad melody, when Mr. Capel himself entered. He was beginning to speak crossly till he saw Philip, whose keen sense of the proprieties made him feel terribly awkward at such an introduction. But this new superior of his was the last person to notice such a thing. He was a tall, large man, with that coarse sensual physiognomy which ignorant people think "jolly" or "good-natured;" one of those men who, though clever after a certain fashion, spend life in skulking or scamping their work, in the firm belief that all human nature does the same at its sincerest bottom, and that any sign of energy or industry is but pretension Mr. Capel took up his place in front of the grate, as if he did not notice that it held no fire, and Sibyl's music did not cease for her father's attempt at conversation with Philip. " Let me see, to-day is Wednesday ; no use your coming to the office till next week. Begin well on Monday morning. Grand thing to begin well, eh ! whatever happens after ! And by the time you are as old as I, the mere beginnings will amount to a good item in the general account. Did you see the letter your old governor wrote to me about you ? Said I should find you quite an acquisition—only wished that he himself could have given you a sphere worthy of your talents. But I don't suppose there was anything more amusing than work going on down yonder, was there ? Like music ? So do I. But now Sibyl, stop that 'linked sweetness long drawn out,' and give us a good rattling song."

"Father, how can you ask me to degrade my powers to play those common things ;" and on went the 'Reverie.' "Oh, yes, it is all very fine," said Mr. Capel ; "but how can I know what it is all about, unless I am told? 'Reverie,' indeed. But what about? His lady-love that wouldn't take him or his butcher's bill that he can't pay?"

"Why, the music ought to tell you what it means," said Dora. "Does it not show you pictures? I saw one then—a lake among the hills and two people walking in the twilight—and there was a third one somewhere out of sight."

"Whatever the music brings into your mind is what the music means for you. Eh, Miss Dora! Thank you, it's not often you condescend to give me a lesson in art, I hope you don't expect a fee ? What is it ? 'Whatever the music brings into your mind is what the music means for you,' that's it. Well, since I've been here it has come into my mind that I have not finished the plan for old Squire Rogers' new stable at Bickley and that I'd better go and do so. So I suppose that is the message the ' Reverie ' has for me."

"Dora despises such bathos, as well she may," said Sibyl.

"Yet it would not be at all despicable if every one heard a meaning that put him in mind of his duty," observed Hetty, coming in, duster in hand, and speaking in tones just a little severe. "There are two gentlemen asking for you down stairs, father. The office bell-rang twice, but I knew you could not hear it in this noise."

"I'm off Hetty," said the architect. I'm a lucky man, Mr. Lewis. Each of my daughters is a personification of something fine. Bessie is Goodness—Sibyl is High Art, and Hetty is Common Sense. Bessie is a saint. Hetty is a strong-minded woman—Sib is—"

"Your favorite isn't she, now, daddy?" and the beauty sprang up from the music-stool and caught her father by both his arms.

"You have no right to stop my mouth, Miss. You only do so because you think I'm going to speak some unwelcome truth. I was about to say, 'Sib is a woman.' You're just that and nothing more, Sibyl."

"And that is the highest compliment," said Dora; "that includes everything."

"Ha! ha!" laughed Mr. Capel, turning back into the room which he had half quitted. "That includes everything, and a precious deal more than you know anything about yet, Dora."

"And so you call music, noise, Hetty?" said Sibyl, putting aside the half-finished, sorrowful "Reverie," and dashing straight into a lively "Caprice."

"Noise means sound out of season," answered

Hetty; beginning quietly to dust and re-arrange the ornaments on a little what-not.

"O Hetty, Hetty!" laughed Sibyl; "if then

> "The man that hath no music in himself,
>   And is not moved by concord of sweet sounds,
>   Is fit for treasons, stratagems, and spoils,
>   The motions of his spirit are dull as night
>   And his affections dark as Erebus.
>   Let no such man be trusted,"

what must such a woman be? Remember this is the judgment of your idol, Shakespeare."

" Remember he puts that judgment into the mouth of a man who gratifies his own will by marrying a *Jewess*, though he thinks a Jew is something less than human, and that this man speaks it in compliment to the delicate æsthetics of a girl who deceived and robbed her father," returned Hester.

" Dear me, Hester!" said Sibyl ; "you have evidently thought the matter sufficiently near home to be worth a good deal of thought."

" I have heard it so often from you," Hester answered.

" And so you have made your own natural deficiency the means of discovering a new dramatic beauty in Shakespeare," pursued Sibyl.

" That seems better than to use one's natural gifts to prey upon others' deficiencies," Hetty retorted, the color in her cheeks mounting a little higher.

" Now don't get excited, dear sister, mine! Do

you feel there is any disgrace in not having an ear, that you resent it so tartly?" asked Sibyl, mockingly.

"I am not so sure that I have no ear, though I don't play myself, and do not care for your music," said Hetty bitterly; "but I know that you think there is nothing else worth having in the world."

"And if I do, who am I, that my opinion signifies?" asked Sibyl, "you have good company on your side. Lizzie is worse than you are. I do believe one might strike two notes together for hours without jarring Elizabeth's nerves."

Elizabeth has wonderful endurance," said Hetty, quietly, "she knows little of harmony except to live in it.

But there is more of it in her voice than yours,"

> "How sweet to hear a charming woman
> Talk of what she doesn't understand!"

hummed Sibyl, provokingly. Can't you leave me my little empire all to myself? It is such a little empire, quite beneath a model Minerva like you."

"You know you don't mean that," said Hester, in parenthesis.

"I can never guide the soul or sway the intellect," Sybyl went on unheeding, and the only sign of irony in the beautiful face was a wicked little elevation of the eyebrows—"I can but touch the heart. I cannot carry on a discussion like my learned sister. I cannot write immortal verse like my cousin. All I can do vanishes as I do it, leaving but a fading echo in some indulgent memory. I can play with some

expression ; just a little more maybe than those interesting young ladies who learn music at ten shillings
a quarter. I can sing they say with some feeling.
O Hetty, Hetty, if only you were not so clever, if you
were foolish just at one little corner, so that I might
stand on a level with you, sometimes! If I could only
pierce your fine hard masculine mind and reach a
warm womanly soul in you, my sister! I know what
you are going to say, Hetty ; that only soul can find
soul. But I do hope I have a little, though it be a
little silly soul that will trick itself so fantastically
that some wiseacres mistake it for a dead wax doll.
You know I have a little soul, don't you, Dora, dear?
I am not sure about papa—he only likes me to laugh
at and tease. I think I might be worth something
more, if people would only believe it."

"I cannot think how you can talk so, Miss Sibyl,"
said Philip ; "I, for one should say you had a very
noble soul." Poor Philip ! He was not used to
young ladies of independent manners and speech.
The girls he had known were quiet girls, who seldom
went out to quiet tea-parties without their mothers, or
said ten consecutive words to any man who was not
their brother or at least their cousin of some degree.
He had never heard a young lady quote Shakespeare,
or make a metaphysical study of herself; and utter
novelty generally strongly attracts, or forcibly repels.

As he spoke, he stood near the music-stool and
Sibyl looked up at him with those dark eyes of hers.
Surely not the eyes that had looked at him so super-

ciliously the evening before; not the eyes that had laughed so exultingly in the mirror. Soft tender eyes these seemed, though still out-looking eyes that admitted none to their own secret. Philip thought there were tears in them. Oh, how lost she must be in that dull house, with that hard father, and the homely Elizabeth, and this stern, common-place Hester, and nobody at all to appreciate her, except perhaps the little sickly cousin, with her somewhat cankered temper! It is always plain practical people, who would never find out that they were not understood themselves, who are the first to pity others, and to believe that anybody who feels unappreciated, must be worth any amount of appreciation; unnoticed gems, rather, than is generally the truth, chips of rubbish, whose safety lies in their not being altogether worth the trouble of throwing away!

Hester had finished arranging the china, and she quietly took up her duster and went away without another word. Away to her bedroom,—the back room on the third floor, overlooking a dull, damp yard. Sibyl and Dora occupied the two rooms on the front, because those looked out on the trees, and Sibyl and Dora could not exist without beauty. Sibyl's door was open, and as Hester passed, she saw the unsmoothed bed, the rumpled night-attire, the messy toilet-table. Not even the full glow of the autumn sunshine, nor the golden green trees disclosed by the ill-drawn blinds, would make that disorderly chamber a shrine of sweetness and light.

Sibyl's room had the dawn, her sister's the sunset ; or rather it would have been at sunset that glory would have visited it, only that the yard was too narrow to admit more than a tinge of pale gold, suggesting the splendors beyond, about as dimly as a city graveyard may figure the country to some poor child who never goes out, even with a school excursion. Yet Hetty liked her room at that dim sunset time. It was certainly very quiet. Not with the hush of country chambers where birds twitter at the window-sill, and the low of cattle comes up from the meadow beyond the purling river, which after rain, sings in that sweetest note of God's grand instrument, the sound of gushing water. This was silent with the sepulchral stillness of high-up city rooms. There were times when Hetty felt as if she would like to stay here always, working on some eternal seam. Reading the Bible morning and night, and keeping Sabbath by putting up her work, taking down Thomas à Kempis, or Jeremy Taylor, listening to the church-bells, and praying for the people who obeyed their call. The room would not need much change to become a typical nun's chamber, with its white bed, strips of green carpeting, rush-bottomed chairs, and Ary Scheffer's two pictures of Monica and St. Augustine, and Our Lord and the Tempter, set in narrow black frames. There was but one sign of outer life at which the veriest ascetic need have demurred ; and that was only a small, richly-set portrait in oils, hanging over the mantel-piece. It was the portrait of a lady, about twenty years of age, dressed in white muslin, with a rosebud in her hair—her left hand wearing the plain gold marriage-ring. The face was pretty, but more unformed than should be that of a child of twelve, and the white neck had a peculiar set, as if the little brown head was very light and perhaps somewhat turned by its new matronly dignity. Altogether, it made one wonder what her husband had made of her.

It was the late Mrs. Capel.

But this was not the sunset hour, and Hester's room was dull enough, as she entered it, and Hester's heart felt fierce and hard. Yet she was used to tilt with Sibyl, and to come off worsted, because her best weapons were those which did not touch her sister, while her sister freely used others that she would scorn to take up. She was used to her father's estimate of her. She was used to that peculiar pain which powerful natures feel, when, in those close relationships, where feelings grow unanalyzed, they find unconscious fear beginning to spring in place of spontaneous love. Hester had long since half-accepted the character which was fastened upon her. Very likely it was true that she was austere and cold and too clever. She knew Lizzie did not think so, but then Lizzie was so kind, that she always thought everybody better than they were. Yet down in the depths of her heart, there was a voice which cried out that Lizzie was right, and that she could love and worship, not only Cromwell and her other dead

Puritan heroes—not only Shakespeare, and such others who are as stars shining above us, but also men and women, stumbling by her side along life's way. But then nobody but Lizzie would ever believe. She felt sure that even this Mr. Lewis, who looked so sensible, was beginning to dislike her and her sharp words, and did not notice that she had not spoken tartly until she was unfairly provoked, and ought not to be provoked? Lizzie seldom was. Their father never spoke a truer word, than when he lightly called Lizzie a saint. Yet Hester could not reconcile herself to be like Lizzie, whose philosophy of life seemed best summed up in the old Mexican adage, " Thou art born to suffer, endure and be silent." There was something in Hetty, which would ask troublesome questions, such as, " If endurance be so fine a discipline, has one a right to keep it all to oneself? Is it not a leaving others' sins undisturbed, that we may use them as steps to raise ourselves into Heaven?"

CHAPTER III.

HETTY sat down by the window and looked dreamily out at the dreary yard. It was not when she was in this mood that she fancied it would be happiness to stay there always and be quiet. It was strange that such a wish should ever come to so young and energetic a girl, with life's book so blank before her! When its story has begun soon, and the opening chapters have been stormy and the leaves blurred with tears, and torn by passion, one can understand the weary attempt to shut the volume and put it away. Yet have you never felt tired beforehand at the thought of a long up-hill walk at sultry noon-tide? And at other times, under the pressure of necessity, have you not braced up your nerves and started off with an extra briskness, to get over, and return to rest with a quiet conscience? And this was how Hetty felt to-day.

"I wonder if anybody thoroughly likes this life," she mused. "I don't believe Sibyl does, or she would not be so restless. You don't say that anybody has a healthy appetite who only eats dainties. And that's the way with her. She drags herself through the bread and butter of common days, only to reach the sweets of a concert, or a party, or a visitor. I don't know whether papa is happy. I think not. He just gets through, somehow. I never heard papa speak of death. And yet mamma died. One would think that would make death so familiar that papa would speak of it quite naturally, much as he speaks of his father's old house, where he was born. Poor papa! And Dora is never happy. Dora enjoys misery, and says there is something far better than happiness. But I fancy that happiness should come hand-in-hand with that something better. If there is anybody contented, I think it is Lizzie, actually Lizzie, who never does anything from morning till night, but look after the house, and plan so that all the bills shall not come in at the wrong time, and who uses fully half her own allowance, to pay for odds and ends that ought to be included in the general household account. When I've heard clergymen giving "proofs of the existence of a future state," I've thought that Lizzie's life is the best proof of all, for if there's one thing that I'm always sure about, it is that God is just, and that he will make things even some day.

Hester was not yet a Christian, nor was she a mere Pagan worldling. She stood just where the grand old patriarchs stood, who knew that their Redeemer lived, and that he was coming to save

2*

them, but who mixed his conquest by suffering with strange visions of a material kingdom. She knew all about Jesus of Nazareth, but it was as people might, who heard of him in the Jerusalem gossip nineteen hundred years ago. She was seeking him, though vaguely, as a blind man might, who, hearing of his strange cures, did not question much more about him, but only wondered if he would cure him too. Do you suppose there was any such who never found the Healer? There must have been many sick left uncured in Jerusalem, on that dark day of public execution in Golgotha, but depend on it, they were only those who thought the Physician but a quack, or were sure he would have no power in their very peculiar cases. For Christ knows the foot-fall of those who seek him, and for every step they take, he takes ten to meet them.

Suddenly Sibyl burst into the room. " Papa has a business appointment in Waterloo place," she began breathlessly ; " and so he is going to drop Mr. Lewis at the National Gallery on his way, and I and Dora are going too. Lend me your lace neck-tie, for mine is a perfect wisp! There's a darling! I ought to have ironed mine yesterday, but forgot it. Is my hair right behind? Just look at these gloves! Nasty, shabby brown things, I shan't put them on. I'll take my best primrose pair. What is the good of having nice things if one does not wear them? Lend me your umbrella, dear pet. Mine has lost its snap. What is yours, an alpaca? I never knew that before.

What a miser you must be! Very much obliged to you, all the same, dear, but I won't take it. I won't take any. I know we are going in a cab, because papa is late already. So perhaps we'll have one back, or if not, I'll take my chance that the weather will be fine, though it does look rather cloudy. What a sight my room is! I just looked in now, and came away here in disgust. If any visitors come, don't let them see it, unless indeed you choose to tidy it, like a dear orderly angel as you are. I don't see why we should ever arrange our own rooms at all,—what is Popps for?"

"Popps has quite enough to do with the heavy work," said Hester.

"Then there's Mrs. Edwardes," returned Sibyl. "I don't believe she half earns her money, as a smart woman might—now, do you, Popps?" she asked, as that young person appeared, about some household duty.

"Well, she do rather creep and crawl," said Popps, "them fallen sort of people often do. I'd rather have somebody as was a-risin' in the world, myself. Not as Mrs. Edwardes ever talks about what she has been, like the one who was afore her, who was forever a-rilin' me, a sayin' 'when she'd a good house and servants of her own,' till at last I told her, that I'd be ashamed to own that I'd been such a fool as not to be able to keep 'em, instead o' lettin' myself down to earn eighteen pence a day and my dinner, to say nothin' o' being that dirt mean as to ask, if there weren't no tea leaves or drippin' to spare! Mrs. Edwardes now is quite the other way; she holds her tongue and goes about a-sighin', till it worrits me so, that I says, 'one would think that you had something a-boilin' in your mind, and you was a letting off the steam.' But we must all have patience with each other, and if Miss Lizzie wasn't the sort of lady to give work to a poor dazy, come-down sort of body like her, most likely she wouldn't have been the sort to take a poor girl like me out of the ragged school."

"And now off you goes, Miss Sibyl;" Popps soliloquized, as the two sisters went down stairs together. " You're a fine bird, aren't you, with your gay feathers ; but you're one o' the sort that looks particular bad when you're a-moultin'. With all your airsomeness, bishop of Chilchester for the benefit of the funds of the Monican Sisterhood. Next Sunday would certainly be time enough for Bracket Court.

Elizabeth Capel had risen at seven o'clock that morning, and had taken her usual brave share of the housework, so that even Popps was free to go to her chapel's morning service. " Two sermons on Sunday are not too much spiritual food for a well-disposed girl who has to work hard all the week, and is not enough educated to get much benefit from books," thought Elizabeth, as she dusted the rooms that she had carefully set in order the night before, so that Sabbath work might be reduced to its minimum ; and then she went up stairs just at the right moment to prevent sharp words between Sibyl and Hester, fastened a refractory curl for Sibyl, pinned Hester's skirt in precisely the right way, went down with them to join the gentlemen in the parlor, ran up stairs again to fetch Dora's gloves, when she found she had left them in her own room after all, kissed the three girls as they passed out at the street door, and hoped they would have a good sermon, for she had heard that the bishop was an earnest charitable man, though he was inclined to favor the curates who wore crosses on their backs. And then she closed the door and went back alone into the quiet house.

Very quiet was the old Bloomsbury house. And as she went into the little back parlor, a ray of autumn sunshine stealing through the evergreens which she kept to enliven the window-sill, carried her mind suddenly back to a little churchyard in Kent, where she had stood one bright afternoon, ten years ago, on one of the few holidays of her existence. She had been on a picnic, not with friends, but with the teachers of a Sunday-school where she herself had found time to take part in those less responsible days. She had not been on intimate terms with any of them. She did her teacher's duty regularly and faithfully, but made so little fuss about it, had such a trifle of money to spend on rewards, never made an important bustle to find a substitute while she took a long summer holiday, that Miss Capel was thought nobody at all, except on wet Sundays when she took everybody's class as well as her own. No, not with one of them had she been intimate. But women who may not love at hand are free to worship afar off.   Lizzie Capel had dreamed her dream, and only a dream, which had never for one moment rounded off into a reality. Lizzie Capel knows what she thinks is the finest type of man God ever put into this world.   A man nearly six feet high, with square solid shoulders, and a healthy honest-eyed face set in a framework of crisp brown curls.   A man who could fell an oak or nurse a sick baby.   Lizzie Capel knows all about such a one, and feels quite sure what he would do in every circumstance of life, though she only knew him as the solitary teacher beside herself, who never missed one attendance all the year round, and never got beyond a lifted hat, if he met her without the school door, or a pleasant "Good-morning" within.   Never but once. They had a little conversation among the mossy graves in that Kentish churchyard.   She had strayed away by herself, and was sitting on the low stone wall looking at the sunset, when he came up behind her. And he was so pleasant!   And only a month after she was asked to contribute towards a testimonial in appreciation of his labors, previous to his departure for New Zealand.   She gave half a sovereign.   Surely he had known of this journey that evening in the graveyard.   She wished that he had just said a word about it.   But why should he?   They had merely taught in the same room twice every Sunday for years.   So she gave half a sovereign towards the morocco Bible which they gave him, and she signed " Elizabeth Capel " to the parting address. Hers was the last name on the list—and her writing did look so bad on the vellum.

He had reached New Zealand in safety; she learned that, because his mother wrote to the school-superintendent to say that she had received a letter from her son, and that he sent his kindest remembrances to all his old friends. About a year afterwards the Sunday-school was broken up, and that was all. Quite all.

Would it be better or worse for Elizabeth Capel if she realized how some quiet, self-contained men watch and value a woman, without a word ? if she knew that there was a certain rash inclination suppressed in that manly heart as it beat heavily and fast under the yew trees in that autumn sunset? if she knew that the last name under that memorial was the first to meet his eyes ? if she had seen him give it one long kiss ere he buried it down at the bottom of his great emigrant's chest, so that it should never turn up to waken memory with that bitter sting which men dread so much? if she could have understood how when, years after, a colonial bishop married him to a wealthy settler's daughter, there came between him and his rather showy bride, a pale vision of a neat, gentle English girl, with an open Testament in her ungloved hands, sweetly teaching little children how "Jesus Christ came into the world to save sinners !"

Neither better nor worse. For Elizabeth Capel is one of those for whom, "fearing God and keeping his commandments," all things and any thing, work together for good and become but steps into heaven.

And she paused with her eyes on the evergreens standing in the light, seeing not them, but a manly figure, with kind blue eyes looking into hers. And she smiled to herself at the memory, not mockingly, but thankfully, thinking how good it was for a woman to love a good man.

It is sad to think of a life so blank and plain, that it is proud of such a single gold thread as this? Nay, nay. Is it the grand end of love that men and women should keep house, and pay taxes, and bear children? Is it not rather that it should teach them some lessons which Elizabeth Capel has surely learned better from one line of its sweet song than many a woman does, who hears out the whole melody, amid a clashing discord of trousseaux and settlements and pin-money? Better a dead-white rose, shut in a Bible, than a flourishing field of stinging nettles. Will you still pity Elizabeth Capel? Do you pity the saints in heaven?

She sat down to read the Bible. It opened at the thirty-seventh Psalm. Unless she had a very express purpose, Elizabeth Capel always read where the Bible opened; why, she could scarcely have told, but it was with some feeling, that God's will was in every circumstance. And so she began, reading half aloud, in a low monotone, and her thoughts made a running commentary about how vexed and passionate she had felt once, years before, when her father had praised the superior style and elegance of a neighbor, like herself a widower's daughter, whom she privately knew to be in the habit of helping her draper's bills out of the household allowance. Poor thing! Elizabeth sighed to remember the ruin that came of that gay girl's marriage, till at last, the once admired belle of the Square had sold matches in the streets on rainy days, when gentlemen's hearts were likely to be softened to give a penny for half its worth! Poor thing! poor thing! and Elizabeth's heart was so sore to think how bitter had been her girlish indignation against her, that she half forgot it had its root in justice. And how strange it was, that there was something more in common between her and the Psalmist, than all the difference of date, and place, and rank, and capacity; so that the same truths came so exactly home to the trials and temptations of both! A very commonplace fact, but a very comforting one for commonplace people, whose speech can never set forth the secrets of their own natures, but must humbly wait for the crumbs of sympathy that fall from other men's tables. Never mind, mute brother! the very foremost talker at the banquet needs just the same food as you, and longs for the same dainties, and though you must be satisfied with his leavings, yet shall the Master of the Feast take care that they suffice you.

Suddenly Elizabeth's eye fell upon the explanation why the Bible had opened at that Psalm. Close on the binding lay a little strip of fancy card-board, with which Hester had been making book-marks a few days before. She too had been reading there. And Elizabeth sighed. For she knew her sister, and could guess how her hot young heart read the words in a spirit of bitter prophecy, rather than of calm hope. Elizabeth's scheme of life was very simple, undisturbed by the contradictions and paradoxes that perplexed Hester. With her it was enough that God governed the world ; therefore the world must be governed well. Satan might meddle, but his might beneath God's, was as a fire-brand put out by the sunshine. She was like a simple villager, accepting and obeying the edicts of the prime-minister, not mingling with the village politicians who will have their little argument over every proclamation, and cavil at words of which they utterly mistake the meaning. Yet among such, there may be a few souls with something far more than the easy talents of doubt and denial, some who will wait and watch and learn till they arrive at the same consenting faith on a higher level of knowledge. But let not those be too sure of their right to the leader's place, so readily assigned to them by their humbler brethren. Christ said, " Blessed are they that have not seen, and yet have believed."

Elizabeth knew how Hester pondered over the facts that Sibyl, who spent most money and did least work, and never suppressed a whim, nor let a wish pass by unspoken, was yet the favorite of a father, who was always justly complaining that his too small income was constantly decreasing, and who looked so gloomy over the necessary household accounts, that

she herself was fain to spend her whole ingenuity in
poor little shifts to keep them down ; how both their
father and Dora considered Sibyl's dresses and sur-
roundings, unexceptionable in fit, dainty in texture,
and delicate in hue, as sheer necessities to her artistic nature, and keen perception of beauty ; never seeming to understand that others might have the same
inclinations, quite as strongly, only not stronger than
their sense of duty ; how Dora's nerves were always
jarred by Hester's plain-spoken truths, but not
by Sibyl's irresponsible frivolities, which provoked
them.

Hester's outward life lay alongside of Elizabeth's.
She too found out the shops where dresses might be
bought a little cheaper than at the old family draper's.
She too said, that they might as well be made up at
home, and that she and Lizzie were often glad of
some such definite occupation.   She too read reviews
of books she could never buy, and notices of picture-
galleries that she would never attend.   She too, ate
bread and butter that the cake might go further, and
found out that she liked long walks, that she might
save the omnibus fare.   But what Elizabeth did as a
matter of course, as barest duty, almost too simple to
be done for God's sake ; but, by his great goodness,
accepted as done unto her fellow-men, Hester did
fiercely, defiantly, self-consciously, proudly aware that
by such strength of will, such self-restraint and self-
denial, she was taking out her patent of nature's no-
bility, caring not much for either duty to God or ser-

vice to man, but carefully seeking, inch by inch, to add to her own moral stature, while her heart protested, with a practical application of terms which made the gentler Lizzie to shudder, " Behold these are the ungodly who prosper in the world and increase in riches ! " She could accept the Psalmist's self-analysis only so far as her own went with it; she could not take his conclusion until she had made it hers by experience. All this Elizabeth knew full well. So she sighed as she closed the Bible. And then she read Massillon's sermon " On the Happiness of the Just."

Popps was the first to return from divine worship, and there was nobody but Elizabeth herself to answer her modest single knock. Popps used the upper door on Sundays. That was one of Elizabeth's homely domestic rules. She had never argued it out to herself, that it was well to surround the holy day with such little pleasant distinctions. She had only thought it was but fair, that all such trifling arrangements should be made on the side sure to be agreeable to the servant. And Popps stepped in, attired in a blue merino dress, a drab cloth jacket, a brown bonnet with green ribbons, and a pink bow in the front. Poor Popps was surely indemnifying herself for the many long years when dirt was the one tint of her whole apparel. And Elizabeth, remembering the squalid shivering girl who had come to her Sunday-class seven years before, neither smiled nor scoffed at the gay conflicting colors ; only wished that she might hope every such ragged child would improve as much.

Presently Popps came into the parlor to set out the dinner-table. Elizabeth had not quite finished Massillon's sermon, but she closed the book. She was not one of those who think that all profitable spiritual communion must be held with the holy dead. She always remembered that God perfects his praise in the mouths of very babes and sucklings.

"I hope you had a full chapel, Popps;" she observed.

"Oh yes, Miss," answered Popps, and such a good sermon! The text was in the seventh verse of the seventh chapter of Ephesians : ' As to the Lord and not to men.' It seemed as if he were a-preachin' right to me, for he made out as how one work is as good as another in the Lord's sight, and, said he, ' If those as has the getting ready o'meals and the keeping tidy o' houses did their dooty more often as they ought, then there'd be a deal of what's thought God's grander work, that wouldn't be needed at all, because men wouldn't be so often tipsy, and girls wouldn't go so much astray. He said that what we calls great services to God, is just that one or two good people have to do at a stretch, what a great many oughter a' done natural, in the regular way of business.' And he said over a bit of poetry, that I wish was in the hymn-book, for I'd like to learn it. You can get a deal of sense packed up in a verse or two, can't you, Miss? The jingling words at the ends of the lines hold the meaning together, like the pegs on a clothes-line. I wish I could remember it. Something about sweeping a room."

"Was it something like this?" asked Elizabeth,

> " From God all things a glory take,
>   No task so low and mean,
>   But with this tincture, ' For thy sake,'
>   Does grow both bright and clean.
>   A servant with this clause
>   Makes drudgery divine,
>   Who sweeps a room as to thy laws,
>   Makes that and the action fine."

"Yes, Miss, that's it. I'd give anything to know it straight off like that."

"I'll find the book where it is," said Elizabeth; "and then you can learn it."

"Thank you, Miss, I should like. D'ye know, I wish Mrs. Edwardes had been with me this mornin'. I thought the sermon might ha' cheered her up. Seems to me as if she always thinks her life isn't worth a-livin', and she's just a-dragging herself to the end, because she can't help it. D'ye know, Miss Lizzie, I don't think she ever sets foot in either church or chapel. I b'lieve she just sets by herself all Sunday in that little bit of a room of hern' a-look-ing out at the dead wall. I can't think why she went to live in such a jail! ' Quiet and 'spectable' she calls it! I'd rather live in the narrowest court, I would! I likes life, Miss. I says where there's a lot of people there's sure to be some of 'em good enough for you, whoever you are!"

"And you don't think she ever goes to church or chapel?" said Elizabeth, her conscience accusing her with some neglect that she had never made sufficient acquaintance with this out-lying member of her household, to discover that she was not justified in her charitable conclusion that this decent middle-aged woman was likely to be far before herself in the school of Christ.

"No, Miss. I'm quite sure she does'nt and hasn't for ever so long."

"Then, Popps, we'll ask her to come to tea with you next Sunday, and when you propose going to chapel afterwards, she'll be almost sure to join you. Perhaps she had to go away from her own chapel when her husband died, or couldn't bear to go by herself when she was first a widow, and so got out of the habit." Elizabeth wanted every good work to be done in the way of neighborly kindness, not with a conscious purpose to convert.

"Well, Miss, I think master an' the young ladies 'll be home soon. I only hopes their Bishop has given them as good a sermon as my minister, that's all. It always seems to me so sleepy-like in them fine churches."

"Not in all, Popps," said Elizabeth. "It was a Church of England clergyman who wrote those verses your minister used in his sermon to-day. I'm very fond of the Church of England, Popps, although I go to chapel so often."

"I'm not saying it's not very good," said Popps;

"only chapel's the place for me, and it makes me speak up for it kind o' bitter, when folks (like the lady that had our class after you left) says that those as go there are guilty of a sin—something that begins like scissors,—I can't say the words, Miss, and I don't know what it means, but I can tell you that they mean it uncommon nasty. There's the family come back!" and Popps bustled off to answer the stirring rat-tat-tat.

They all came crowding into the little dining-room.

"Tired to death!" exclaimed Sibyl, throwing herself into the easy chair. "Well, it wasn't much of a sermon after all! I mean the Bishop is nothing of an orator. But the music was very good, and the congregation most aristocratic. I wonder who those ladies were who sat to your right, Dora? I saw they had a coronet engraved on their prayer-books. Did you notice the wall-flowers on their black-lace bonnets, Hetty? I never saw artificial wall-flowers, before, and they make such a stylish and novel autumn effect."

"I was greatly struck by the memorial-window in the side aisle," said Dora. "Did you observe it? A path with the shadow of a cross thrown over it, and strewed with thorns; at either side, hedges with wild roses growing just out of reach of a little child walking on the prickly path between them, and at the end of the way a great gate, with the sun behind it, and an angel watching through its bars, to be ready to open it when the pilgrim should arrive. That was my sermon Sibyl."

"'Then you mean to say that you believe the Thirty-Nine Articles are not intended to be taken according to my views?" This was addressed to Philip by Mr. Capel.

"No, Mr. Capel, certainly not. It is my full belief that"—and the two gentlemen walked up and down the passage to finish an argument they had begun in the street.

Elizabeth looked at Hester, and Hester looked back at Elizabeth.

"I should like to have had a little talk with some of the sisterhood of St. Monica," said Hester, softly. "There were some happy faces among them—like yours, Lizzie!"

3

CHAPTER IV.

A PORTRAIT AND A PUZZLE.

N Monday morning Philip sat down to his desk in the office.

He had felt in a kind of feverish excitement during the few days since his arrival in London. The novelty of everything around, from the bustling streets to the pretty Sibyl, with her sweet glib tongue, the unwonted leisure and the utter absence of all his old landmarks of life, had made him as one in a dream. He had not felt even surely rooted in his own mind. In that short time he had come in closer personal contact with more varying ideas, more differing modes of thought than in his whole life before. A close worker in the office at Ribbock, and a diligent student at home, he had made no acquaintances beyond those that he found ready to his hand in his mother's small circle—a circle whose dimly defined individualities were all alike saturated with the dogmas and idiosyncrasies of the Rev. Mr. Williams, the old Independent minister, who had earned a small grade of Popedom by forty years' diligent service and tenacious self-assertion. In fact, Philip had felt altogether so loosed from his moorings that he was fairly glad to find himself once more among familiar ground-plans and diagrams. However different the world seemed growing, here was his work for him to do ; and what a stay work is ! Not employment merely, for that may be local and temporary, colored by the changing skies of our existence, but our own work, that which we do by the sweat of our brow, that we may eat bread ; that which we must do to-morrow, though we may bury the desire of our eyes to-day; that which we must steadily pursue to-day, however much we are tempted to dream of the bliss that may come to-morrow. This work may be likened to the stake whereto our lives are bound. It may cramp us a little sometimes, but where should not we wander without its chain? We may fancy how we could enjoy ourselves without it, how free, how spiritual, how lofty our natures would become, while we are only as free and lofty and spiritual as we are just because of it ! O worker ! repining at the same dull task that waits you day after day, look at those who, having no need for the bread that perisheth, and feeling no hunger for that which perisheth not, work not at all! Would you be as they ? Are they so free, so spiritual, so lofty ? Does not the Devil deceive them into turning his tread-mill and calling it sport ? Is not work the homely stool whereon we may climb to peep into our Father's treasuries ?

By the middle of the week, Philip was his own so-

ber self. Life was no longer a mere hurry of fashionable crowds, a delirious sense of uttter novelty. It was
the old practical world again, wherein young men must
be punctual and concentrative ; where, too, there
were absorbing professional interests, that made one
quite eager for the office, quite able to forget that the
sun was bright in Regent street, and that Hyde Park
was a pleasant place even in the dull season. He had
now fairly unpacked his boxes, and the very look of
the familiar books, and other proprieties had had its
steadying influence. It is not easy to keep oneself
the same person as one was yesterday, without some
outward assurance that one really is the same. If you
would find the river of Lethe, take nothing in your
hand, and go and seek it, away and away, where no familiar household bell no well-known mark on the wall,
can startle you back into yourself. But remember
there is no certain antidote for that deadening draught,
and that in blurring the form of the woman who played you false, or blunting the sting of the dire mistake
you committed in some black passion, it will also dim
the memory of the mother who taught you your pray-
ers, and cloud the recollection of the little cousin who
died when she was young, and sent her love to you,
just the moment before she went to sing in heaven.
Well for a few that some forgetfulness may be pur-
chased even at so high a price ! Only beware of starting on such quest without due cause.

Still, though Philip returned to his old allegian-
ces, and did his professional duty, diligently, and call-

ed at the house of the minister of Bracket Chapel
only to learn that he was out of town—yet he did not
the less find it very delightful to go up to the drawing-
room in the evening and enjoy Sibyl's music and join
in the family chatter. In the course of a few days, he
almost unconsciously learned a good deal of the Capels' history. On certain points Mr. Capel did not
leave him to this chance information, but frankly told
him that the business was not so good as it had been,
that he himself was not equal to improve or even to
keep it up, which was his reason for taking an assistant with a prospective interest in its prosperity, and
that he himself had some small private means to fall
back upon.

"Not much, but an old man don't want much," he
said. "I'm tired of business, and shall get rid of it
in a year or two when some of the girls are off. I did
not think I should have to stay in it so long."

Philip found that Dora was an orphan, left so in
infancy, and wholly dependent on her uncle, who
bluntly put it, "That she was quite welcome, he only
wished she'd do his kitchen more credit."

Philip could not altogether understand this new
principal of his. Was he selfish or unselfish? Was
he reckless or only careless? He might let the orphan sit at his table and share alike with his daughters, yet he could not cross his own indolent nature
to make fitting provision for any of them. What there
was, any one might have, only he could not trouble
himself to make it more, and, if it grew less, each

must shift for himself. This father of a family seemed to Philip to be of the typical bachelor nature, to whom domestic comfort is but a fancy name or bondage, who likes to come in and go out when he likes, even at the cost of cold wretched meals, eaten amid the uninviting ruins of the general repast; a man who would walk easily through life, who would go straight when the path was even, but would not level for himself; and if he came to a rut, would fell the very tree that should shelter those who would come after, and make a temporary bridge of it for himself, and go on, and forget about it. And yet, just because of his jovial manner, Philip was ready to give him the excuse that he meant nothing and did not even know the weakness in himself; forgetting that a man's first duty is to know himself, and that the sins of such culpable ignorance are registered against us, to be confronted some day, just as the damage done by a drunkard is scored against him for his soberer hours.

Among the girls in the drawing-room, Philip gathered particulars of the domestic past of the family. One evening the post brought him a letter from his mother, and as he read it, culling sundry little incidents about the weather, and such other public property, by which we may give a private epistle the coloring of a social event, Sibyl (who always ventured to be rude, because she believed that she could do so with a grace), took up the envelope and Hester, looking at it over her shoulder, remarked:

"What nice writing!"

"Do you think so?" said Philip, gratified. "Mother always considers she writes so badly."

"It is not writing-masters' good writing," Hester returned. "It is a writing that knows a great deal more than can be taught at school."

"Do you believe there is any character in hand-writing?" asked Sibyl.

"I don't know; I never thought about it," Philip answered ; thinking to himself that he had not seen a scrap of her calligraphy.

"There is character in handwriting, just because there is character in everything," Hester observed.

"Then I'm afraid there is not much in your own, Hester, love," said Sibyl. "Papa says it is like a common clerk's."

Philip knew it ; he had seen some letters she had copied for her father. It was a firm, plain black hand, without one unnecessary flourish—not so much like a common clerk's as like an uncommonly good one's. Philip had looked at the manuscript with genuine respect; and now in his simple manly sincerity, he said:

"I shouldn't draw your conclusion, Miss Sibyl. The useful qualities that are necessary to what you call ' a common clerk,' are sufficiently rare among ladies, to be highly characteristic."

Hester raised her dark eyes in a quick grateful glance. So this young man could be just, and justice was the very quality for which she was always looking in vain. And she appreciated it all the more, because she instinctively felt, what Philip himself did not distinctly know yet,—that he was not prepossessed with her, and that it went against his grain, even thus slightly to contradict Sybil.

Sibyl pouted. What, this raw youth from the country had opinions which he dared to set up against hers ! She was used to utter any absurd dogma, and to find all opposition suppressed for the sake of her pretty face. Rather tame, that sort of thing, after all. The rider likes best the horse which needs most breaking in. The general prizes most the fortress which took the longest siege ; and the vain beauty cares most for the conquest which employed the whole artillery of her charms. There is a delight in effort. It would be quite a new thing to try to talk sense under peril of reasonable reproof.

"Isn't it strange?" said Dora, suddenly rousing herself from a long dreary gaze into the fire. "Out of us five, only you, Mr. Lewis, have a mother, or know what it is to have one !"

"Is it really so ?" Philip answered.

"Yes," said Miss Capel. "I think you have heard that my father once had an appointment as architect and surveyor to a large estate in Italy. That was when he was first married. It was not a healthful district, and as soon as each of us was a few months old, we were sent to England to be brought up by an aunt of papa's. Mamma died about a year after Hester was born, and then papa gave up his post and came home."

"Was Mrs. Capel English?" Philip asked, just to show a civil interest.

"Oh yes!" said Miss Capel. "She was the orphan daughter of a gentleman in the East-India Company's service, and she was an only child. So that relations are very scarce with us. We never knew any except our great aunt, who is dead now, and Dora herself."

Hester had left the room in the midst of this colloquy, and now returned with a picture. It was the portrait that hung in her bedroom. She put it before Philip, saying; "That is mamma, painted during her honey-moon." It was her form of thanks for his vindication of herself.

Philip took it, and put it in a good light, and the wayward vain face smiled into his. "She must have been pretty," he said, and could not conscientiously say more. Then he looked up at the three sisters, then back to it again, with a sudden eagerness, like a person whose mind half catches the solution of a problem.

"It is strange," he said; "but it seems familiar to me."

"Perhaps through some resemblance in us;" suggested Sibyl.

Philip again glanced from the picture to her. "It is like you, something," he said; "not a bit like Miss Capel or Miss Hester. But you look almost younger than this portrait, while I seem to know it as an older face,—as quite an old face."

3*

"Some chance resemblance," observed Dora. "You may chase it through your memory as long as you like, but how can you recall it when, very likely, you only saw it opposite you in some omnibus or railway carriage?"

"But doesn't it haunt you, not to be able to remember?" asked Hester.

"There are matters above our philosophy," said Sibyl. "Once I saw a picture that struck me as like somebody. I could not tell who it was like, and I looked at it every day for a month (you must know it was in a broker's shop in Great Queen street), but could never fathom its mysterious familiarity. Years after, I was introduced for the first time to somebody with that very face. .I think coming influences, as well as coming events, cast their shadows before!"

Philip looked up at Sibyl and caught her eyes as she spoke. Was it his sheer masculine vanity that made him feel sure that he was the "somebody."

"But was it a coming influence?" asked Hester. "Come, Sibyl, for the sake of the science of mental mystery you must answer our questions. Did the coming influence ever arrive?

"Yes—no—not yet—I don't know," said Sibyl; hastily rising, and looking out of the window. "There's such a glorious moon!"

"Hester," said Miss Capel, "will you take mamma's portrait back to our room, in case papa should come in?"

"Oh yes!" and Hester obeyed, instantly.

"Never speak of it to my father, if you please, sir," said Miss Capel. "He cannot bear any mention of our mother. It is such a pity, because it prevents us knowing anything about her. But it is the turn that great sorrow takes with some natures."

"I shall remember," Philip answered reverently, and thought to himself; "but I wish that picture did not puzzle me so. I should say I had seen it somewhere, grown wrinkled and with gray hair!"

CHAPTER V.

"FAIR AND HONORABLE."

ELIZABETH CAPEL spent much of her mornings in the kitchen. She did not expect one girl to make six beds, keep ten rooms in order, attend to three fires, do the marketing, and prepare the dinner without any assistance except a charwoman on washing and scrubbing-up days. What sort of livelihood do our fine ladies think they could make themselves, when they demand such energetic genius at the modest rate of board and ten pounds a year!

It was Saturday, the Saturday after the family visit to St. Monica's. Elizabeth went down as usual. Popps was cleaning the kitchen grate. It was not generally done on Saturday, when there was quite enough to do without that. But Elizabeth took no notice. She knew that, in the long run, one keeps nearest the general groove, by permitting occasional departures therefrom. So Elizabeth took down a bowl and began to pare the potatoes for dinner. It might spoil her hands, but then Popps could never keep hers clean enough for Elizabeth's dainty ideas of cooking. "And nobody looks at my hands," Elizabeth thought; "a little pumice-stone afterwards and they are well enough!"

"It's an awful hot morning, Miss," said Popps, giving the fender any amount of friction.

"Well, I have on a shawl because I feel it cold," answered Elizabeth; "but you are doing warm work, Popps."

"Oh! I was hot afore," she returned.

"Why, you have scrubbed out the kitchen already," said Miss Capel, getting a mat to guard her feet from the possible damp. She was never so troublesome to other people as to catch the slightest malady she could avoid. "How ever have you found time for that so early?"

"Oh, I got up!" answered Popps. "There's times when one can't rest, and then what's the good of laying a-bed? If one gets up and slaves away, perhaps one may expect to get a bit of peace when one really wants it."

Elizabeth went on paring the potatoes. She felt something in the air. Was Popps thinking of "bettering herself?" She did not begin bitterly to reflect on ingratitude, and to moralize that the old charities and patiences are bought out for a pound or two more a year. She had tried to make Popps a good servant, expressly that the girl might get on. She had an ambition for Popps. Fancy her rising to be some nobleman's upper-servant; and coming, a comely, middle-aged woman in a good black silk, to call upon her, when she was an old lady! How nice it would be! Elizabeth almost smelt the sweetness of the nosegay that Popps would be sure to bring from her master's grand garden!

Popps dropped the poker, and, in picking it up, knocked over the tongs.

"There's a spirit in the things!" she cried, setting them up with the sort of shake that nurses give to naughty children. "And now, Miss, what had I better do next?"

"Why, you have not washed up the breakfast-dishes yet;" Elizabeth suggested, mildly.

"My—no more I haven't! If I didn't sheer forget 'em!" And Popps got out a clean towel, and proceeded to wash the cups with extra care and deliberation, as if to defeat "the spirit" that might have transferred its quarters from the fire-irons to them.

"Miss," said Popps, all of a sudden, in a very quiet tone; "do you think there's any harm in a gal thinking of getting married?"

"Harm!" ejaculated Elizabeth in astonishment. "Of course not. God means most people to get married."

"I didn't know whether you'd think so, Miss," said Popps, in a relieved manner. "The girl next door said you'd be sure to set your face agen all such rubbish; being single yourself."

"But marriage is anything but rubbish. And who is thinking of marrying?" asked Elizabeth, amused.

"Oh, I don't know! Not me, I'm sure. I'd always something else to do than think about such things. There was never any of the boys waiting about for me at the school door, as there was for the other gals, was there, Miss?" said 'Popps, all in a flutter. "But if it's ordained, as they say, that every woman has one chance in her life, whether she takes it or leaves it, then I suppose what is to be, will be, Miss."

"Very likely; Popps," said Elizabeth.

"And there's that Tom Moxon, the carpenter's man, always coming, talking his nonsense! I've told him to go along with him, ever so often, but he won't, and he's even took to coming to chapel—he has. And there's his mother goin' about talking how bad he looks, and what gals deserve that makes fools of a decent young man. She's a making a fool of herself, I reckon!"

"What nonsense does young Moxon talk?" asked Elizabeth, with all appearance of gravity.

"Oh! about how nice it is to have a home of one's own, and having nobody to love him, and how his mother's ideas of things an't his'n (shouldn't I like to tell her that?), and how he thought what a good wife I'd make, the first time he saw me, that day when he came to mend the dresser drawer, and I was a turning the blue and black striped skirt you gave me, and wouldn't it be better for me if I had somebody to take care of me? and that last always rouses me up to tell him that I never knowed an old maid that didn't get on very well, until she let herself be gulled by some brother or nephew or something in the shape of a man ; and then he says back, 'that's in the nature of women, if they haven't a husband to look after them.'"

"And is that all he says?" Elizabeth inquired again.

"Well, Miss," and Popps industriously rubbed up the slop-basin, with her back towards her mistress; "he kep on that way for a long time and just whenever he came to work, or when I run agen him by chance in the street. But last night he met me as I was a-coming down Liquorpond street, and says he, 'I wants to speak serious, once for all. If its agreeable to you, I'd like to come a-cortin' ye, fair and honorable. When a working man's come to be three and twenty,' says he, 'its's time he was a-planted out on his own account, if his timbers is to be anything like full at cutting-down time.'"

"And what did you say, Popps?" asked Elizabeth.

"Oh, I laughed him off, Miss! I wasn't agoing to say nothink till I spoke to you, Miss. I wasn't agoing to give my word all of a suddent, as I'd nobody but him to consider."

"And what do you really think, Popps?" Elizabeth inquired.

Popps was facing her now. "Well, I don't know, Miss," she said. "He's a good sort of young fellow, that I do believe. He ain't a teetotaller. but he never takes but his half-pint at dinner and supper. You'll

not see him hanging about the Public, Miss, an' he
gets his thirty shillings a week regular all the year
round, and he says he is putting by to start in business for himself. There's a many begins worse off
than we should be, Miss."

" But do you like him, Popps?" said Elizabeth,
gently. " Do you think you could love to obey and
serve him—that is the chief thing for you to consider."

" Laws, Miss! what's the good of saying anything
about that?" returned the maid. " It stands for so
little. Allays puts me in mind of Old Mother O'Brien,
the apple-woman, who was forever a-talking about
doin' this, that and tother to please her 'Master,'
while all the time the old man did not know his very
life was his own. And there's our oilman's wife, just
the same, and a-telling the people over the counter, as
how her husband never spends an evening away from
home' and I'm sure he hadn't need, for she's always
a-looking after the other men! I mind what you said
to me when you took me as servant, Miss. Says I,
'I'm feared I don't know nothin' about the ways of a
gentleman's house.' Says you, ' Popps, you've done
very well in all the duties God has given you yet, and
I don't doubt you'll go on the same.' That's how
Tom Moxon ought to feel, an' if he can't trust me, he
can just leave me."

" Then how do you mean to make up your mind?"
asked Elizabeth.

" Please, Miss, as you don't seem particular agen it, I'd like to try him ! "

" Very well," said Miss Capel. " You mean you would like to know him a little better first."

" An' he oughter to do the same. ' Ditto,' as they say in the bills. He ain't never seen me in a temper yet, Miss."

" Perhaps he never will," said Elizabeth. " I hope not."

" So, Miss, you won't look upon it as a certain sign that I must be a-neglectin' of my work, if some of them old ladies who has nothin' to do but watch other folks, tell you they sees me a-talkin' to a young man, and they'll warrant I'm a-coming to no good ! You'll know who it is, an' all about it."

Elizabeth sat thinking. This house was Popps' home,—the only home the girl had. Was it right that it should have all her honest work and faithful interest, and give nothing in return? Were all its obligations fulfilled by board and lodging and the ten pounds a year? There was a ray of sunshine coming into the hard rough life now ; should it not be made as bright and pure as possible ?

" You may invite Mr. Moxon to take tea with you every other Sunday, Popps," she said kindly ; " beginning from to-morrow."

" Mr. Moxon ! " Popps bridled. How respectable it sounded !

" Mrs. Edwardes is a-coming to-morrow, Miss," she answered. " You told me to ask her, and I asked her yesterday, and I ain't a-going to put her off for Tom. It would be a bad look-out to begin by disappointing a poor body as doesn't look as if she had many treats."

"Mr. Moxon can come too, if he likes," said Elizabeth. "It may make it less strange for his first visit. When is he to get the answer, Popps?"

"Please, Miss, he said, he'd look in this afternoon, on his way home," answered Popps, demurely.

"Then if you will tell me when he comes, I will just step down and speak to him. And I hope it will go on comfortably, Popps, and that you will both be very happy."

Popps did not say even "Thank you." As Miss Capel glanced at her servant as she passed out of the kitchen, she saw grimy marks round her eyes. The black-leaded hands had wiped away a tear or two.

"God in heaven bless her!" said Popps, talking to herself in her excitement. "And to know what a bad cold in her head she caught that blowin' evening when I left the areay door open to say some foolery to Tom on the steps! I'd fancy it was downright wicked even to think of leavin' such a hangel, if the werry Bible didn't tell us that a man shall leave his own father and mother to cleave to his wife, which Tom hisself answered me with, when I made believe to put him off with why didn't he keep to his poor old widow mother,—wouldn't she be lonely without him? Tom's very smart with his answers, and says fine long words straight off. I likes smart men. It's a pleasure to hear 'em talk, even if you don't quite make it out. And won't I tell the girl next door that I have got leave to ask my young man to tea, just like any lady! 'Old maids is so spiteful!' says she. Is they, indeed? If a virtuous woman is far above rubies, as Solomon says, what's the value of a wise man as knows her when he sees her? Too high to be very common, I'm thinkin, and that's why Missis never came across him!"

CHAPTER VI.

IBYL had been out for a walk before dinner. She came home half an hour late, and looked as if she had been walking very fast. And when Elizabeth innocently asked her, where she had been, she only answered by the pert inquiry, "Where do you suppose?" But Sibyl got up and kissed her sister the very next moment, and Philip Lewis thought what a sweet nature it must be, that was so very prompt to atone!

Sibyl and Dora spent the evening together. They often did. Sibyl practiced her music and Dora read poetry, and they both carried on an interjectional sort of conversation. But this afternoon, Sibyl was self-absorbed, and answered "Yes" and "No," as if she scarcely heard what her cousin said.

"Sibyl, I have written a poem, which I have not shown you yet," said Dora.

"Have you, dear?" she replied, her fingers wandering over the notes of the piano in a way very different from her usual crisp and brilliant execution.

" And I have sent it to the West-End Magazine, and I expect an answer by the last post to-night ; " Dora went on. " I think they will take it this time, Sibyl."

" If they are wise, dear," she replied.

" You don't ask me to show it to you," observed Dora, wistfully.

" I was just thinking how naughty it was of you to send it away without doing so," responded Sibyl.

" But I've kept a copy," said Dora triumphantly. I'll read it aloud to you ; for if you tried to puzzle through my writing, it would lose all its beauty. It is called 'A Broken Idol,' and I do think it is the best piece I ever wrote ; " she added, wistfully, and then began to read :

> " You are the shadow of a vanished form,
>   Your simple majesty to me is more
>   Than aught else of earth's beauty ; calling back
>   The face that smiled in dreams I dream no more !
>
> " Methinks that in my heart you soon might stand,
>   Close to the spot whereon the other stood.
>   That idol, broken now ! Ah, many gods
>   Of many hearts are only gilded wood !
>
> " You are so like ! I think I might forget
>   You are not she, that age has touched my brow,
>   Only I see the glances that I won
>   You shyly turn upon my grandson now.
>
> " And so I recollect that all is changed.
>   Mine are October days, yours, laughing June ;
>   At the grave's door I chant my psalm ; you sit
>   And sing youth's old song to your own sweet tune.

> " Be true to him who joins his voice with yours ;
>   Give him a holy treasure in your name.
>   Yet did he know what I know, he would fear
>   Lest it should prove the spirit were the same ! "

" What do you think of it ? " the poet asked, anxiously.

" Oh, it is very beautiful ! " said Sibyl.

" I don't think you care for it," sighed poor Dora.

" I'm sure I do," said Sibyl, pettishly.

" Don't I say it is very beautiful ?   If you will not believe me, how am I to convince you ? "

Dora said no more.   Sibyl was not thinking of her or her poetry just then ; that was all.   But why was there not something in it so sweet and so burning as to compel her to listen?   The trees were growing and the beasts were feeding when Orpheus began to play, but then they left off to follow him !

Dora lay back on the sofa and looked up at the bit of grayish blue sky which she could see between the window curtains, and it came to her with a great pang,—one of those pangs which are always birth-pangs—that her powers of expression represented the whirl of emotion within her, much as that little bit of grayish sky represented the glorious firmament, with its golden dawns and its opal sunsets.   The poor little orphan had within her a real spark of that creative spirit which foresaw the swift rivers and the mighty hills, while yet the earth was without form and void.   She had never seen a mountain, but she knew more about them than Philip Lewis, who was born among them. She had only seen the sea twice, off Brighton, but she knew that it has a secret, like a dumb man who goes moaning what he cannot articulate and sometimes rises in wrath because people cannot understand! Dora felt a longing in her heart for something—she sometimes thought it was to be a poet. She felt something leap within her to hear the praises of the dead who left words and works to live after them. Oh how hard it was to find, that not even Sibyl could feel interest in her poor work! Not even Sibyl—generally so full of sympathy! Poor Dora! her genius had not yet that insight which often refuses to take things at their own valuation. Sibyl found sweet words and tender tones very easy, generally, and used them as freely and disastrously as paper-money circulates in a country which has little bullion. But there are moods when even sweet words cost something, and Sibyl could not afford them then. Poor Dora! It is certainly trying to find a stone where we expected bread; but the worst part of the trial, is our own folly in looking for a loaf in a quarry!

But, like all geniuses (and there are many more geniuses than the world hears of), Dora caught one sweet blossom from the prickly bed where her heart had fallen. "There must be so many more who try and fail like me!" she thought. "So many who mean so much and can give out so little! It must come to something, somehow, for God is never wasteful."

She lay there quietly, and Sibyl went on with her crooning music, and Hester entered with a bound, which landed her in the easy-chair.

"So, somebody has a sweetheart!" she exclaimed.

"What do you mean?" cried Sibyl, starting up, with a vivid flush upon her face.

"Popps—the carpenter—he is down in the kitchen and Lizzie is talking to him. She has just been telling me all about it."

"What a ridiculous thing!" said Sibyl, sitting down; "the idea of your coming in crying out about that. Just like you! And did I not always say there would be some such end to Popps! Elizabeth spoiled her. The only way to keep these girls in order is to keep them in their place!"

"Some such end?" laughed Hester. "Why, you don't know how pleased Lizzie is. The sweetheart is to have permission to take tea in the kitchen, tomorrow."

"Well, I never heard of such a thing!" Sibyl exclaimed in scorn. "One would suppose the girl was at home! And what impudence of her to dare to tell about a beau! And he coming to tea, using the tea and sugar and bread and butter! Who else allows such goings-on?"

"Is not a servant a woman?" asked Hester.

"A servant is a servant," said Sibyl. "If you or I were governesses, Hester, do you suppose we should get such indulgences?"

" Perhaps not ; but we should be very glad if we did," returned the other.

" We shall not find our own lives so easy that we need to lay them down to be trodden under foot by other people; " Sibyl went on.

" O, Sibyl ! never mind that just now," Hester said, with a laugh. " Here's a bit of sunshine come into the house to-day. Don't talk about the rain that may come to-morrow ! "

" Sunshine, indeed ! " scoffed Sibyl. " Not sunshine for you ! What has it to do with you, I should like to know ? "

" I don't know," said Hester ! " Perhaps nothing has anything to do with any of us. I suppose it need not affect us, if every face but our own was bathed in tears, and the very leaves came out black on the trees ! "

" And I am not so sure it is sunshine for anybody," Sibyl pursued. " The carpenter's man gets a pound or two a week, I suppose. And they'll have a dozen children, and he'll take to ill-using his wife, and getting tipsy, or else he'll have an accident, and she'll have to go out charing, instead of living in a nice house and having good meals and ten pounds a year to spend all on herself. Elizabeth ought to be ashamed to encourage such madness. If she really wishes the girl well, she ought to tell her that she can't stay here unless she gives up all such folly; and if she won't, let her go, and ten chances to one, she'd have to leave the neighborhood, and that would put an end to it naturally."

"Do you think 'out of sight' is sure to be 'out of mind,' Sibyl?" asked Dora, rather sadly.

"With these common people, yes;" said the young lady. "Is it likely the young fellow would go about by himself, and stand mute at the corner of the street, when there were a dozen girls better than Popps to speak to? What can he see in Popps? What is there in her for him to see? What do you suppose they can talk about together? Just their wages, and their savings and their work, and perhaps the Sunday's text."

"True enough," said Dora; "their souls are shut in such thick husks of ignorance, that they cannot get near each other; and how can there be tender love without soul-fellowship?"

"Well, I don't know," observed Hester; "but it seems to me that one's wages and savings, not to say one's work, and the text, are as good topics as the last new novel, and the latest song, and the choicest scandal, and everybody's income except one's own. And how should you like to hear an aristocrat speak of you and your grade, as you are speaking of Popps and hers, Sibyl?"

"Oh, that is quite different!" said Dora. "Given a certain elevation, and all mankind are equal."

"I can't think how you can talk such nonsense, Hester," cried Sibyl, in indignation. "Put it to this simple test: what is there about me that would prevent me from marrying a nobleman? Don't I know how to dress myself if I had the means? Don't I know how to behave? But just fancy me marrying this carpenter!"

" Well, I should like to see it from the nobleman's stand-point," said Hester.

" I never before knew that you worshipped mere rank," remarked Dora; with an emphasis signifying that Hester had hitheito held one position in her good opinion, but had now forfeited it.

" I don't, I don't!" she protested eagerly; "but I believe there is only one equality by which you can make any rule, and that is universal human nature, which is the one stratum running under all sorts of cultivation."

" But you set up rank as something above admitting genius, or learning, or energy;" said Dora.

" Or beauty, or grace, or refinement!" cried Sibyl.

" It does not matter what I set up," answered Hester, with a quiet laugh; " for it admits them every day, if well balanced by the safe ballast of wealth. But as far as I can see, it makes as particular exception in their favor as Sibyl would, if, out of marked love for some individual merit, she married a working-man."

" Don't use such absurd illustrations!" sneered Sibyl, with a toss of her head.

" Here comes Lizzie!" said Hester, who was sitting opposite the open door, and could see the stair-case—" Lizzie with some chrysanthemums in her right hand and a letter in her left."

" The chrysanthemums for myself—the letter for

Dora," explained Lizzie, entering, and handing the packet. "See! It is lucky to be kind to a young courting couple. Moxon has brought these for Popps. I went down stairs before she expected me, and I heard her saying, 'Offer them to the Missis, Tom. A flower is good enough to give anybody.' So Tom said, would I be kind enough to accept them— and I said I was only too happy; flowers being very welcome in London houses at this dull season : but I added, ' Popps must have one or two,' so I put a few into the kitchen spill-holder, and here are the rest."

Dora, who had opened her letter, now hurried out of the room.

"Moxom has just gone," Elizabeth went on. "He is so grateful for the permitted fortnightly visit. 'It does seem rather hard to only meet in the dark streets and all sorts o' weather,' he says; 'but it's what most of us has to do, and it's to be hoped that those who meet with such kindness as yours, will deserve it, ma'am.' And so I've got over the first proposal of marriage that ever I had any responsibility about ! "

"I'm sorry you show yourself so simple, Elizabeth," said Sibyl.

"If a sweetheart of yours asked Lizzie's good graces, you would like her to deny them, wouldn't you ? " asked Hester.

"It will be time enough for you to talk about my sweethearts, when you see them," said Sibyl, tartly ; "nor do I suppose they will care for anybody's good graces but my own ! "

"Is there anything the matter with Dora?" asked Elizabeth—"She hurried out of the room so abruptly."

"She had a letter, hadn't she?" said Sibyl, carelessly. "Depend on it, it was from the editor, respecting a poem. She has been sending some verses to the West-End Magazine. Of course, they won't take them."

"Why not?" asked Hester. "Have you seen them?"

"She read them to me," Sibyl answered; "but I was not in the humor to be appreciative. I don't think they were good."

"We had better go down to supper now," said Lizzie. "Call Dora, Hester."

Hester went to her chamber and knocked at the door. There was no answer; so presently she opened it gently, to see if her cousin were there. The room was in total darkness.

"Dora," she said, "are you here, dear? It is supper-time."

"I don't want any supper," replied the girl, in a voice that was peevish with the tears that choked it.

"Was that a letter from an editor?" Hester asked, groping toward the couch whence the answer came.

"Yes," said Dora, shortly. "There was no need to ask what it was about!"

"I'm so sorry, dear," Hester whispered, bending over her. "But think how rich you are compared with me! I can't be rejected, because I can't write, darling. If I could write or sing, Dora, I would be most happy to write or sing for myself, if other people did not care to hear me. Then I think they would listen by and bye, or else be very sorry when it was too late!"

There was a stifled sob among the pillows. Hester bent down hurriedly and the cheek that she kissed was wet. She could not have spoken so in the light.

Meantime Elizabeth lingered in the drawing-room behind both her sisters. She took her Bible from her pocket, and then she drew towards her the glass with the chrysanthemums, and her fingers hovered over them to select the smallest. It was a tiny white flower. Hastily she drew it out and laying it between the leaves of the Holy Book, pressed to the clasps, and went her way down stairs to rejoin the others in the dining-room. It was a relic of a Happiness which God had let her help to perfect. That was something to remember!

She did not know that she had laid the blossom on the words,

" Inasmuch as ye have done it unto one the least of these, my brethren, ye have done it unto me."

CHAPTER VII.

ESTER found it necessary to go into Sibyl's room before she retired for the night. Her sister was there, standing before the mirror, gazing at something in her toilet-drawer. But she shut it with a jerk when she heard Hester's step.

Hester's errand took her to the wardrobe. Sibyl sat down on the bed and watched her. Sibyl was not undressed, but she had taken down her hair, kicked off her shoes, which lay at right angles in the middle of the apartment, and donned a cashmere toilet-jacket, to which Hester had a particular objection, because it had a false color—magenta—and because it had always a greasy mark round the neck, where Sibyl's locks strayed during the half hours that she regularly trifled away every night and morning.

"Doesn't it seem hard that Popps should have her ridiculous proposals, while we have none, Hester?" Sibyl said, at last; throwing herself back on the pillow.

"It is a very good proposal for Popps," answered Hester ; "so perhaps if you had one as fitting to you, you would call it ridiculous too, and be as discontented as ever."

"I suppose you would call it a fitting proposal for me, if Mr. Lewis made me an offer?" Sibyl remarked. "And I suppose it would be. I believe Miss Winter, opposite, is setting her cap at him, and she has some money of her own, too. But he would never look at her. At least, not if he could get anybody else to look at him. I don't believe he has noticed her existence."

"And she may be as unconscious of his;" put in Hester.

"She will have a humdrum time of it whoever she may be—the woman who marries Mr. Lewis;" Sibyl went on. "He has his mother to look after, and he could not make much money out of his profession for years and years to come. Still I suppose it would be better than to be a governess (with a sigh) ; and I believe Mr. Lewis would make me an offer if I chose. Somebody one doesn't care for, is sure to be ready enough! Heigho! Hester, I don't think I'd care to marry at all, if I had a thousand a year!"

"Well, if we're to mix money matters in such a question," said Hester, impatiently ; "then I think an old maid is happiest when she has her own living to earn."

Sibyl did not seem to notice this remark. "I could be quite happy if I could go about and have

4*

plenty of company, and all sorts of nice things to wear," she said : "and if I could do that, without having somebody dictating to me, and believing me to be under his rule, I should like it all the better. But I shall never get anything nice unless I marry. And although there must be so many good chances in the world, they do not seem to come to me. There's that Mr. Willis ; it is very fine for him to be always coming here, talking to papa and looking at me. What is the good of that I wonder ?"

" I thought you said you hated him, and thought him a perfect bore," interrupted Hester.

" I don't care for him, but his share in his father's business can't be worth less than sixteen hundred a year. If he made me an offer, I don't suppose I should refuse it, and I daresay I should get on with him as well as with anybody. I should like him for the comforts he had brought me. Love in a cottage isn't my style, Hester. It would soon wear out my temper and my looks, and they are all that any man would care for. Who would even look twice at me Hester ?"

There was just a touch of genuine sadness in her last words.

" O, Hester," she said, presently ; " I could be so good, if I had but half the chance that some girls have ! If we had been but a little better off, so that I might have gone into society, where some tolerable man with a good income might have taken a fancy to me ! I should have made him a good wife—as good as most—

as good as he'd deserve. And I would have had you
to stay with me, and taken you about, till I had got
you off, too. And everybody would have said that I
was a most excellent woman. And yet I should not
be really better than I shall be now. There's my
music," she continued ; " if I could be a great singer
or a first-class performer, earning plenty of money
pretty easily, and everybody making a fuss over me,
I'm sure I should not want to give it up to be some
nobody's wife ; to look after his house, and to think of
nothing but him. But I shall never be anything particularly clever. I've had all my trouble for nothing,
apparently. Just to be a teacher, traipsing through
the streets from one house to another, and invited to
parties to play, when nobody else is inclined ! And
all for about a hundred pounds a year, or very little
more ! Not enough for one set of enjoyments, and too
much for another. For if I can't have really good
clothes to wear, and servants to keep my house in
order, I think I would rather live in one room in some
place where I needn't bother to be tidy ! "

" Well, it is a pity you don't count even your music
a blessing, after all the money, and all your devotion
to it ; so that father and Dora and even Lizzie seem to
think, that it is quite a grand sacrifice if you ever give
an hour to anything else," said Hester. She spoke bitterly. Sibyl's confidences always embittered Hester.
They forced her to feel that her estimate of her sister
was not uncharitable. And this was the sympathetic,
romantic artistic nature ! Hester was ready to shake

the dust off her feet at a world, where such base coin
passed current! Poor Hester! too angry with her
short-sighted fellow mortals to remember that her
Father in Heaven had provided a special balm for her
special pain, by the promise of an everlasting home in
a kingdom, where the simplest shall be so wise, that
the "vile person shall no more be called liberal, nor
the churl said to be bountiful·!"

CHAPTER VIII.

THE NAIL ON THE FLOOR.

 LONDON kitchen, even on a bright June day, is not a cheerful place, much less so in November, when scarcely the faintest ray of sunshine can struggle through its depths, and even the poor window-plants have ceased their struggle with adverse circumstances, and withdrawn their shadowy screen from the wearisome panorama of muddy feet.

But a light honest heart makes brightness and beauty about it. And, after all, brightness and beauty are but comparative things. Angels who know the crystal sea and golden city may pity the fairest sunset landscape that ever moved mortal poet to tears; while that same poet smiles half in contempt at poor Popps, enraptured with her shining covers and spotless plates and dishes, with the scarlet print iron-holder, bought the night before in Leather Lane, and with her whole library, a gilt-edged Bible and Bunyan's Progress, and about half a dozen smaller volumes all ranged along the window-sill. Popps usually kept the books in paper covers, but to-day they appeared in their native glory of scarlet and blue. "What's the good of having things nice, if you don't show them when it is worth while?" soliloquized Popps, as she stripped them. "And if they're too good for Tom to touch, then who's to ever touch 'em, I want to know?"

Popps had permission to take some of a simple tea-cake with which Elizabeth usually regaled the family on Sundays. But she could not be satisfied to be such a very passive party to the entertainment of her Tom. So she had laid out sixpence in the purchase of six half-penny bunns and three tiny slips of short-bread. And so the tea was set on the kitchen-table at four o'clock.

Tom Moxon was the first to arrive. He had tried to be so, since there are some meetings which are most agreeable when unwitnessed. Tom was a slight young man; dark, with a pale strongly marked countenance, and deep set gray eyes; and instead of making himself look common and snobbish in ill-fitting black, his Sunday garments, in make and material, were such as would afterwards suit his working-day duties. Tom had been the cleverest scholar in the National School, and they had wished him to become a pupil-teacher, but that career had sides which did not suit the lad's taste. Now Tom Moxon belonged to a Mechanics' Institution, and had books from the library. And there was more than one girl in the parish who set it down as a new instance of man's bad taste, when Mrs. Moxon spread it about, that "her Tom was as good as settled with Elizabeth Popps, at Mr. Capel's."

Mrs. Edwardes was not long after Tom. His face lengthened a little when she appeared, but Tom had an unsophisticated notion that Popps would think the better of him for civility to a poor elderly woman. So he set a chair for her close to the fire, and politely waited to take her bonnet and shawl, when she unfastened them.

"We'll have tea directly," said Popps, bustling; "for we might as well have it in peace before they want their'n. Will you bring up your chair, Mrs. Edwardes, or will you like to sit where you are, mum?"

"Oh, I'll bring in my chair!" answered the visitor, and rose, and Tom gallantly brought it in for her.

"Well, they're nice lookin' visitors, so they are," thought Popps, slyly glancing at them, while she measured out the tea. "Tom looks like a working-man, and a gentleman at once. A precious deal more like that last, than them little whipper-snappers that pass here of a Sunday afternoon in their tail-coats and beaver tiles, and their bits of brass chains and cigars. And as for Mrs. Edwardes, there's something very genteel about her. It's a good gown she's got on, though I'll warrant it's worn out it's price and that collar of her's u'd be very pretty, if it were a bit fresher, like. If I'd such a bit of good lace, I'd not grudge washin' of it. Well, I hope I shan't show off any bad habits. I've always tried to notice how the young ladies does at table; but sitting by one's self, one's werry apt to get like a greedy pig."

"I saw some of the family after I parted from you this morning, Bessie," said Tom. "They were just coming along Holborn as I turned out of Brownlow street ; the youngest Miss Capel, and little Miss, the cousin and the flashy one, along with the gentleman that's just come into the business. If he is sweet on her, he needn't be, I'm thinking, Bessie."

"Why not ?" asked Popps, while Mrs. Edwardes observed :

"Flashy is not a nice word to describe a young lady."

"Well, I mean she's a dashing girl, and what ninety-nine men out of a hundred would call a regular beauty."

"And don't you ?" asked Popps, happily confident of a negative answer.

"No I don't. I can see nothing in a face except what it stands for. Give me a good woman, an' I know she'll grow better looking every year. But I wouldn't trust that second Miss Capel—no, I wouldn't take her oath, where I'd take half a word from some women." This with a look which pointed the compliment.

"Don't talk about swearing, if you please, Tom," said Popps, primly.

"I don't think you have any right to pronounce such judgments," remarked Mrs. Edwardes, quite earnestly. "What reason have you to say such things of Miss Sibyl?"

"We've all a right to our own opinions, I think ma'am," Tom answered civilly; "but nobody need take 'em for more than they are worth. He must be an uncommonly poor friend that would be set against anybody by what another said."

"But people oughtn't to speak evil without reasons for it," said Popps; "and then they should tell the reasons, and then it ain't evil, it's truth."

"Very well, Bess," returned the young man; "you know I've always said the same of your second young lady, having no reason, but my own judgment. But yesterday I was on a job, mending the seats in St. James' Park. You know what a day it was; fog, not thick, but as yellow as a guinea, and the ground under your foot like a sponge not wrung out."

"I hope you had on that nice comforter I gave you, and didn't play any fool's tricks of sitting on the grass," put in Popps.

Tom went on without heeding this parenthetical solicitude. "There was nobody in the Park, to speak of, and all of a sudden I saw a young lady coming down the walk. What made me notice her was her walking so slow for such a day. She'd passed me before I saw her, and when she'd got to the end, she turned back, and then who should she be but this here dashing Miss Capel."

"Presently a gentleman came petting across the grass. A great, tall, swell fellow, and he went up be-

hind her, and overtook her just behind me. And
' How do ye do?' says he. And she gave a little cry,
quite as if she was startled, like, and, says she; ' Isn't
it dreadful on this damp path, but I've been to Pam-
lico and came across as my nearest way home,' and
then went pattering along as if she grudged putting
her feet upon the gravel. And he went with her."

"Did she see you, Tom?" asked Popps.

"See me!" echoed Tom, indignantly; "Why
she's the sort that would as soon notice a tree from
another like it, as a working man!"

"Ah, so she is," Popps assented. "It's wonderful how soon you make people out, Tom. You know
her better than me as lives in the same house. Mrs.
Edwardes, you don't seem enjoying of your tea; will
you try a bunn?"

"Thank you, but I can't take any more," said
Mrs. Edwardes, and pushed her chair a little back
from the table. "Still I don't think you need make
so much out of the little incident in the Park, Mr.
Moxon. Of course the gentleman was a friend. Perhaps more."

"An' as for her making believe she wasn't waiting
for him; why, it was only natural, considering," rea-
soned Popps. "Not as I like Miss Sibyl a bit, but
I likes to make all the excuses I can for folks ; 'cause
then I can judge 'em pretty smart when I can't make
any more!"

"Yes; I know all that, and I'd be the last to
think evil o' some people," said Tom. "If I was to

see the youngest Miss Capel doing the queerest looking action, I'd believe she had good reasons for it. She has an honest face."

"You like her, do you?" asked Popps. "Well, I daresay she's good enough, but Miss Lizzie for my money, all the days in the year!"

"Miss Lizzie would never do even a queer-looking thing," returned Tom. "Miss Lizzie's a real good lady, but there's some bits of duty in life that she'd never see to be her duty. It would be easier for her to go on bearing burdens herself, when it would be the right thing to throw them off. The young one is made for hard work. There's the same look on her face that I've seen on the old men who come to our meetings who were among the first to agitate for Reform and Repeal. She's got the eyes that see the root as well as the plant. As for this Miss Sibyl, I don't want to think evil of her either. She's just trying to serve herself in her own way, and if you put it to her fair, I don't believe she'd deny it. She thinks everybody's doing the same, and she's pretty near right for that matter. Only what makes me bitter against her is, that if she was a servant gal, she'd be called a regular bad one, and turned off without a character; but because she's a young lady she's only attractive and beautiful and all the rest of it. You'll find that sort of inconsistency as strong in religious people as anybody else, and its these ways that makes infidels of ever so many fine honest fellows. There's some such that work at our place and they say to me,

'Moxon, can you deny that nearly all your rich parsons are friendly enough with rich people, that they'd be always nagging at if they were poor. They're always pitching into the vices that we're likely to get into,' says they, ' but how often do they say anything about hypocrisy and insolence, and screwing down the workman to the lowest farthing, so that he can't help himself in any pinch, and then glorifying themselves by giving him the rest of his just earnings as a heavenly charity!' 'If this is religion,' says one of 'em —and he's a chap with a weak hand, and keeps a a half-idiot brother off less than full wages—" if this is religion, Tom, I'm sure there's something better somewhere.' "

"But then it ain't," said Popps.

" But how are they to know that? It's what they so often find when they go to look for it."

" Haven't they Bibles, and can't they read?" asked Popps, promptly.

Tom shook his head. "That they can," he answered ; " but they've had it drilled into them that it's all on the rich folks' side, and when you've once had a wrong meaning set to words, it's hard to read them over to any other tune. I think there's some that turns round fiercest of all, and says they don't believe in a God, while all the time it's the libels on him that they can't abide ; and there's others that go to hear such speechify, although they don't half like their bitter railing at what they don't know anything about, except by the ugly mask that men have put over it,—yet they do want to hear bits of justice and truth or what seem like 'em."

"Well, I'm satisfied with what I find in the Bible," said Popps.

"So they be, but they can't see it all yet," Tom returned.

"Perhaps they've some sins between it and them," said Popps. "Perhaps the Bible says, 'Give up something,' that they don't want to give up."

"Yes, that's it," Tom assented ; "but then according as they've had it preached to them the ' Give up' is all on their side, and not a bit on t'other, and they say at once, ' that is not fair."

"Well, it seems to me that they must be werry blind if they can't see that the Bible's always a-taking their part against tyrants and oppressors," Popps returned. "Why just look at Moses and the children of Israel ! "

"They're told they must look at that in a spiritual sense," said Tom ; "meaning the deliverance from sin."

"Well, it do stand for that too, most beautiful," answered Popps. "But still God did tell Moses to bring the people out of their bondage. So he must have meant it was right. 'Tisn't likely he'd do evil to make good in a spiritual sense. You'll not get a sound kernel out of a rotten shell ! "

"What do you think of all these matters, Mrs. Edwardes ? " asked Tom ; thinking that she had sat in silence too long.

She was sitting with her face towards the window. The gas had just been lit in the street, and its yellow glare fell on her white countenance, and out of the lights and shadows thus cast on the pinched features, developed a curious expression of pain and terror. She half started to find herself addressed, and nervously wrung her hands, as she replied :

"Oh, I don't know ! It's hard to believe, but it's worse to doubt. Whether the Bible is true or not, they're the happiest that keeps to it. You may fancy you have got enough light in your own soul to guide your steps, but when you drop the Bible, you find it all came from there, little as you thought it, and it soon dies out by itself."

" She's been a well-brought up woman," concluded shrewd Tom ; and looked at her with increased interest ; but she had changed her position and her face was in total darkness now.

"We're in hopes you'll come to chapel with us to-night, Mrs. Edwardes," said Popps. " I think you'd be sure to like our minister. He's such a nice old gentleman."

There was just a moment's pause.

" Thank you, but I cannot go to-night," said Mrs. Edwardes. " I want to get home as early as I can."

" But service is over a little after eight," pleaded Popps. " We go in at half-past six. Do come. It will be so companionable like, won't it, Tom ?" appealing for his concurrence in the invitation, in case Mrs. Edwardes was refusing in good-natured observance of the adage, that "two are company and three are none."

"Oh, Mrs. Edwardes will come!" said Tom. It's not a close place, although it's crowded. My mother, who has asthma ever so bad, goes regularly and never takes any harm."

"It's very good of you to ask me," replied the charwoman, suddenly rising; "but I can't come—it's no use, I can't come."

There was something in her manner which checked all further petition.

"Well, I must go and see after our teas," said Popps. "You'll keep Tom company till I come back, at any rate, Mrs. Edwardes."

"Oh, yes; I can do that," replied the other, sitting down again, and relapsing into her usual indifferent manner.

Popps stirred the fire into a cheerful blaze, and thriftily observing, that they could talk by that as well as by candle-light, left them to themselves. Tom stole many a glance at his companion. She sat before the fire, motionless, with her hands folded in her lap. Tom looked at her face, and he had an idea that he did not quite like it—that he should have liked it less, if he had seen it before it was faded and lined; but it was such a worn, defeated face now that it seemed cruel to criticise it.

Tom did not speak. He could be fluent enough with his energetic kindly Bessie. But as is often the case with quick close observers, his keen knowledge (wherever sympathy was lacking), checked all show of outward sociability. Nor did Mrs. Edwardes speak. So that they had not exchanged a word when Popps returned, and then it was time for her and Tom to start for chapel. Mrs. Edwardes put on her bonnet, and went off first. As she passed the office-window she looked in and saw the gas was turned on, and two people were standing at the desk, bending over a great book. She actually stood still and peered in to see who they were, and what they were doing. It was Philip Lewis and Sibyl, and the book was a Bible, and they seemed searching references.

"False! false!" she groaned. "The treachery is in the blood! 'The fathers have eaten sour grapes, and the childrens' teeth are set on edge.'" And she suddenly turned, and fled down the street with a wild speed, at strange variance with her usual heavy step.

"She's a queer body, isn't she—that Mrs. Edwardes?" said Popps, cheerfully, linking her arm in Tom's.

"That she is," he assented, "there's more in her than meets the eye. And I don't know if we should like her better if we could see it all. She's turned some sharp corners in her time, I reckon."

Mrs. Edwardes went home. She lived in the back attic of a large old house in a blind alley near Hatton Garden. It was the only dwelling-house among half a dozen warehouses. A very dismal house—where the door always swung ajar—because there was nothing within to tempt the meanest thief of that squalid neighborhood. A very quiet house ; many of the rooms having fallen to such depths of decay, that they were left to the tenancy of rats and spiders—and to such gloomy abodes, young married couples, with cheerful swarms of children, do not come. The bachelor-landlord, a miser, lived in the parlors, with two black cats and a pet ferret. The habitable part of the first floor was used by two widows who adhered to the place for the sake of some parochial dole. And the front attic belonged to a man employed in the dissecting-room of a metropolitan college. He took tea with the widows occasionally, but with none of this lively household was Mrs. Edwardes on similar terms of intimacy. She came in and went out, and paid her rent. She might have died in her top chamber, and unless her employers had inquired for her, nobody would have missed her for days. Not one of the other inmates had entered her room since she rented it. Nobody but herself knew how black were the carpetless boards ; how thin and poor the bed upon the floor ! Nobody saw how her farthing rushlight guttered over the filthy candlestick, and befouled a cracked table that was foul enough already. And she never noticed. It was wonderful how she could come forth neat and tidy from such a wretched hole. She must be so, if she was to be employed at all, but accepted no such necessity for any such care over her room. There are women who will make comfort and beauty in a pauper ward, or a convict's cell. There are women whose hopes and energies are so vital that they will spring in life's saddest places, and make them fair and endurable ; being in themselves the best pledge of a better life, where the wrong will grow right, and the crooked straight. How could immortality mean anything to this poor woman, while her own soul seemed dead within her?

She sat down. The only seat was a chair without a back, which she never missed ; her usual attitude being to lean on the table and rest her head in her hands.

It was the first time she had made a visit for a long while, for years and years. And what good had it done her? There were horrors in her heart that long seemed dead, yet they could have been but benumbed, for she felt them stirring now. She thought she had forgotten so much. That she had drank such a deadly draught of monotonous solitude, that her soul might go to her grave in its dull opiate calm. But no !

She had worked one wild fierce wickedness in her life. That was long ago now, and when she herself and all around, had been so different that of late the memory of the sin came to her but vaguely ; almost as the believers in transmigration may fancy a sheep might dream of the carcase it tore when it was a blood-thirsty tiger. She had sowed the wind and reaped the whirlwind, and she and her sin had seemed alike dead and lost. Once or twice, even in that wretched room, she had stood at the window looking at the stars, and thinking that she only had suffered

for her own crime, and that there was something in
her that did not shrink even from the unknown
torments of the revolving wheel of eternity. She
had tested herself with a long pondered test, and she
had not seemed to break in that trial. Fool! fool!
She could see it all now! What was it in her that
had craved the ordeal? Can the corpse ask the
galvanic battery to prove how useless it is? It was
the lingering life in her that had sought the electric
touch, and lo, before she was aware, she was once
more a moving woman in an acting world!

And her sin lived too! It looked up and smiled,
not a bit changed, and only loathsome and horrid now,
because she knew what it all meant. Mrs. Edwardes
sprang from her chair and paced the room with such
fierce steps, that the rats raced down the crumbling
walls, and startled the windows from their evening
nap.

She went to the window and looked out. There
was a thick fog in the air, and as she leaned from the
window, she could not see the dead wall that she
could almost reach with her hand, nor yet the pavement of the yard below. She knew that pavement
well enough, and the coping over the basement-
window. There was a story that when the house had
been a well-to do family mansion a little child had
tumbled from this very window, dashed against that
coping, and laid a stark corpse on the flags below. It
would be but the deed of a moment, and the fog
seemed mercifully to veil the horror of it. If there

was a God, surely she had lost him already! She leaned out breathless. And a church clock chimed through the mist. Surely something from within the room touched her. She turned with glaring eyes. Nobody was there, but her gown was certainly pulled. Yes—only by a nail sticking out of the floor! She stooped to release it. The spell was broken.

" Misery here or misery there," she murmured, as she went back to the table ; " so I'll wait and see it through."

And at that very moment in a church scarcely a stone's throw off, Lizzie and Hester Capel, looking over one hymn-book, were singing

" Depth of mercy, can there be
Mercy still reserved for me ?"

CHAPTER IX.

WHAT NEXT ?

LIFE went on quietly enough in the old brown house in the Queen's Road. Every week brought a letter with the Ribbock postmark, and every week took away one with the Ribbock address. Philip Lewis told the folks at home all the news, how well he got on in the office, what slight business acquaintances he made, what friends visited the family, what lectures he went to hear, how he had settled himself under the minister at Bracket Court, thinking he might as well accept the instructions of his old preacher's friend for one service on Sunday, since some of the household generally gave him an invitation for the other—in short, he told them everything except what gave significance and soul to all—that he was in love with Sibyl Capel.

Did he know it? Perhaps not as soon as did Sibyl and Hester. Sibyl knew it from the beginning. In short it was only what she had expected. Hester knew that it was among the possibilities which her sister had mooted to herself, before the stranger arrived. Sibyl had observed how nice it would be to

have a beau so circumstanced that he could be useful
and agreeable for a long time, without any necessity
to make a fool of himself and spoil everything. Marriage with a man in Philip's position might be a necessary evil at last, but let it be kept off as long as
possible. So Hester knew that her sister's snares
were set, and she had to stand by and watch the game
step into them.

Anything will do for a man to fall in love with!
It is the painful perennial truth of that story of
Pygmalion and his statue, which makes nearly every
modern poet give us some version of it.

Just a point where two natures touch, and then,
the barer the one is, only the more room it seems for
the other's fancy to do its sweet and wonderful
work.

There was Sibyl's music ! Now there was a dumb
genius shut in Philip, and he felt that the noblest part
of him cried out in the poor straggling discordant
notes that ventured out under his fingers, during the
secret practicings, when he had pushed the mat
against the chink of his bedroom door, and stuffed his
pocket-handkerchief into the keyhole. And what a
burst of melody came from Sibyl's magic touch ! So
his poor logic concluded what a soul she must have !
What grand ideas, what tender emotions must be
there !

Don't laugh at him, you wise people, who know a
great deal of society, artistic, literary and musical.
You have been behind the scenes, and seen the strings

that move the puppets. And very likely you wish you had never gone there, and would give much to have back the old delusion ! And yet no ! It must be a poor soul, which having once seen the truth, would fain shrink back from it into the false.

He was but a commonplace young man who tried to keep the fifth commandment, and wished to get on in the world, and had very strict notions of his own narrow groove. Particularly about womanly proprieties and how young women ought not to be out alone after certain hours, or to go near sundry localities ; what books they should not read, how neat they should be, and how regardful of all the beauties of existence. He was prone to lay down little rules which would fetter all true womanliness, to put the letter above the spirit, to forget the dissimulations and evasions and traditional renderings, which always come in to keep such legal regulations, and in the very keeping to defeat them.

He did not like clever women ; he did not like masculine women ; and he gave that name to any who did man's duty when God set it for them. He liked to see woman in her true place—at the domestic hearth, living for her husband, training her children. He liked woman as the teacher of the young, the consoler of the sorrowful, the ministrant to the sick and dying.

Such whole truths in themselves—such half truths as he uttered them ! Especially as he sat and looked at Sibyl while he spoke.

His was a good honest soul in its own small way. But it was not tall enough to look over the fences of its own narrow experience, and see the broad meadows beyond. His mother's virtues had been those that grow indoors, in those household economies and industries which patiently make the most of a little that was yet sufficient. Let women be like her, he dogmatized, and never asked himself why the same flowers do not flourish in all climates!

And how gracefully Sibyl did those little bits of household duty which rise to the surface! How adroitly she carved the fowl, which poor Lizzie, tired and nervous from a morning's fine ironing of ruffs and cuffs (two-thirds of them Sibyl's), was beginning to haggle. And how deftly she re-habited an old winter dress, paying as much for the fresh fashionable trimmings as did her sisters for the whole of their new serviceable linseys. Whenever a fit of depression made her glad of some satisfactory excuse for her melancholy, how tenderly she lamented over Dora's delicacy and sufferings! And nobody but Hester noticed that when her spirits were high, in anticipation of a promised party, she danced a jig and sang an opera air, in the room above that in which her cousin was then lying in the tortures of acute nervous headache. How she talked of every little duty before she did it. and after it was done, just because her treasure of good deeds was too small to part with one coin uncounted, and so got more credit for doing once

in her life such things as her sisters did twenty times
a day, and never thought about again !

The very shadow of the substance of domestic duty
was so foreign to her nature that it bored her dreadfully. She felt herself quite a martyr under it. But
the fact was, everything bored Sibyl. Admiration was
the bread of her life, and the old curse was upon her,
and she ate it in the sweat of her face. Some bores
were lighter than others and that was all. As in most
callings, so in hers, the slighter work often brought in
the larger remuneration. The comparatively pleasant
toil of evening dress, and an imposing performance on
the piano, and a little flippant talk, would bring in
the return of twenty compliments, and perhaps a hundred admiring glances ; while a week's enforced attention to unnoticeable neatnesses, and to the topmost
amenities of the family circle might barely win one
sweet speech from Philip. True, it might be sincere,
which would be a high make-weight with some women.
But not with Sibyl. What did it matter? it was only
the less florid for that. When she was a child, she
had always bought colored sweetmeats. They were
prettier to look at—never mind the poisons. But still
it was all a weariness to the flesh, and after her gayest
reunion, if Dora or Lizzie venture to ask how she had
enjoyed herself, her reply never went beyond a peevish " Pretty well."

And yet Philip Lewis sat and talked of the holi-
ness and beauty of woman's true mission—and looked
at Sibyl Capel !

5*

Hester's problems grew very hard that winter. She had set a high value on Philip's just word about her handwriting. If she could only have known it, it was better to her than all the compliments were to Sibyl. It was such a trifle ! But it always seems as if the best bits of happiness are made up into the smallest parcels. For days Hester went bravely in the strength of that just word. But gradually she found out all that it had not yet meant. All Philip's little theories could not shut his eyes to facts. He saw that all women did not walk in what he deemed the one fitting path. He did not deny that some such outsiders did good works and great deeds. And he was one of the first to give them a meed of pitying respect or respectful pity, much in the spirit with which kind people pay dearer for manufactures imperfectly made by the blind. But he shut his gates upon them nevertheless. If they did not walk only in his way, they might not walk there at all: They were not true women according to his notion. They might have only done the task that was fairly put into their hands, but according to his theory the genuine womanly nature would sooner have left the task undone. A woman's charm was tenderness, not strength, said he. And he could not perceive that they are the halves of the perfect whole, and that tenderness without strength is likely to keep as safe and sound as a kernel taken from a nut, and thrown in the gutter of Cheapside.

Strange, pitiful too, what bitter stress Hester's

heart put on Philip's want of insight! What did it matter? What was he, that his judgment should weigh aught? Ah, but we are human, human, and that means so much! It may be but a jeering finger, pointed in the street at a man who is straining soul and body for his country's sake, but the greatness of the nature will not save its pain ; only the pain will not scare it from its work. For the bitter word and the slighting smile mean more than the scoffers know. They come to the brave struggling heart as the latest note of that fierce yell which began with " Crucify him ! Crucify him ! "

And so the winter wore away. The only breaks in the quiet family life were Sibyl's attendance at two or three concerts or parties. The perusal of Dickens' Christmas number formed Hester's sole Christmas felicity. We all of us know such seasons. They seem like great blanks in our lives ; like long lanes whose end we may never reach. Time is surely running to waste, think the young children who always want to see a flower the day after the seed is sown. But the older folk fold their hands, and are content to wait. One or two events make us satisfied with monotony.

Evening after evening Sibyl toyed with her music, and Dora lay on the sofa ready to listen whenever she was in the mood to play, and Philip often found his way to the drawing-room, although for form's sake, he occasionally started for a walk, but generally found the weather not very agreeable and came home in remarkably good time. And, evening after evening, Lizzie and Hester sat in the parlor and worked. They got through their dressmaking and household mending, and actually treated themselves to some embroidery; long strips, which would absorb the leisure half hours of many months. And sometimes Hester used to wonder to herself what would come to pass before those embroidery strips were finished, or at any rate, worn out? Once she hinted as much to Lizzie.

"Why, nothing at all, I hope!" the elder sister answered, quickly. Change was a stranger to her, and Lizzie was shy of all strangers! "You shouldn't forebode about the future, Hetty."

"I'm not foreboding," defended Hetty. "May it not be something pleasant? Perhaps Sibyl will be married!" she added, half mischievously.

Popps put her head into the room. "There's a gentleman been asking for Master, Miss," she said. "I said he wasn't at home, but the young ladies was, but he wouldn't wait. He'll call again, he says. And he's left this. You'll see something on the back, Miss, he wrote it up agin the door-post. I think he'd ha' liked me to ha' gone into the office and got him a pen and ink, but I let him rummage out a pencil of his own, for there was all the coats and umberellers about; and how's one to know who's who, when there was a swell-looking young man only yesterday, as couldn't make no better excuse for his double knock than that he'd got some lucifers to sell, and it u'd help ·

him a trifle if I'd buy some. I told him them was small profits for a gentleman in kid gloves, which he'd better pawn and buy a broom and take a crossing, meaning no harm, but only recommendin' him to take a way that I know you can get a livin' honest ; when he turned ugly, and said a lot of impidence as made me precious glad I'd not laid on a penny with him, as I was half inclined at first."

"Then do you think this last caller was an impostor?" asked Hester, stretching out her hand for the card.

"Oh! how do I know?" returned Popps, cautiously; "gentlemen has different manners, but I doubts 'em when they call ye ' my pretty girl,' a-standing in the dark ! Not but what it u'd be worse in the light, true or not true. Takin' insults is no part of a servant's duty as ever I heard." And Popps departed.

Lizzie took the missive, and over her shoulder Hester read aloud :

"Mr. Anthony Fiske, of the old times at Ligney. See, I am not too vain to feel that I may need recalling. Don't be disgusted if I call in again late, when *un pere de famille* will surely be at home. I would not trouble *Mesdemoiselles*, your daughters."

"The old times at Ligney ! " said Lizzie. "Then he must have known mamma. That was where she died."

"Fiske? It's an English name, surely," commented Hester. "At any rate, he writes English well enough Why need he stick in those French words? "

"I'm sure I don't know," Lizzie answered. "But I don't think there's anything very nice in the larder; only the cold shoulder, and the cheese that I meant to toast if Mr. Drew or Mr. Drake came in with papa. But a friend one hasn't seen for twenty years is different. I'll send Popps for a pair of soles. She can fry them before she goes to bed, and they can be kept warm till midnight."

"I dare say Mr. Fiske won't come back to-night," said Hester, laughing. "He'll drop in upon some other dear old friend instead."

"Then papa can have one sole for his own supper, and the other will do cold for my dinner to-morrow," answered Lizzie.

CHAPTER X.

A GENTLEMAN AT LARGE.

IZZIE was still down stairs, on household cares intent, when Mr. Capel came in. It was rather early for him. He was one of those men who habitually pass the hat-rail unnoticed and saunter into the parlor, great coat, walking-stick and all, seeming to need half an hour's rest after any pedestrian exertions before they can put themselves into comfortable condition for in-doors society. But he caught instant sight of the card lying on the crimson table-cover.

"Mr. Antho—confound it! Here's a pretty go!"

Hester looked up in astonishment, but she was used to such ejaculations and only thought her father was vexed at missing his old acquaintance.

"You'll find a message on the back, father," she said; "he is even coming again to-night to take the chance of finding you at home."

Mr. Capel put off his hat, and set it on the table, whence Lizzie, coming in, removed it to the hall. And he walked up and down the hearth-rug while

Lizzie looked at him wistfully, thinking that however silent people may be, things and circumstances will speak. "The old times at Ligney"—what chords must that simple phrase have struck! About the sweet early married life, which Lizzie, bound by no single disenchanting fact, had imaged wholly out of her own pure ideal. Even about his own old self, for of course, papa had been very different then, all his little peculiarities and weaknesses had surely grown in the shock of the sad loss figured by the grave he left at Ligney. Lizzie had often thought that it would be better for him if he could break the spell and speak about this sorrow; but perhaps that thought was born only of her own fond longing to hear something of the dead mother in the far-off resting-place that none of her children had ever seen. She had fancied about that grave sometimes. It would surely be in some little Protestant burying-place, perhaps beside a Waldensian chapel. There might not be another stranger lying there. Not another grave where anybody went to water the flowers, or to hang a wreath of immortelles. Poor, lonely mother! well, if she was able to afford it, when she was an old woman—(not before, for it could never be in her father's days, and of course they were not to close till Lizzie was quite an old woman), then she would make a journey to Ligney and see the tomb, and get the Protestant pastor to promise that he would see it always kept neat and bright, if she sent a trifle for the gardener.

And Mr. Capel walked up and down the hearth-rug, musing.

What a pity it is for our comfort that the same circumstances which induce us to kill our own inner conscience, generally provide us with two or three exterior consciences, which in this very little world of ours, with its paltry divisions of Europe, Asia, Africa and America, are sure to find us out, and jostle against our beautiful equanimity! What railway accidents and shipwrecks and South American revolutions, and New York-editor-duels have been going on for more than twenty years, and this Anthony Fiske wandering to and fro on the face of the earth all that time, and had never found a permanent provision in any of them! We can have a pretty good idea why his call is so persistent. Purses will grow empty. And his stay at some London hotel may have outlived the temporary security that mine host sees in a carpet-bag. What will he look like, this Anthony Fiske? But he will not disgrace us in that wise unless he is indeed wofully changed. Ha! he had a card ready to leave, and we may engage the pencil he wrote with was gold, or at least, silver, with an onyx seal, and the Fiske crest. 'Tony always knew the world, and that was how he got the best of it. 'Tony would keep everything pleasant—at least as long as he could. And things must be very bad if 'Tony couldn't.

There was a light long airy double knock. " I dare say this is Mr. Fiske," said Hester.

" Here's the gentleman agin," said Popps, throwing open the parlor door.

The gentleman followed close at her heels.   He
meant to come in, and he meant to be very welcome,
and he meant to feel so, and he was not going to permit any complication or delay that should in the least
damage the dear self-delusion.

"My dear old Fred—once more!" and Mr. Capel's hand was seized and shaken with an energy that
rattled the superficial good-fellowship of Mr. Drew
and Mr. Drake down among the very dregs of friend-
ship.   This was intended to represent the light and
warmth of " Auld lang Syne."

" And this is one of your daughters? the eldest?
—no, the youngest!   Dear, dear, dear!   how time
slips away to be sure!"

" Sit down, Fiske, sit down," said Mr. Capel;
" there will be something coming on for supper, presently.   And do you mean to say you have never been
in London before this?"

" Well, yes," admitted Mr. Fiske; " but only for
very short times.   Why, you know, Capel, my poor
mother was buried in St. Andrews' churchyard—ah,
years before I knew you at Ligney, Capel—and yet
my visits to London have been such that I have never
had leisure to visit her grave yet, though I would
naturally have gone there at the first opportunity.   At
the first opportunity, quite naturally, Capel!"   And
a sigh that began theatrically, ended genuinely enough,
whether paid by filial affection or by some fresher

anxiety, glad of a more sentimental garment to cover its coarser pain.

" Where do you put up ? " asked Mr. Capel.

" Why, that's just what it is ! " cried the visitor, with vivacity. " You see I've never been in London alone. At least, I was once, but then my destination was provided for me, without any responsibility on my part, (he did not add that it was in Cursitor street, and there were bars to his chamber window, though Anthony Fiske could almost have persuaded himself and anybody else that they were only put there in paternal solicitude lest the interesting lodgers should precipitate themselves into the street, in an over anxiety to see what was going on around the corner). " That's just what it is, Capel ! Do you suppose I would disturb you in the bosom of your family at this hour for nothing ? No, no ! I want you to recommend me where to go. Somewhere comfortable, and moderate and very quiet. Especially very quiet. I might have put up anywhere for the night, though they do say London is such a dreadful place, but I don't believe it ! "—in a tone rising from the confidential whisper of prudery to the bright assertion of innocence. " But Capel, what do you think ? Here's an incident that would do for a novel. I've a great mind to insert an advertisement in the *Times*, that I have such an article—warranted fact—to be disposed of, for a small consideration. I came up from Derby this afternoon. I go into the Railway-buffet to obtain a cup of coffee to refresh me after my journey. I take out my purse,

I do not for the moment notice that it is a small bead affair, which I keep for stray coin, instead of the substantial Russia I ought to have for travelling. I open it. I find only half a crown and a half-penny! I feel for the Russia—in this pocket—in that pocket. It is in neither. Horrible situation! I find myself alone in London with half a crown and a half-penny—and where is the Russia I should have brought, and containing the money I ought to have? Where is it? I do not know."

"That last is true enough, I dare say," said Mr. Capel to himself, and added aloud; "Where have you stowed your luggage, Fiske?"

"My dear fellow, I haven't brought any. I came up to meet a gentleman who ought to have arrived from Jersey yesterday. An hour's conversation would have done my business with him, and I should have been back in Derby by this! But I find a telegram from the dilatory fellow that he will not be in London for a week. So I shall have to take another journey to and from Derby; whereas if I had only brought the purse that I ought to have brought, I'd have made a stay here, and renewed all my old memories—for I'm a Londoner born, as I daresay you've forgotten, Capel. But as it is, I want you to oblige me with the name of a hotel, or any decent lodging, where they will trust a friend of yours for a night or two, Capel."

"You might as well stay here," said Mr. Capel, bluntly. "My new assistant has got the regular spare-room, but I think there's some sort of garret un-occupied, and I dare say the girls will find some bits of furniture, that you can make shift with. My two elder daughters, Fiske," as Lizzie and Sibyl entered.

"Capel, how kind of you! Good-evening, madam. Good-evening, madam. For your parents' sake, I cannot look upon you young people as strangers. But Capel, it is too great an obligation! How can I make myself so troublesome to the young ladies?"

"Tut, it won't trouble them, Fiske. They're glad of something to do."

"Happy to do kindness and to show hospitality, perhaps," said Mr. Fiske. "Well, I think I should feel so myself—if I had a house of my own—which I've never had yet. I've been a poor wandering un-settled fellow all the days of my life, Miss Capel. It was all very well when I was young, Miss Capel; though I'd always a sort of feeling that it should come to an end, and I always meant to settle before I grew old. But now I must just venture into my neighbor's fields, like Ruth, and glean after the reapers; and now and then, some good soul like your papa here, makes me free of his hearth for awhile, and then I glean even among the sheaves."

"I did not know you were so well up in Scripture history," said Mr. Capel, with a coarse laugh.

"I am not, I am not, Capel; and more's the pity. But I read the whole book of Ruth on my way up in the railway train. What do you think, Miss Capel, I found a Bible in the carriage—one of the Society's Bibles. I suppose it dropped from somebody's portmanteau. I was the first passenger, so I took possession and read all Ruth and all Esther and some of Revelations."

"Did you have any fellow-travellers?" asked Mr. Capel; "if so, they must have thought you remarkably pious."

"I'm afraid they did," said Mr. Fiske, with a sigh. "It's very hard to be thought better than you are. It makes you wish you were, you know. There was an old lady in the carriage, with some ginger biscuits, and some sherry in a sarsaparilla bottle. She offered me some. She didn't offer any to a young man next me, and a very nice-looking young man he was; but then he was reading some book in a colored paper cover that he'd bought at the railway-station."

"And did you accept?" inquired Mr. Capel.

"Of course, I did," said Mr. Anthony Fiske, with great energy. "A man who refuses another the pleasure of doing a kindness is one-third fool and two-thirds brute. Very good sherry it was, too."

"It took some faith to drink out of the sarsaparilla bottle," said Mr. Capel, making a grimace.

"Oh dear, no! And besides, if sarsaparilla itself was offered me in the way of kindness, I couldn't refuse it."

"Ha, ha!" laughed Mr. Capel. "Don't you remember all the filthy decoctions you swallowed to please that old *bonne* who undertook to cure you of your ague at Ligney?"

"Well," said Anthony Fiske, gravely; "and I was cured, and I know it was not the filthy decoctions that did it, either. It was just patience, and excellent nursing, and good living. But if I hadn't swallowed her pet potions, would that good old *bonne* have given me a fire in my bedroom without an extra charge? Would she have put all the neighboring dairies and orchards under contribution for my nourishment? I had her doctoring reputation in pledge, and she was bound to do her best to redeem it. But she was a good old soul. If I'd a fortune, Capel, she was the sort of woman to whom I'd give a little annuity. Meantime, I hope she gets on very well, I hope she does. And I'd advise all travellers never to refuse her doses. But to return to the events of to-day: There was a young married lady in my carriage with three fine little boys. Very fidgety they were. I let one of 'em sit on my knee to look out of the window, and the others cried all the time because it was not their turn. Their ma wanted to buy them some bunns at Leicester. She did not dare take them all with her to the buffets, else she wouldn't have got back in time. So she asked me so nicely, if I'd just look after them while she went. I knew she thought she could trust me after seeing my studies, Capel. A pretty-looking woman she was, and quite young."

"What a joke if she'd never come back and you'd arrived in London with a flourishing family, Fiske!" laughed Mr. Capel. "I should have been rather afraid of taking such a charge myself."

"Oh, no, you wouldn't!" said the other, confidently; "You always did talk as if you were very suspicious, but I don't believe it, Capel. Nobody has ever deceived me. To be sure, it wouldn't matter much if they had. If she had left those boys with me, I might have been very sorry for them, but I could not have done anything but take 'em to the workhouse. But people have not known that, and I've trusted them all around, and no harm has ever come of it. I like to trust and to be trusted—it's a very pleasant feeling. It seems to me it is quite worth being deceived sometimes, for I'd rather be a fool than a knave, if there's nothing between the two. What do you say, Miss Capel?"

"Oh I think so, decidedly!" she answered, daintily portioning out the fish-supper, "and I think people generally know whom to trust. You'll hardly ever see a child ask the time, or the use of a high knocker, of a person who will not attend to the request. This morning when you were out, Hester, a little boy asked you to read an illegible address on a letter, didn't he, dear? Well, I had watched him from the window and he had stood still and let about fifty people pass him before he spoke to you."

"That's always happening," said Sibyl. "In Red Lyon street the other day a little ragamuffin asked her 'to ring the top bell three times;' and in Mecklenburg Square, yesterday, two charity children had let a ball through the railings, and they came up curtseying; 'Would Miss mind giving it a hook-out with her umbrella’—straight opposite the Winter’s windows—I was never more ashamed in my life. Nobody ever troubles me, thank goodness!”

“You’re too fine a lady,” said her father. “The top bell would soil your delicate kids. They can see that you are the cat in mittens who catches no mice.”

“I believe it’s an unconscious exercise of physiognomy,” remarked Mr. Fiske. “Without knowing it, they watch for a face with a certain expression. Under these circumstances they seek an expression of beneficent will and—and—general gumption. People may ridicule physiognomy if they like, but, as Lavater says, ‘All men estimate all things whatever by their physiognomy; and physiognomy, whether understood in its most extensive or confined signification, is the origin of all human decisions, efforts, actions, expectations, fears, and hopes.’ I consider physiognomy to be a genuine science, and, even taken as most people can only take any science, as a mere hobby-horse, it will carry you safely as far as you need to go, and if you will override it, you deserve to be taken up by the Society for the Prevention of Cruelty to Animals! How I know so much about it,” continued Mr. Fiske, descending from his stilts, and relaxing into easy familiarity, “is, that I once lectured upon it.”

“Well, I don’t believe in physiognomy,” said Mr. Capel, “and here’s a case in point: You and Hester are asked for the same little favors”—and yet I’m

sure you couldn't find two people more different-look-
ing."

The visitor raised his faded eyes, and fixed them
on Hester, and then shook his head gently. "Very
different indeed," he answered, "as different as may
be. And I'll tell you what, Capel," he added, resum-
ing his vivacity, "our kind offices are asked with a
different feeling ; hers, because they can see she is
ready to do them ; mine, because they think I've got
nothing better to do ! She'll be asked to give more
than cheap little favors some day. I shan't—unless by
a fool. I'm only made for odd jobs. In the moral
world I'm like the man who shuts up shops, and
sweeps up the snow, and don't even mind clearing
your doorstep when the maid is ill. It's a comfort to
me to hope, that such may make life a little pleasanter
to better people—the oil that makes the wheel to go
round without cracking, eh, Miss. Capel!"

"How ridiculous of the man to keep appealing to
Lizzie, who never has anything to say for herself!"
thought Sibyl.

"Now, girls, you had better go and see after Mr.
Fiske's room," interposed Mr. Capel. "Sibyl, you
might as well stay with us. Lewis is not here to-
night, and so you needn't go off, making believe you
are going to help, for I know you won't."

"I'm not making anybody to believe anything,
sir," said Sibyl, haughtily. "I am not needed to help
and am going to bed. When Mr. Lewis comes in you
can tell him all about it, if that will be any satisfaction

to you. Good-evening, Mr. Fiske," and she passed that gentleman at the door of the room, whither he had followed Lizzie and Hester, protesting against the trouble he was giving them.

He bowed to her—he had shaken hands with the others—closed the door behind her, returned to the fireside and seated himself opposite to Mr. Capel. He sighed as he sat down, and a very faded and defeated little man he looked.

"Well, Fiske!" said his host, shortly.

Fiske smiled feebly and wriggled in his chair. There was in the motion a half ludicrous resemblance to the cringing movement of some poor dog, obedient to a rough master's call ; "Here Brute ! "

" And so you've been giving lectures on physiognomy, have you, Fiske!" pursued the other. "Of course, I can understand that sort of thing implies a very flourishing state of the funds, eh, Fiske ? "

" That was on the Cliff at Margate only, last summer," answered Fiske, ruefully heedless of the ironical inquiry. "They didn't answer well. The public on the Cliff is not the public that cares for science, put it as popularly as you may. The Ethiopian serenaders had it all their own way. If I'd been able to engage a room, it might have been different. Nobody listened to me, and what I got, I believe was given chiefly in the spirit of an old gentleman who put a shilling in my hand, saying, that he was sorry to see what a well-taught man might come down to, and he hoped it was not through drink ! I found out he was a carcass-

butcher in a large way at Smithfield. And he called
a scientific lecture a ‘Come down!’ For science is
science after all, Capel, whether it’s in the Royal
Institution or on the cliffs at Margate!”

“Now, what did you care for science?” asked
Mr. Capel, laughing. “All you wanted was money.”

“No, no, not all;” don’t say all, observed the guest ;
“If I’d only thought of money, most was to be got by
blacking my face and going in for the banjo. One must
have money that one may live—but money is not all.
No, Capel. There are some things that a gentleman
will never do, as long as he can help it!”

“I hate business myself,” said Mr. Capel. “I’d
sooner live your life than mine now. Only you were
a fool to lose your money. I own I am more fortu-
nate there. I had a little money too, as you may remember. I’ve bought an annuity of a hundred odd
per annum. I did that years ago, and so, being secure from the workhouse, I have never bothered myself to save more. Not that any extra has come my
way. I’d be living on that annuity now, and enjoying
myself in peace and comfort, but for the girls.”

“I wonder that Miss Capel has not married,” said
Anthony Fiske, reflectively.

“Miss Capel? Bessie?” echoed her father.
“What should I do without her? The cat would keep
house as well as the others. Of course, Bessie never
thought of marrying. She’ll stay with me. She’ll make
my income go twice as far as it would, if I was left to
lodging-house keepers and such thieves.”

“But if she outlives you?” suggested Anthony Fiske.

“Oh, what’s the good of borrowing trouble?” The clouds we look for never come, answered Mr. Capel.

“Well, if I had my life over again, I’d do very differently,” said the visitor, shaking his frizzled locks.

“So would I,” assented the host.

Anthony Fiske looked at him wistfully. “I’ve thought so sometimes,” he said sadly. “I’ve thought if Edward Capel had only known how the silly, pondering, loving heart, of the sweetest girl that ever was, was goading itself to madness, with his wildnesses and negligences, how different he would have been! I’ve often wished some idea of it had struck me, and I might have done good where I did rather evil. For I’m afraid I often tempted you from home and steady habits, Capel. I’m afraid I did.”

Mr. Capel laughed contemptuously. “The mistake lay in my marrying at all,” he said. “I was not made for domestic bliss.”

“No, no, don’t say that,” interrupted Mr. Fiske. “You might as well assert that everybody that can’t read is an idiot who couldn’t learn. Let us hope we are all fit for something more than we attain. Else what am I, Capel?”

Mr. Capel didn’t think the question worth an answer.

“We might as well go to bed,” said Mr. Capel. “It is past midnight.”

They both went up stairs together. The master of the house made no pretense of showing his visitor to his room, but just paused at his own door, until he heard the guest had found his.

It was a gloomy suspicious face that looked back at Mr. Capel from his toilet-glass. "I wish Fiske had never been born," he thought to himself. "But I don't care how much he knows or how little. He can stay here for two or three days if he likes. I'm not going to let him think I'm frightened of him. But if he thinks I am going to keep him for the benefit of his silence, he's very much mistaken! If he chooses to talk over old stories with the girls, and they make a fuss, and she—as perhaps she may (they may be in league together for aught I know)—Well, I don't care! Things must take their chance. If they turn out uncomfortably, there's my annuity, and I'll go and live in the country!"

And in the meantime Anthony Fiske was making himself at home in the little sloping-roofed garret; had taken off his watch-chain and trinkets (there was no watch); had taken from his pocket the Bible he had found that morning; had read two or three verses by the light of his tallow-candle, and by so doing had awakened a long-dormant memory of himself, a little boy in frocks, proud to spell out his portion from a daily text-book; and Anthony Fiske shut the Bible very quickly, and was beginning a sigh but turned it into a yawn!

CHAPTER XI.

THREE LOVE STORIES.

MR. Fiske made himself quite at home, and Philip Lewis was not a little perplexed by the new arrival. Mr. Fiske was a man, and so there was no glamor about him to deceive poor Philip, who soon reckoned him up and wrote him down in his mind as "a worthless adventurer." All the more so, because Sibyl took a great dislike to the visitor, and lost no opportunity of saying as much to the young assistant.

Mr. Fiske did not often go out with his host on his evening rambles. He sat at home and chatted with the young ladies. He was very amusing, full of stories and hits of character, gleaned they little knew how. It was wonderful how gay Hester's laugh rang out at some of his sallies. Unconsciously, even to herself, he made the world seem a pleasanter place, and life an easier thing than hitherto. He would have been a very dangerous companion for most young people, this man, looking upon the world as a place where one must just push along " somehow,"

with a light-hearted knowledge, born of experience,
that there can never be a day too dark for one ray of
sunshine, and that no depth of misery is so forlorn
and cheerless as it seems to those who look into it
from their outer sunshine. There was a rich vein of
cheerfulness in the shallow soil—a vital wealth that
would have raised this man to the highest beauty of
life, if his hard lines had been drawn by duty, and not
set by the thoughtless selfishness of his youth. In
that curious division of qualities, which, after all perhaps makes existence endurable, there had fallen to
the share of this man, of no solid principle, of no
single sterling merit, this creature of chance, and of
his own shriveling necessities, those quick impulses,
that perennial flow of kindliness, that happy instinct
of turning up the bright side which everything has
somewhere—blessings which many a "righteous man"
must go lacking from his cradle to his grave. Anthony
Fiske knew this, and the purest feeling he ever had,
was the simple self-abasement with which he was ready
to own that what might be such beautiful virtues in
some, were very tarnished graces upon him. "They
are like my watch-chain," he would say to himself;
"people think there must be something fastened to it,
but there isn't."

Yet the experience derived from the society of this
man was good for Hester, to whose strained vision
life seemed like a relentless machine, with a mechani-
cal faculty for picking out the best material to be
crushed first. It is unhealthy to be cribbed and cab-

ined in narrow cells, and the healthiest will suffer most for the loss of the exercise their strength demands. Hester had latent powers of insight and observation that might stand her in good stead in a wide range. But a constant microscopic observation of our meals, our garments, and the air we breathe, is scarcely wholesome. And Hester's life was cribbed and cabined in a very narrow cell. She had read and read and read, until her head was as dazed as a poor prisoner's may be, with counting the nails in the dungeon door. She had imagined beauty, much as he tries, with a rusty spike to carve a Madonna's head on his stone wall. Her affections had narrowed and intensified like his love for the solitary mouse that shares his crumbs. And now, in the dead wall, a window was suddenly opened, looking out on the meadows where God clothes the lilies and feeds the ravens! Never mind that its glass was darkened and soiled! Let us thank God when we get his sunshine bright and pure, but we shall scarcely attain to that thanksgiving, unless we thank him first for what comes through imperfect windows. Let us never be afraid to bless God for the good that reaches us through the worst of men. The good, so far, is his good. Whatever is good is his. It is his witness in that otherwise dark soul ; a witness which, we may trust him, not one in this wide world is left without. No, not the vilest drab, or coarsest drunkard in yonder black alley—nor yet the farthest heathen, ignorantly serving his fetish. Original depravity? Natural goodness ? Let us leave off our little wrangling about these things which are so easy to quarrel over, because their whole secret is neither on this nor on that, and let us reverently remember, who said, " Let both grow together until the harvest."

Dora, too, sat more in the parlor than she had been accustomed. She did not dislike Mr. Fiske, though she cared little for his odd stories. Dora could not catch the pathos and poetry which quite unconsciously lurked in many of that gentleman's sketches of human nature. Not that Mr. Fiske never aimed at being pathetic and poetical, but when he tried, he became merely ridiculous, especially to Hester. Hester knew better; she saw through this—she only wanted his facts, and she had an instinctive knowledge of what was fact. She knew what was all tinsel, and she knew what was a real thing, disguised in it—the difference that must always be between the best marionette and the worst actor. She knew better than Mr. Fiske himself. She threw such new lights on his old experiences that he was quite startled. She had showed him cause for contempt where he had respected,and for honor and admiration where he had given a kindly abject sort of pity. But his thoughts had always been such surface thoughts, that any shrewd adverse commentary tore them up at once, roots and all. A man's habits in one respect, are his habits all through. If he shuffles in his step, depend upon it, his brain shuffles too. Originality and independence of mind are not for such as this Anthony

Fiske, who, having no field of his own in the world, must follow the most cracked and rumbling wagon, because the richest gleanings are in its track. There is no mind more slavishly conventional, than that of your free Bohemian. He can see nothing but his own dirty standard, which is only thought original by weak minds because it is a change from their good old household banner of Right and Decency. Something of this was in Mr. Fiske's attraction for Dora.

Here was a man who had not walked in any beaten track. Thus Dora put it. Anthony Fiske himself, with his sad candor, would rather have said that he had walked in a road where all tracks were beaten out by particularly weary and heavy feet. And so Dora sat more than ever in the parlor, helped to that conclusion by the fact, that the more attractive the drawing-room became to Mr. Lewis, the duller seemed the society there. No marvel that third parties wonder how lovers can have patience with each other! They cannot see them unless themselves are there!

They were all in the parlor; Mr. Fiske, Lizzie, Hester, and Dora; two sisters at work, Dora, doing nothing, and Mr. Fiske winding some cotton for Lizzie ; the skein stretched on two chairs and he standing up to perform the task. Mr. Fiske had been narrating an incident of his morning's walk ; how he had chanced to see the gentleman who had been articled in his stead in his uncle's office ; how he had been stepping from a handsome set of chambers in Lincoln's Inn, into a neat brougham, where sat a lady and a little girl, such a darling little girl ; with long, fair curls, and she kissed him as he got in. Mr. Fiske dwelt upon that. Looking down the door-list, Mr. Fiske saw the familiar name of his old comrade, " Frank Clinchman, Solicitor."

" 'That's the way the world wags," said Anthony Fiske, as he finished the narration. " The Clinchmans were decent people, I believe ; but I daresay the old tenant-farmer father would open his eyes at those chambers and that brougham ! He was dead before Frank Clinchman came to London, and earned fifteen shillings a week in my uncle's office, and lived off it too. He used to be a dreadful guy sometimes, poor fellow ! I used to make fun of him then, but I can understand it now. As soon as he got a guinea a week, he began to help his mother. Even before that, he had sent her presents ; for our old housekeeper told us he got her to go with him to choose a shawl to send home at Christmas time. But oh, he was dreadfully mean ! for when we started an oyster-supper at half a crown a head for the first of August before we began to take our turns of holidays, he backed out because he said he couldn't afford it ! Half a crown once a year ! If that's the way people go a-head, let Anthony Fiske stay behind ! "

" But I don't call it mean to grudge ourselves that we may give to others," said Hester. One of the blessings that this poor rag of humanity had brought to her, was that somehow she could always speak out her mind to him, and many an impulse which, shut up in silence and darkness corrodes into mere bitter feeling, if clothed in words and sent out into the sunshine, will grow into strong and beautiful thought. "I call it mean to grudge anybody but ourselves. To expect liberality but to give none. To keep ourselves always on the debtor's side, and everybody else on the creditor's."

"Well, so it is. I don't suppose anybody would deny that, if it is stated fairly. But Frank Clinchman never said anything more than 'Couldn't afford.' 'And how is one to think of things?' Poor Frank! I feel that he must have had a hard time of it in those days."

"But he has a good time now," replied Hester, half mischievously.

"Yes, to be sure; and do you know, after all, I do think he saved money for himself when he was ever so poor, for he had enough to pay for the stamp when my uncle offered him his articles without any fee. Oh, but he was really a great screw! He used to keep a private diary—one made out of the spoilt law papers, writing on the blank side. He left it on the desk once. One of the fellows read it, and fine fun it gave us."

"Read a private diary, Mr. Fiske?" asked Dora, in a tone which gave meaning to the inquiry.

"Well, you see it was lying about, and perhaps the clerk did not know what it was when he took it up, and then he just read, you know. It's the way things happen. There was a list of Clinchman's expenses. Three shillings a week for his bedroom, and so much for every meal. If he spent a penny more one day he made it up the next. But to just show you he didn't grudge himself unless he chose, I must tell you he gave half a crown a quarter for a sitting in church."

" The people who have fewest luxuries are always begrudged one," said Hester. " And, besides, if he could pay at all, he had a right to do so, as much as to pay for the use of his bedroom. What he gave shows he didn't take a front pew ! "

" But the greatest joke of all was when we found the ' Miss Spillman' in the entries : ' Met Miss Spilman at week night service : ' ' Left Wordsworth's poems at Miss Spillman's according to promise : ' ' Went to the *Times* office to insert an advertisement for pupils for Miss Spillman.' Then later, ' Met Margaret Spillman at week night service, walked home with her, took a little round, for a pleasanter way, it being a fine evening ; ' then, ' Went with Margaret to see the skating on the Serpentine ; ' and at last : ' Walked with Maggie in Kensington Gardens. Long confidential talk. I proposed. Dear girl ! ' You may be sure we never forgot that ' Dear girl ! ' "

"And do you think she was the lady in the brougham ? " asked Hester, interested.

" I suppose so. I heard they were married at last, after waiting ever so long. She was a daily teacher, and lived by herself in an attic in Lambs-Conduit street. I forget who found that out. There was a great nettle geranium at her window, and we used to think it fine fun to walk by of an evening, and see her sitting behind it, at work. She had dark hair, and so had this lady—only growing a little gray."

" Well," Mr. Fiske went on after a moment's pause ; " Frank Clinchman travels in his own brougham, and I walk at both ends of my omnibus journey to keep down the fares. And I suppose there is something in ourselves that explains all about it. But yet there's some luck in the matter. Why, my cranky old uncle offered him his articles just to spite me for turning him up. Clinchman might have grubbed out his whole life in ninety offices out of a hundred without such a chance coming to him ! "

" But if Mr. Clinchman had not waited patiently, living on fifteen shillings and a pound a week, and so on ? And if he hadn't the money ready for the stamp on the articles ? " asked Hester, archly. " There is no such a thing as luck, Mr. Fiske. It's a fancy name for being always at your duty, and so sure to be ready when the good time comes."

" There's a good deal in that," said Mr. Fiske, reflectively. " But still I've known people stick steadily to their post, and just leave, and that only for another sort of duty, just before the luck came. I can give you an instance of that in this same affair of Clinchman's. He was taking a salary of a hundred pounds a year when my uncle gave him the articles. Up to only one month before he was getting but eighty. And how did he get that last rise ? I will tell you : The clerk before him was named Richard Wriksworth. He was a little younger than Clinchman, though his superior, and he had been in my uncle's office one way and another for ten years. He was a very quiet young man. I can engage it was not he who read Clinchman's diary, and made fun about Margaret. He had a widowed mother, too, who had some small annuity, and though I don't doubt he was careful enough, he was not obliged to make those penny and half-penny scrapings, like Clinchman's. And yet I don't know whether the difference was not rather that we did not notice him so much ; he was so very quiet, and rather delicate, and so sincerely pious that I fear our ways of going on— thoughtless young fellows' ways, Miss Capel—must have been a real trial to him, sometimes. He used to read good books, and I've always a respect for good books for his sake. I've seen nasty, stingy, canting old women reading the very same volumes, and seeming to find comfort out of them to continue to be their miserable selves. But I've said to myself, ' Never mind, Anthony, one of the best men that ever breathed found good out of those books. I hope you'll take to them yourself some day, 'Tony.' Richard was engaged, too. We seemed to take that quite naturally. I never remember any particular joking on that score ; perhaps because it never seemed to be made a secret. A nice, merry little grig of a thing she was, too, a little puss of a thing. She used to come and meet him of an evening. I don't think Wriksworth's mother made herself quite pleasant. I saw the three together once or twice, and then the little lassie was uncommonly prim and proper, quite different from when I'd seen her walking down Holborn, with her two hands clinging round Richard's arm. Wriksworth was one of those men who keep their love safe shut in their hearts, like wine in a cellar, cool and fresh, till the right time. And I believe that little Puss knew well enough she had got the key, and that the right time had come. Well, Wriksworth had an offer of another situation at twenty pounds more a year. Thinking of his duty to little Puss, he told my uncle all about it, hoping he would offer the same after such faithful services. My uncle wouldn't ! At that time he thought he had bagged me. So Wriksworth left, and Clinchman stepped into his shoes, and a fortnight after that I went away, and another fortnight later Clinchman got his articles."

" And did you ever hear any more of Richard ? " asked Miss Capel.

" Oh, yes. Naturally enough, when I first left, I often went hanging about Lincoln's Inn, to see my old chums. I used to see him and the lassie meet and go away together the same as ever. But they never married. The work at his new office was a great deal harder than he had been used to, and he, being such a nervous man and making conscientious duty of everything, took to tic-douloureux every day for a year, and then went off suddenly in a brain fever. There was a quarter's salary due to him when he died, and that, and all he had saved, he left to little Puss, who was worse off than an orphan, having a drunken father, and nothing to depend on but a stall in the Pantheon Bazar. She lived somewhere in Clerkenwell, and that was how she had always taken in Lincoln's Inn so handily on her way home. And, do you know, Miss Capel, that years after, when I was strolling in that neighborhood, I saw her coming down Little Queen street just as she used to, and when she reached the corner where he had always met her, she paused and turned back, and went trotting off the way they'd always gone—not stalking like a ghost, but looking in at the shops, just as they used, drapers' sometimes, but picture shops and booksellers' always. She was just the same little puss of a thing—only she had a sort of look as if she knew a happy secret that had some good to everybody only each must find it out oneself. I think she believed he met her still—somehow. And I wouldn't say he didn't—Miss Capel?"

"Oh, surely Mr. Fiske! For there can be no parting where there is love on both sides. And so I often think the separation of death is not so bitter as the severings in life." But as she said it, Miss Capel did not give even so small a sigh.

And then Popps brought in supper.

The summons of the gong was only obeyed by Philip Lewis. "Miss Sibyl does not want anything!" he said. He was very silent and absent during the meal. Hester remembered that afterwards.

She went up stairs before Lizzie, and looked into the drawing-room as she passed. The gas was turned down, and Sibyl was not there. She went on to the third story. Her sister's door was open, and the candles lit on the toilet-table.

"Is that you, Hester?" cried a voice that seemed half-smothered in pillows.

"Yes it is," said Hester, by no means inclined to go in until she was fairly called.

"Come in, then—I want to speak to you."

Hester went.

Sibyl raised herself on the couch, propped up by her elbow. "Philip Lewis has come to the point," she said. "I wish he hadn't. Why couldn't he leave well alone?"

Why couldn't Sibyl keep her confidences for somebody else?—For Lizzie, who was angel enough to have patience even with this form of human nature? There was a hot rebellious throb in Hester's heart. It was too hard to have first to hear of Sibyl's speculations, and then of their successful result now spoken of as if what she had aimed at had rather been thrust upon her. Should she be false and speak sweetly, or should she be true, and expose herself to the charge of feminine jealousy and malice? Hester did not even ask herself the question.

"You know it was only what you meant him to ？" said Hester.

Sibyl laughed. "If you think that women have it

all their own way, why don't you try yourself, my dear?" she asked.

There was a moment's pause.

"Well?" said Hester.

"Well," echoed Sibyl, mockingly.

"You know what I mean," said Hester, impatiently. "If you are not going to tell me anything, why did you call me in?"

"Do you think I have rejected him, Hester?"

"You should. You know you don't care for him!"   .

"That's the way you jump to conclusions, my darling! Mr. Lewis does not think so."

Another silence.

"No, Hester, I have not rejected him. I'm sure you would be sorry if I had, for I know you think him a very excellent young man. I told him I was sure you would approve of the match, and that when he knows you better, he'll wonder how he had the bad taste to pass you by, preferring me. Of course we shan't be married for years. And everything will go on exactly as before. There will be no difference!"

"That means that if you can find what you call a better chance, you'll take it," said Hester.

"Well," answered Sibyl, composedly; "as I said to Mr. Lewis, nobody knows what changes years may make. As long as we both like each other, all will be well, and if time brings in any difference, I'm sure we'd both be the very last to keep each other to a bargain that would be only in letter and not in spirit.

Living in the same house there will never be any letters or nonsense. I'm not going to wear any engaged ring. He wished it at first, but I brought him to reason. (I think I could bring him to anything.) 'What's the use of it?' I said; 'it just makes all the girls hate one, and doesn't keep the men from flirting with one—not one little bit—rather the reverse!' It is a very comfortable, common sense arrangement."

Like her father's annuity, it was Sibyl's provision against emergencies.

"An ounce of reality is worth a pound of romance," she said.

Hester wondered if they had the same weights and measures in heaven!

Sibyl now got upon the tack that offended Hester worse than her worldliness. She grew plaintive.

"I know it might have been different. I know I could have loved some people better than I can ever love Philip. I know who might have been my one true love. But it was not to be. In this world we must take things as they come. I stand at the window sometimes and look out at the trees in the moonlight—and think—and think—"

"You'd be better employed then if you went down to the drawing-room, lit up the chandelier and played a symphony to Mr. Lewis! I wish you both joy of each other!" and Hester's patience slipped wholly out of her control, and she left the chamber in a manner more energetic than graceful.

Was the world a lottery in which Clinchman and Margaret put in their hands and drew out joy, and Richard and the little Puss, sorrow—and others a bauble truly, but yet just what they wanted—while blank and bitterness remained for the rest—that silent *et cetera* to which Hester's impatient young heart despairingly doomed itself?

Poor Hester! She forgot that Clinchman and Margaret could not have seen the end from their beginning. And what is the end? Is not all in this life only the beginning? Richard Wriksworth knows all about that now. And the Lizzie Capel's and the little Pusses are as happy as contented heirs who know there is a noble fortune laid up for them, when they leave their School of Discipline, and have a joyful Coming of Age in their Father's House.

CHAPTER XII.

DOWN STAIRS.

POPPS was in her kitchen. It was one of Mrs. Edwardes' days, and that silent woman had just entered, and was hanging up her shapeless bonnet and flimsy shawl. If she had not been shut up in her own heavy heart she would have noticed that the girl was very quiet, and during all her little arrangements had kept her face carefully turned to the dresser. But Mrs. Edwardes did not notice anything, and quite unconsciously went off to her work in the scullery.

Then the girl turned round with a sharp, volcanic sob. Oh! life may tear us with many wounds, but scarcely one of them has so sharp a pain as the first pricks of a nettle in the posy we thought all roses. One may barely see the mark it leaves, but the poison may be conveyed through the very pores, and the pain will rankle!

"I thought it was all a-goin' to be so nice," sobbed Popps, to herself, "Why shouldn't I? There seems plenty o' niceness goin' in the world, only perhaps it's like granny used to say, we can see the lumps o' cake that others is eating, but we don't know whether the flavoring is to each of their likings. Maybe every one gets the wrong bit! And yet I'll not believe that—no, I won't. It's just a drop o' essence of that apple which Eve eat, and it sets our teeth a-scrapin,' it do. I don't see why I was to give way directly, that I don't,—and yet I wish I had!" And there was another sob.

Somebody had heard it. Hester had entered the kitchen, so quietly that Popps had not observed her, till the sob was fairly out, in all its passionate vehemence. Then she turned again to her refuge, the dresser, and rattled the dishes with commendable activity.

Hester did not believe her ears. She turned brightly to the maiden, thinking the sound was far more likely to have been an incipient laugh. Hester was always in sympathy with simple honest mirth. There were capacities for great gladness in her own nature, a sure sign, had she known it, that the wounds in her heart, were certainly curable. To look at her, nobody would have guessed those secret wounds—a deception as blameless as the pure and graceful beauty of many a gentle woman, dying of hideous cancer. Strangers called her "light-hearted." Lizzie thought her "the life of the house;" and the very mirror told her that she was a wholesome bonnie lassie, in the human garden; something like the hawthorn among flowers. Hester wondered at her own face. An un-

happy hungry look might come for a while, but it flit-
ted, it never fixed there. One solution of this mystery might have been found in the fact, that she did
not enjoy being miserable. She did not cultivate discontent, yea, she rather hated it ; and though, like
much in this life, it seemed to follow the more the faster she fled ; still her attitude towards it was always
flight. She was not one of those people whom we can
scarcely imagine happy in any world where the Devil
and Death and all their discordant legions are no
longer at hand to be contended with and lamented
over. She wanted rest. Not because she was too
weak to combat, but because there was too high met-
tle in her, patiently to endure contest without victory.
And the time for victory was not yet. The other explanation of the broad clear brow, with its brave out-
looking eyes, and the sensible mouth, just a smiling
curve in the firm lines, lay in the truth that some
countenances are retrospects and others, prophecies.
There are women in our great cities, into whose deeds
the sun dares not look, yet whose foul blaspheming
words pour through lips, still as soft as they were
when they murmured the catechism in the village-
school; whose faces remain the same fair, childlike faces
that their mothers used to kiss in the early evening
twilight. The rosebud fell into the gutter, but you can
see what it used to be. And there are other women,
living reserved monotonous lives, in whose faces you
see something that promises a rare blossom some day,
in this world if the weather favors—somewhere else,

if their spring is late. I think any wise man would
have turned round to look at Joan of Arc while she
was still the serving-maid at the inn. Such faces are
like bulbs, which a child might throw away ; but the
botanist picks them up and knows their value !

So she turned to Popps, ready to develop and re-
spond to what she thought must be an irrepressible
giggle. But the sturdy red hand was lifted to dash
away a tear. "Why, Popps !" said Hester, in sur-
prise :

" Its no use, Miss ; it isn't anything, it's only the
nasty way o' the world, that's what it is. The sooner
one's out of it, the better, that's all. But one's sure
to get one's fill, as one's passin' through." And, re-
straint being removed, Popps, sobbed heartily.

"'There's nothing the matter with Tom ?" asked
Hester.

"No, Miss. Leastways nothing much. It is not
much to have a cold in the head ; but its troublesome
enough an' may turn to anythin'. And so with other
sort o' matters."

Hester could scarcely refrain from a smile at the
homely illustration. " Come, Popps, tell me all about
it," she said.

" Well, Miss"—and Popps gulped down a great
sob—" you know next Sunday's Easter Sunday. You
must leave your winter things off sometime, mustn't
ye ? And I'd made a new bonnet. I'd went all along
Oxford street looking into the bonnet shops, not as
I'm such a fool as to think that sort would become

me, but just to get an idea, as Tom calls it. I thought I'd have my last year's cleaned, for the straw's good, though a bit browned, and I thought I'd like pink ribbons for a change. An' I saw a nice bit o' artificial ivy to sell for four-pence, and I'd a piece of good black-silk fringe that I thought would go fine around the curtain. And I put on clean aprons two nights a runnin'," said Popps, with a fresh burst of grief, "so as I shouldn't dirty it while I was a-doin' of it. And this mornin' as Tom came in to see what makes the back airy door scrape so, I showed it to him."

"And didn't Tom like it?" asked Hester, finding that the damsel's grief had come to a gulf of bitterness, over which a leading question might assist it.

"First o' all he said, what did I want a puttin' on finery on Easter morning? It was an old Church of England superstition, and he was out o' patience with dissenters for stickin' to the manners and customs of those who were always looking down upon 'em, just as if they couldn't leave 'em to themselves, and make ways of their own, and not half the time think a very weddin' wasn't all square, unless it was done by a parson in the parish church. Well, I answered him fair enough, I'm sure. I said the Church of England has a deal o' good in her and has done a lot of good, and my Miss Lizzie herself belongs to it. (Maybe what I said would have come sweeter like if I'd said that I'd been put in mind o' these very things just lately by Missis, when I was a-runnin' down of it myself)," admitted Popps, parenthetically. "I said I wasn't always thinkin' o' the Church of England, and wasn't a goin' to put myself out o' my way to spite them as wouldn't notice I'd done it. And then"—and then the sobs broke out afresh.

"And then?" echoed Hester, catching up the falling link.

"And then he said the bonnet put him mind o' the sweeps on May-day—and that he had no patience with such fal-de-rals, and he shouldn't care to go out with me in it—and then I said back 'twasn't me that asked him to go out with me, and I'd always been quite happy a-going by myself."

And the sobs came thick and heavy.

"You dear, silly Popps," said Hester kindly, with just a ray of playfulness to lighten the sympathy; "what did you care for the bonnet? You had only thought to please Tom. And you might have made that very bonnet please him more than anything if you'd said, "As you don't like it, Tom, I'll alter it.""

"But Tom oughtn't to ha' spoke so hasty!" sobbed Popps.

"No, he oughtn't. And, of course, he is ever so sorry for it now. Why, Popps, dear, aren't you sorry for answering back? and how much harder it must be to know one spoke sharp first!"

The sobs grew a little quieter. But Hester was giving comfort with which her own heart could not wholly go. It was not that she felt it must be hard to take reproof from a dear hand, or to sacrifice our own notions to the little whims of those whom we love. But ought not they in turn to love us enough not to ride even their superior taste rough-shod over our poor attempts to please? Hester could understand how it was. She had gone to one or two lectures at the celebrated Mechanics' Institute, whose classes Tom Moxon attended. She had seen the well-dressed middle-class girls with whom, while there, he was on a certain footing of equality. Tom might not like to meet such, when in company with a bonnet like poor Popps'. The chances were ten to one that they would not think this offending head-gear at all out of keeping with the "working carpenter." He had nothing to do with them, beyond perhaps a civil "good-evening," given with a profound feeling of encouragement to a young working-man who endeavored to improve his mind. Naturally, he would become less "interesting" when he had a wife of any sort, in Popps' bonnet or otherwise. If Tom preferred such reflected light to genuine sunshine—well, there was painful truth in poor Popps' retort, "'Twasn't her that asked him to go with her!"

All this Hester felt, but not one word of it did she utter. She would not bring forth weapons which, in the face of this actual conflict, she somehow felt might not be the very best. She could see that it was not herself, but Tom, that Popps wanted to justify; and that her keenest trouble was, that she couldn't quite make herself wholly wrong, and him utterly right.

Hester could find nothing to say but this: "Give

me the bonnet, Popps, and let me see what I can do for it."

Popps had only time to snatch it from the bandbox, before a man's step on the kitchen stairs made her hurry off to hide her crying face in the scullery. It was Mr. Anthony Fiske, with an empty water-bottle in his hand. He came down humming:

> " Sae bide ye yet, and bide ye yet,
> Ye little ken what may betide ye yet."

"O Miss Hetty!" he said, "I beg your pardon. I thought there was nobody here, not even the domestic genii. For I've been ringing my bed-room bell for the last half hour, and so found leisure at last to remember two good old proverbs, that it would have been better had I oftener borne in mind, 'Help yourself and your friends will love you,' and 'if you want anything done, do it yourself.' And in point of fact, why should a lazy fellow like me take a hard-working girl like Popps up the house, to fill my water-bottle?"

"Because it's Popps' duty,—and I know she would wish to do it," said equitable Hester. She has not heard the bell, and I am sorry you have the trouble to come down stairs," and she made a movement to take the bottle herself, that Popps might be screened from the curious observation of the visitor.

But Mr. Fiske gallantly resisted. " I have been down here before and I know where the filter is," he said ; "and it's quite a treat to me to see a kitchen and kitchen offices. They seem so homelike. You may pay for drawing-rooms and dining-rooms at any hotel, but you can't pay for admission into the kitchen. There are things you can't have for mere money, Miss Hester. Things you can have as free as air if you seek them at the right time. I only wish there was some royal road to experience!"

And he went off into the scullery and as Hester went up stairs she heard Popps scuttle away, and make a precipitate dive into the coal-cellar beyond. On what little links do great chains sometimes hang!

Mrs. Edwardes was standing before the sink, cleaning out the saucepans, that dirtiest and most repulsive piece of domestic industry, which is such bitter discipline to many a trim active maid-of-all-work. Only a little patch of sunlight could ever enter the scullery, and in that little patch she stood. It could not brighten her. There was no point on which it could seize in the dull, coarse dress, the strangely dead hair, with its thick flecking of white, or the yellow-pale face. She did not even lift her eyes to meet it.

Mr. Fiske stepped on gayly. He had resumed his song—

"Ye little ken—"

Why did it die so suddenly on his lips? And he stood still, like one struck with a swift, nameless terror. Surely that place was too homely and the hour too bright, for ghosts!

Mrs. Edwardes turned and faced him. Whatever the horror was, they both saw it, only what had startled him, did not come quite so sharply upon her! For a moment a ghastly youthfulness seemed to sweep over her gray gaunt figure. The rigid lines of her face broke up, the mouth trembled irresolutely, and the eyes fell. Only for a moment, but time enough for Anthony Fiske to step forward impulsively. Time for nothing more. The sternness flashed back, and the gray eyes looked up with that strange repulsion in them when it seems as if the spirit shut itself behind a screen where it can watch, and yet defy watching. Then she turned again, and lifted another foul vessel in her polluted hands.

Anthony Fiske stole away. As he went up stairs he crept by the wall, drawing his hand along as he went. He went straight up to his own attic chamber. The window was open, and the room was bright with sunshine, and gay with the spring-twitter of birds outside. He drew a long gasp of reviving, as we might on regaining the fresh air, after a visit to some damp and dismal charnel-house. He set the water-bottle in its place, and never once noticed that he had not re-filled it. Then he sat down by the open window.

The sounds of common household life went on around him. He heard quick foot-steps on the stairs, openings and shuttings of doors, little cheerful domestic colloquies. But he sat and wiped his brow, and breathed hard and heavily. How would you feel, reader, if in a friend's house you innocently opened what you thought to be a china closet and found instead—a skeleton? A skeleton, too, on whom some lingering lock of hair or poor rag of raiment, revealed that these were bones which you had once seen clothed in youth and beauty?

Anthony Fiske sat quite still. He could not think. Only his mind kept snatching at little memories as we seize swift glimpses of some of the pictures in a rapidly turned-over portfolio. Now a vision of a house among vines, himself outside in the sunshine, a helpless invalid on a couch, merry laughter from within, and a tall slight figure that came through the low window opening upon the terrace. A tall slight figure, in a pale green robe with white trimmings. Such a pleasant cup of tea she brought him. And she stayed there with him till a voice called from within. And it felt lonely after she was gone. The sun went down suddenly and all the sky was gray, and a foreign waiter came to lead Monsieur Fiske to his chamber.

Then a gaily-lit room, full of beautiful and richly-clad women, one of them sitting a little apart ; who did not care how the passing feet trampled the velvet robe that lay unheeded round her. A white woman she was, with a wedding-ring on her hand, and as fair a woman as any there, whose smiles would have been courted readily, had she smiled, and who would have been moved to smile, had her watching gaze ever wandered from one fresh stalwart figure that moved to and fro everywhere, except towards her.

Then a painted saloon and plenty of candelabra. A balcony outside, and an odor of cigars coming in

7*

with the moonlight. The sort of place where you might as well expect snowdrops to grow, as virtue ; many men and several women, with rouged faces, hard eyes, and high glib voices : the door just left ajar, and a white face coming through the dark and frightened eyes running over the groups till they caught sight of a couple at the far end, the man's face in full view, the woman's only sideways, shaded by a veil that made it look almost pretty. It was ugly enough in reality. Anthony remembered that. This poor scrapegrace, Anthony Fiske, had never thought a woman pretty if she was not good.

There was one more picture. This was of a very early morning. Himself wandering aimlessly among the vines, while a carriage dashed along the road below him. He had thought nothing of it at the time, only he had fancied that he knew one of the boxes in the dickey, and had half wondered in a casual way, which of his Ligney friends was going for a trip. It was but a small box in brown holland, with red edgings. A very small box. It could not have held dresses. Certainly it did not hold that pale-green robe with the white trimmings, which Anthony Fiske saw afterwards in the possession of the barmaid of the Auberge. It had grown old-fashioned, and was soiled and crumpled, but he had seen the girl remodeling it with her busy foreign fingers. " It will vash, Monsieur," she had said. " And it is an ill wind that blows no good, as you Anglais say, for my vages are very small, and *ma m're* is a widow."

There was a loud double knock at the door, and then a bluff voice in the hall, and Sibyl's light metallic laugh, announced that some pleasantries were passing between her and her father. Anthony Fiske stepped out upon the landing and listened. When he heard the office door close and then silence, he stepped down stairs. "Anthony Fiske had often spoken when he should have held his tongue," he said to himself, "but he will never hold his tongue when he ought to speak. Capel cannot know of this, and he must be told. It is too horrible!"

He knocked at the office door. Mr. Capel cried, "Come in," cheerily. He was seated behind his desk, his face aglow with comfort and satisfaction. He had spent the morning with a builder, who had just paid him a tolerable bill, and they had dined together at a hotel at seven-and-sixpence a head exclusive of wines. But the radiance died when he saw Anthony Fiske's terror-stricken face. He did not see it as terror-stricken, only as concentrated. "He has lived on me for a fortnight already," he thought, "and he thinks it cannot go on much longer without some explanation between us, so the whole artillery is about to explode! Now for it! I am ready?"

"Capel," whispered Anthony Fiske, "don't— don't put yourself out—but—if you only knew—what —WHO is in your very house!"

"I can get full information as to the inmates of my habitation at a somewhat less cost than your board and lodging, Fiske," said Mr. Capel, turning round on his stool so suddenly that his forehead nearly touched the other's bent head, and caused him to start backwards.

Mr. Fiske, quite innocent of any predatory intention, or of anything beyond the sponging instincts of his limp nature, did not understand this speech in the least. Nor had he time then to try to do so, but in the meantime, accepted it meekly; humble-pie, at least, being food that he always felt he honestly deserved!

"But SHE is here! Oh, can't you understand?" he pleaded. "I don't like to say the plain name to you."

"I tell you I know all about it," returned the other with a hoarse laugh. "I never interfere with anybody's right to independent action—I don't. When she ran away, she can't say I ran after her. When she chose to come back in her own fashion, I let her come. As for the girls, Anthony Fiske, you can go and tell them all about it, if you like—I'll not hinder you. It will serve them instead of novels for the next twelvemonth."

Anthony Fiske left his side and came round and stood before him—stood stark upright, with his frisky hair very frisky indeed.

"I don't envy you now, Edward Capel," he said.

He said it as solemnly as a curse. Then he turned and left the room, and heard a brutal laugh behind him.

"If I was as I ought to be, I'd leave this house

this very moment," soliloquized Anthony Fiske. "But when one has not ten shillings in the world, what is one to do? I see one must be frugal and industrious if one is to keep one's own feelings—though they don't eat, or wear out shoes!"

CHAPTER XIII.

MR. CAPEL'S WALK.

MR. CAPEL had only laughed as Anthony Fiske left him. The sudden burst of righteous indignation, and the mock dignity which clothed it, struck him only as supremely ludicrous. That anybody should think it worth while to be angry about anything except a spoiled dinner, was to him an amusing mystery. When he was young, he had himself been weak enough to fly into passions with his tailors, but that was a folly he had parted with for many a day.

Nevertheless the laugh was followed by a dark cloud of gloom. Did he feel the sad loneliness of a black secret kept from those who still gave him their innocent affection? Did he realize the degradation of falling from the envy of even such as Anthony Fiske? Some men, however guilty, would have risen in wrath, and bidden the contemner to carry his contempt at least beyond the threshold that sheltered him. It was no fear of the exposure that might follow a quarrel which deterred him, for whether they quarreled or not, it never struck Edward Capel that Anthony Fiske could possibly shut the skeleton-cupboard without calling others to look. Anyhow he regarded exposure as a certainty.

But what a bother it all was, to be sure!

If people would only take life rationally as he always wanted to do! If they would only be cool! Why need they excite themselves, and force him into excitement? What a blessing it would be, if only *somebody* would keep cool! At point after point, he could see that a stoicism like his own could stop all further worry and flurry. Why couldn't Anthony Fiske know when he was well off, and eat his dinner, and sleep in his garret, without raking up old stories. And when the girls heard about it—as of course they would—why couldn't he trust them to give no further sign than perhaps to ask for some new dresses or bonnets, trusting that so sensible a behavior would merit such moderate reward? Hadn't they enough to amuse them, looking for husbands, and dressing themselves? He believed Sibyl had. If she were the only one it might be all right yet. But those other two were so dreadfully in earnest about everything except what seemed to him to be their own proper business. Yes, it was a disagreeable affair. And just as Sibyl had done her duty as a daughter, by giving him a prospect of getting rid of her maintenance, and so bringing him one step nearer to retirement on the annuity. And what would Philip Lewis say to this goblin of Anthony Fiske's? Philip was another uneasy soul.   Not that Mr. Capel feared he would offer Sibyl her release.   "He does not think such angels as she are to be found everyday," said he, grinning to himself.   But still he would make a fuss, and be another raging element in the storm which was gathering.

Oh dear, dear! how hard it is to care for nothing but comfort—and to be deprived of it after all! Savory meals, soft beds and friendly indifference, why every cat gets as much—not every dog for being a nobler animal, he must keep guard and fetch and carry.   Something is expected of him, and he gets cuffed for his failures.   But oh, it is hard to aim at what every cat gets, and yet to miss it!

Mr. Capel got up and stretched himself.   He should go for a walk.   There were some plans that he had intended to revise to-night, but they must wait till to-morrow.   One could make a capital book of " Proverbs transposed as practiced," and Mr. Capel's contribution to such work would be, " Never do to-day what you can possibly put off till to-morrow."

Though the evenings were lengthening, the air was still chilly, and he was too prudent to go out without his great-coat.   As he was drawing it on, Hester came down stairs with Popps' remodeled bonnet in her hand.   She had found some neat dark-green ribbon, not new, with which to trim it, and had put a simple lilac flower in the cap.   It was very neat and pretty.   The neatness and prettiness escaped her father's eye, but not the ironed ribbon, the coarse straw, and the flower he remembered from last summer. So it was very ironically that he asked if that was her last new fashion?

Hester felt particularly bright that afternoon. The bonnet looked better than she had dared to hope. So she sincerely took her father's words in good part, and th ught that it must be really a success, as he seemed to think it quite suitable for herself, while generally he scoffed heartily at everything that she or Lizzie bought or made.

"It's for Popps,' she answered, cheerfully. "She had not trimmed it very well, so I offered to do it for her. You know she wants to look very nice now, father," she added, archly.

"Oh, indeed!" he said. "Very kind of you, but think of yourself too. What are you going to have for your new bonnet?"

"Straw, with white ribbons and forget-me-nots. We're going to buy them to-morrow, and trim them ourselves," said Hester, carried out of herself in anxiety to return a pleasing answer to such unwonted inquiry. "You like blue and white, don't you, father?"

"Oh yes! I like anything. Have them pretty, though. After all, you're not a bad looking little girl, Hester, if you only dressed yourself like other people. Tat-ta." And he was gone.

Hester went down to the kitchen. It was not always that her father spoke as kindly as this. She was glad of such crumbs of paternal interest, though she would know better than to let them influence her to any little extravagance, that should heighten the weekly expenditure, at which he always grumbled so sadly. Only she wished she had a little money of her own, that she might please him without costing him anything.

She saw him pass the area window. He looked down. Mrs. Edwardes was standing there to catch the waning light for some little task, which she was performing. She looked up, and their eyes met.

Edward Capel walked on mechanically. It did not matter where he went. He turned down the Gray's Inn Road, threading his way among the crowds of young law clerks, just thankfully released from their day's labors. He paused for a moment to look into an old furniture shop. His eyes fell on a little faded gilt clock, surmounted by a figure, which might be symbolic either of Time or Death. The dealer, with less view to the fitness of things than to possible profit to be derived from the divers Irish hymeneals sure to be celebrated this Easter-tide, had labeled it "very chaste—suitable for a wedding present." Mr. Capel walked on.

On and on, down Chancery Lane, and then he turned eastward, and struck through Whitefriars towards Blackfriars Bridge. He did not notice where he was going. He was like a deaf man who accidentally strikes a sweet chord he cannot hear, for he did not even remember that this was the track of his courting days, when he had been a pupil at a famous architect's in Bedford Square, and she who was to be his wife, had been a parlor-boarder in a ladies' school near the old church at Camberwell.

On and on he went, across the river, with the dim evening clouds setting heavy above it, with just one lingering line of light in the far west. Down the Blackfriars road, past the coarse flaunting cheapness of its shops, threading his way among the worn-out, decrepit throng upon the pavements, broken with long hard struggle, and spoiled for earth's beauty, but not necessarily, thank God, for heaven's.

Edward Capel went on ; his mind filled with his own selfish thoughts. He calculated what board and lodging would cost in some quiet country town. Lizzie could not be his housekeeper, after she knew of the secret which Anthony had pulled from its untimely grave. Without any conscious explanation, Mr. Capel felt that he should suffer less from Hester's unmitigated indignation, than from the startled horror of Lizzie's pure nature. No, he must go his own way alone, and they must go theirs. He did not trouble himself to consider the ways and means of that latter clause. Many girls had to shift for themselves, and got on well enough. No sense of fatherly duty had ever come to him. It is not only orphans who are cast straight on the Fatherhood of God.

On and on, till he noticed the fresh sweet odor of budding trees. He was passing the Magdalen Hospital. It was in occupation then, and its old-fashioned front, with its clean windows and rows of greenery, made a pleasant picture in that dreary road. Perhaps some sore hearts outside thought bitterly that it was hard some should find the beauty that virtue missed ; while wiser souls, though as burdened and pressed, thanked God for the trees of the Magdalen hospital, and sent up a prayerful sigh for those sad spirits that could never know another blooming time on earth. Edward Capel looked up at the old house, and the budding trees. "I should think they would pull it down, soon," thought he, "now land grows so valuable near the city."

Crowds were pouring into the Surrey theatre. Mr. Capel paused to look at them. He had been a great theater-goer in his young days. It now struck him that he might go again more frequently, once he was set free from business. "But if I live in a little country town," he mused, "there will be no actors worth seeing. That's the worst of these little country towns. They are so slow. I don't see why I shouldn't stay in London. Just a little way out, Highburg or Peckham, or some other suburb. There must be plenty of people who would be glad of a boarder, at abated terms too, for a permanency. It might be a little dearer, though ; but if Lizzie got over the tiff, and came out once in awhile to look after my things, I think it would come to much the same in the long run.

There were two crowds in the great clearing by the obelisk. One was gathered round two men in a cart offering bargains for sale. Mr. Capel stopped to listen—"Genuine Assam tea," they cried, "only one and four-pence a pound. Isn't there any lady here that drinks tea? Curious thing it is that people always seem ashamed to buy. Come along now, don't be bashful. There's nothing to be ashamed of, if you've got your money ready, and you may be sure we won't deal with you without it. What, nobody speaks! We're not going to chaunt our goods as if it was a favor to buy, 'em, but once more—one more chance. Genuine Assam tea at one and four-pence a pound! Oh, I see how it is, the housekeepers haven't come out yet,—its only the lodgers. Haven't you an article to suit them, Bill? Yes, here's a knife. Now, it's not fancy goods, this isn't, but genuine Sheffield blade, and sound ivory handle. It's not the sort of article as I'd advise any gentleman to go a playing at suicide with. He might find his self—"

Mr. Capel wandered on again, making towards the other group. This was a smaller group, the inner circles of which stood still and quiet with bowed heads, heedless of the blasphemous ribaldry that fringed its borders. It was harangued by a man, standing on the step of the pillar. Mr. Capel did not need to go close, for the speaker's voice rang out sound and clear, in a very different key, to the besotted salesman's. He was a tall thin man with deep set eyes and dark hair, waving in the swift spring breeze that blew round his uncovered head. He knew the policeman would be soon upon him, and he spoke eagerly but not impatiently. Like one who has many seeds to sow, and doubtful soil to sow in, and would fain cast in all, lest haply some might fall upon the right.

"Behold, now is the accepted time ; behold, now is the day of salvation !"

"The Lord is not slack concerning his promise, as some men count slackness but is long-suffering to us-ward, not willing that any should perish, but that all should come to repentance."

"Cast away from you all your transgressions, whereby ye have transgressed, and make you a new heart and a new spirit, for why will ye die, O house of Israel ?"

"For I have no pleasure in the death of him that dieth, saith the Lord God ; wherefore turn yourselves, and live ye."

Mr. Capel walked on again. He knew all about it. He had received a scriptural education. He had dropped church attendance during the years of early manhood ; but now-a-days, he often attended, when the weather was fine, and he was not tired or otherwise disinclined. He thought religion excellent for women who had nothing else to do, or for poor people, who would be more likely to pick your pocket without it. Mr. Capel did not feel himself among the publicans and sinners. Oh no ! who does ? He knew there was an ugly reality behind his respectable exterior, but he believed himself quite as good as anybody else, and was satisfied in that belief.

It is too much the fashion to set down respectability as Pharasaical in itself, whereas genuine respectability is but a convenient colloquialism for christianity.

The distinguishing mark of the Pharisees was their shamness ; " whited sepulchres, appearing beautiful outward, but within full of dead men's bones, and of all uncleanness." Such respectability is the easiest road to damnation.

As he walked slowly away, he heard the crowd strike up the hymn

" Lo, He comes with clouds descending."

He knew the tune, and the words too, for that matter, and heedlessly hummed them as he went along, soliloquising :

" I could certainly get very snug board and lodging for about eighty pounds a year, which would leave fifty for dress and extras—I might do a little stroke of business too, whenever a profitable bit came across me :

"Come to Judgment,
Come to Judgment, come away."

" I can't help thinking what a blessing it is that I put everything into that annuity. It is just the thing for me under the circumstances; I can't be expected to do this and to do the other, when I haven't any ready cash, and yet all the time I am safe myself. Things really do seem to turn out for the best, I was in twenty minds whether I would do it or—"

" Hullo—mind yourself—where are you a-going

to—there now, 'twasn't my fault! I hallooed as soon as I could, and so did my fare; and he'll speak up for me."

It was at the point where so many roads meet, in front of the Elephant and Castle coach station. Mr. Capel had gone carelessly across, humming as he went. A hansom cab had come dashing up Newington Causeway. It was within an inch of knocking him down, indeed it was the sharp touch of the shaft, which aroused him from his reverie, and sent him blindly scrambling out of its way, to fall right under the wheels of a heavy wagon with a sleepy driver, bringing cabbages from Balham to the Boro market.

There was a rush of people. The first to reach the spot stooped low in the twilight, and when he raised his head the cab lantern shone on a whitened and awed face.

"Stand back—stand back"—said he, and the two drivers paused in their clamorous self-vindication, and a little withered widow with a great door-key hanging on her forefinger, wrung her bony hands, and cried, "The pore gentleman's dead! I seed him coming across as innocent-like as possible. Yes, mum, he's quite dead, and no mistake. The p'liceman says is 'ead is smashed in."

"A sudden call, truly," said the clear sad voice of a tall figure that towered over the outskirts of the gathering crowd.

It was the preacher from the Obelisk!

CHAPTER XIV.

ENDS AND BEGINNINGS.

IT was just as it always is under a great shock of affliction ; those who felt least, felt first, and the lightest blow showed its mark the soonest. That was Sibyl's part. There was somebody who must come to the front and pick up every duty that nobody else claimed. That was Hester's.

The poor mangled remains were brought home after the inquest, and, for a week, life went on in the shadow of drawn blinds. A little lame woman was shut in the upper bedroom, dressmaking. Lizzie and Hester took their tasks from her, and stitched away in the twilight-house, for though neither said a word to the other, they both knew she must not be engaged one day longer than was necessary. Sibyl also spent a good deal of her time with the workwomen, who, not seeming to have many ideas of fashion or style, she thought might be all the better for her suggestions. Besides, the dressmaker worked for many of her neighbors, and after the first day or two, Sibyl found that

she wanted more topics than her own lacerated feelings, and the imaginary beatitudes of her departed
parent. After one fit of hysterics in Philip Lewis's
arms, she rather shunned him, with an unconscious
instinct that if he knew too much of her she might fail
in her role of mourner. Nevertheless, his existence
was a great comfort. Not because it afforded that
warm shelter which a true woman finds in simple love,
whether protecting or protected, but because she
thought it was a screen between her and self-depen-
dence.

Mrs. Edwardes came to the house once or twice
while the dead lay there. Popps saw Mr. Fiske speaking to her once in the passage. The charwoman was
told all about the accident by Popps, and the charwoman went through her work, and listened—mostly
in silence.

"I'm afraid the master wasn't a good man," said
Popps—"I don't say he has gone to hell, we never
likes to think that of anybody, and we have no right
neither, for we can't tell what may be between God
and theirselves at the very last moment. The hymn
says:

> ' While the lamp holds out to burn,
> The vilest sinner may return.'

I don't say the master was that neither. If he was, I
shouldn't be like to know it. But I'd never have
thought of him as a Christian, and if you a'n't the one,
why you must be t'other. The master went to church

as much as many gentlemen, but he left Miss Lizzie
to say the grace, and she and Miss Hetty reads a
chapter o'nights in their own room together. The
master never nagged at me, but whenever he was out
o'temper, he seemed to forget I was a human bein' as
had feelins' in my back and legs. An I'd always a
notion that he left places open, and things lying about,
not because he trusted me, but because he thought
one would manage to come at what one wanted, however he might lock it up. But he had a jolly cheerful
way, and he'd poke harder hits at Miss Sibyl in his fun,
than ever Miss Hester would dare in her earnest.
Maybe he'd ha' been very different if the Missis had
lived. It's a comfort we have not got to judge ; and
lor, what different judgments we'd make ! I believe
Miss Lizzie would let everybody into Heaven but
herself, and then be happier than any of 'em, just
waitin' outside, thinking what a good time the others
were having. But when I look at Miss Hetty's face,
as she sits doing her black, I'm certain sure she's
thinkin' of many things."

It was the night before the funeral. The spring
weather was calmly fair ; one staircase window was
open, and the evening breeze crept into the house,
soft and cool. Everything was strangely still. Not
mere silence, but hush, that peculiar hush, which is not
broken by isolated sounds, but absorbs them into itself.
All the mourning was made, and laid up in the bed-
rooms in gloomy readiness for the morrow. Mr Fiske
was out. Lizzie and Dora were in the drawing-room.

always in a far-off heaven or hell?   May there not be
a sweet secret in the meek resignation with which the
most tender love often bears the fleshly absence of
the holiest departed?   God sends our mortal blessings by dear human hands,—who shall say how he
heals and comforts our souls?   Are there not " minis-
tering spirits?"   Is it unlike what we know of God's
way to suppose that earthly loves and labors will rise
up glorified, with the glorified spirits?   There is
another side to the picture.   The world has outgrown
the mediæval idea of the torments of the wicked.   It
has risen on the sign to the thing signified.   It under-
stands that the worm and the fire but typify the
miserable completion of hopeless iniquity, even as the
great white throne and the sea of glass are but faint,
faint symbols of the peace and rest of the everlasting
kingdom.   What of the sinner doomed to read his
career by the fierce light of an awakened conscience,
finding God's story of what might have been, beneath
the black blots of the Devil's facts?   What if Edward
Capel was watching by the decaying ashes of that self
which he had loved better than his own undying soul?
What if he saw the kiss upon the coffin ; and, spirit
reading spirit, knew the unspoken memories of thirty-
three years before?   What if he heard that cry for
pardon?—and was now too much fiend, even to wish
that he had a voice to answer, " The first guilt lay
with me—the first forgiveness must be yours!"

In this common-place world, there, is not much
time for such supreme anguish as was throbbing in

that shaded room. There was some slight sound in the house below, and Mrs. Edwardes started to the door like an alarmed thief. There was a step in the hall; somebody was coming up stairs. She hurried down.

On the drawing-room flight she met Philip Lewis. Instead of walking close to the balustrade or the wall, as she usually did, like one accustomed to step aside, she was in the middle of the stair. Everybody knows how the reproduction of some little outward circumstance will help to reproduce the by-gone mood that was associated with it. And may not the stirring of an old feeling bring back the habits of its first season?

Philip Lewis stood aside to let her pass. He guessed that she was the charwoman, but he had never seen her since the night of his arrival in London, when she spread the supper. The staid habits of his decorous nature prevented him, though an inmate, from making himself so free of the house, as that casual visitor, Mr. Fiske. He went up, as she passed on; but presently stopped, and watched her over the banister.

"Bless me!" thought he to himself; "I do believe the familiarity of Mrs. Capel's portrait was some sort of likeness to this deplorable looking wretch. What a good thing it is I did not say so! Sibyl would have been angry. It is odd what a likeness may be in a most awful caricature." And then he went to his own room, and got out a marking-ink bottle and a clean quill, and wrote his own name in full upon some black-bordered handkerchiefs that he had just bought. For Philip Lewis was a very domestic and neat young man.

Mrs. Edwardes went down to the kitchen for her bonnet and shawl. She found Tom Moxon there; he had only just come in, and it was his first visit since the episode of Popps' smart bonnet. Would he have arrived now, but for the affliction that had befallen the household? Popps was doubtful—but nevertheless véry glad to see him. Mrs. Edwardes kindly left them to themselves.

"It's a sad thing for the young ladies," said Tom; being not yet off topics of general interest. "I suppose they will not live on here. They'd like to keep you though, if they can anyways, I reckon, Bessie."

"An' I'd like to stay, anyhow," she said. "I'm not the sort to rub on well with most misses, specially after being used to Miss Lizzie. I'd take less wages, I would, sooner than leave 'em. It would pay better in the long run than bein' always out."

"It would pay better as things stand," he answered, thoughtfully. "'Tisn't as if it was for all your life; a pound or two less for one year or so is nothing compared with comfort. It won't be longer than that, before we'll marry, Bessie. I'm doing famously; extra money nearly every week. There's no need that you should go gadding into new places, putting up with all sorts of miseries, and forgetting all about me, into the bargain."

"I didn't know but you'd be glad if I did," said

Popps, able to name her pain, as it leaped away from her heart.

"Stuff and nonsense!" he responded, with a kiss which made the laughing contempt into the height of gallantry. "Or if you did, it was because you wanted to think so."

"I shall be in black now, so I shan't be too smart for you," said Popps demurely.

"Oh, bother that!" cried Tom. "If you like I'll take you out for a holiday, Bessie, and you shall carry that bonnet in a bag, and when we're safe away, where the family a'nt likely to see us, you shall put it on, just to show you how little I care about such rubbish!"

"The bonnet's all gone," said Popps; "leastways the trimmings is. Miss Hetty did it over again for me, as neat and nice as her own."

"You dear little woman!" ejaculated the lover.

But Popps looked up at him with something moist in her honest blue eyes. "I shall always be doin' something to upset you," she said. "I don't understand things like other girls do. Now there's Lucy Smith that teaches in the National school, she'd never put you out with being common-looking in her dress, Tom?"

"And don't I want a wife who is something more than bonnet and examination-papers?" cried, Tom in disgust.

"But there's plenty others beside Lucy that's the same," said Popps, dubiously.

8*

"Well, I shall never find out whether there are or not," he returned, heartily. "For I know that you are nearer all I want than any other woman in the world, Bessie. And now, good-bye little woman; I'm glad I've made you laugh again!"

But when he was gone, the smile slowly died away. "Nearer all I want, he said," she mused to herself. Popps was only a simple-hearted girl, and she could not clothe in words the shadow that was floating in her mind. Only, alas! where a pain has once been planted, the soul is always ready for a fresh crop.

"I was a brute the other day," thought Tom, as he went off whistling. "But I've made it all right now, bless her forgiving little heart!"

CHAPTER XV.

DIVERGING PATHS.

IT was over. The blinds were raised. Life moves on again. But in its old track— Nevermore.

The Capels must leave Queen's-Road. They had no relation nearer than a cousin of their father's, whom they had only seen about six times. But he and Philip Lewis, and the family solicitor settled matters between them. The business was indeed small, only some peculiarities of the last part of the connection made it just too much for Philip, single-handed. He would require to find a partner and it was hoped that the consideration for such partnership and the sale of some of the furniture would cover the out-standing debts and all those expenses which gather around the downfall of anything —the sad cost of destruction—like the woodman's charge for felling an old oak.

Hester invested privately in Daily Telegraphs— and read the advertisements first. Dora shut herself up in her bedroom for hours together, the only result being an almost daily book-packet from the postman, which arrival or rather return, Hester and she spoke no word about to each other and generally managed to keep secret from the rest. Future responsibilities were not yet mentioned. All was dark and indefinite.

About three weeks after the funeral, there came a purchaser for the business. The negotiation went on for some days. Hester almost prayed for its conclu sion. She wanted certainty. It was so hard to move towards a novel way of life, amid old customs and associations. Well, but it was settled at last. The incoming partner would take the house too, and most of the heavy furniture, but he did not wish to move in, just yet. They could remain till Michaelmas.

"I wonder what they will do, poor girls," said Sibyl, languidly; leaning on Philip Lewis' arm, as they walked together under the lilacs that were now a-bloom in all "the squares." But the remark was put forth to sound her own future, and not her sisters'.

"I don't know,—but there are many things," responded the young man; "only dear, you can't think what a comfort it is to me that you will be amply provided for by a very slight exertion of your splendid accomplishment which must be an enjoyment in itself. It is as good as a fortune, Sibyl."

Passionate tears rushed to Sibyl's eyes. She had dared to foster another hope. "I hate teaching," she said, pettishly.

Philip's understanding caught the pain, but not

the passion. He stroked the elaborately gloved hand on his arm. "And I am ever so sorry you should have to do it," he said. "If this had happened only about a year later, or if"—he was going to add, if even his slender income had no home-claims upon it—but his mother had had a severe illness, and the expenses had overflowed the boundaries of her annuity, and similar possibilities lay always at hand.

"I wish you were rich," she cried.

There was a pang, that Philip put away at once. Grave and forgiving amid all his commonplace. "So do I," he said, tenderly. "If only for your sake, dar- ling."

"And you will go on living in the house?" she asked, presently.

"I think it is to be so arranged," he said.

"There will be no difference to you," she ob- served, resentfully.

"Don't you think so?" he said, with the silent pang twinging again: "You will not be there."

"But you will be able to come and see me when- ever you like," she retorted ; "though to be sure, by the evening, I shall be too tired to be fit for anything."

"I hope not," he remonstrated. "Why, Sibyl, it won't be for long. It's almost time that you should begin to knit and crotchet the trimmings of the—what do they call it—the trousseau."

"I shall not do a stitch of it myself," said Sibyl, shortly. "I hate that sort of thing—and you can buy it cheap enough."

Philip had his own style of sentiment. He thought a woman might find it very sweet to sit quietly, sewing sweet hopes and dreams into tangible shapes. He had often thought so, on those occasions when his mother had let her boys peep into her stores, and finger the soft old embroideries and laces, whereon she dropped a tear or two; plain, reserved, practical woman though she was. But as Sibyl did not have those fancies, they must surely be old-fashioned or vulgar, for Philip's was that calm and simple love which always rests in the assurance that the beloved must be right.

They walked on in silence. In his heart was a yearning of steadfast and patient devotion which it was not skilled to utter. It is no use to ask what he saw in her to call it out. He had clothed his ideal of woman with Sibyl's beautiful form. He believed in her—and that is the whole secret of all love. And before you despise him for his blindness, pause and ask yourself is there anybody who thinks you are his best blessing? Do you deserve that? Have you not often, with half-remorseful candor told him that it was all a delusion? Have you not playfully held up your faults that you might see them transformed in the beautifying mirror of affection? If you are but wise enough to know the secrets of your own nature, you will thank God that the kind eyes which see it the nearest, look through a softening mist. Nobody deserves love, and it falls like God's unmerited bounties of sunshine and rain on the just and on the unjust. Only, like them again, it cannot fertilize the stony ground while the better soil will justify the fostering providence. Let the ideals of us, in the hearts that love us, be prophetic of what we shall become!

And what was in Sibyl's heart? Nothing at all. But in her mind there was a vision of flounced petticoats and sealskin jackets floating away from her grasp, to make room for a daily teacher's waterproof and umbrella. What was the use of being pretty? She could not have met a harder fate, if she had been as plain as a deal-board. And it might have been so different. There was a definite " might have been," in her thoughts. Her castles in the air, had been built of too substantial material to vanish into that shadowy past which is too subtle to be remembered. She knew of definite somebody whose allowance could not be less than a thousand a year, and whose prospective fortune must be at least six times as much. She knew just the neighborhood, and just the house where people with such an income could live. If she only had it, she knew what style of carriage she would have, and what *modiste* she would employ. And walk ing by Philip's side, her light head tossed a little with the vain consciousness that this somebody had not been at all oblivious of the poor architect's daughter. Between them, there were many gaps of the social chain. He had only condescended " to look in" at the grandest party she had ever attended, where she had been invited at the last moment to fill a gap made by some unexpected excuses. She remembered it all well enough. How negligent she found all the servants! How condescending the lady of the house, how coldly dignified the guests! But never mind that. " Somebody," had stayed till the very end of the entertainment, pointing the compliment by carelessly observing that he was due at a countess' ball—but that it didn't matter. She had seen him afterwards, and in the half-expressed and wholly clandestine admiration of this man with a title and landed property before him, there had been a strange sweet zest, which she did not find in all the honest courtship of the plain lover, with his straightforward offer of marriage. " Somebody" was away in the west of England now, with his regiment. " He must not stay where inclination would keep him, but must go where duty called him"—he had said. Philip had never made such a pretty speech. he would have thought it quite beside the mark, and would have followed duty humbly as a matter of course. If she had only been quite sure that somebody meant something ! But how was one to know ?—And in the interval, poor Philip had made his " bothering" proposal ! But while she held the tame bird in one hand, she stretched out the other, after the wild one in the bush. She did not know this hard truth of herself. She was not honest enough to suspect herself of dishonesty. Only she wished—and wished—and wished. And a wish, may be a prayer to God or Satan. And Satan answers—Oh, most readily ! We need only sigh to him for a crumb of bread, and he will give us beautiful fruit—so tempting—till we bite it, and then !—

It was nine o'clock before they reached home, the last post was going round to the houses. Hester had just emptied their letter-box as they came up, and she opened the door and almost before she touched the knocker :

" Anything for me ? " asked Sybil, sweeping in.

" Yes, one," Hester replied, handing it to her. Sybil took it and looked at it earnestly. She almost fancied—but feared to put her fancy into shape, lest it should not be true. So she held the letter aside, and asked again. " Anything for anybody else ? " Having no duties in her own life, Sybil was always at leisure to peep into other people's ; about as kindly and helpful as your next door neighbor's surveillance on a washing day.

" Something for Dora," Hester answered, and then the little group separated.

It was at least half an hour before Sibyl rejoined Philip in the drawing-room, she did not speak as she came in, nor did she take her usual seat beside him on the sofa, but went straight to the piano and began to play. She seemed a little flushed, and looked so grave and pre-occupied that Philip feared lest she was in some way troubled. That perhaps she had already entered on some secret negotiations for independence. Women were always braver and nobler than men's thoughts. So presently he crossed over to the chair which faced her as she played, and then ventured to interrupt the melody with the whispered inquiry, " Is anything wrong ? "

" No; what did you think ? " she answered, quickly.

" I fancied there might be something in that letter," he said, meekly ; then resolutely determined to save her from the suffering of unshared anxieties, he presumed to inquire who it was from.

" Only a note from an acquaintance," she answered, rather pettishly.

But Philip persisted in his private brain of thought. " Don't you trouble yourself about the music-lessons," he observed, confidentially.   " Just write out a grand advertisement ; in this world, most people accept you at your own estimation, and I will take it to the Times' Office, and you must promise to let me see the answers which you get, that we may judge what are worth your attention.   But don't you trouble yourself, there's a darling ! "

" I wish you wouldn't worry me," she replied. " We are not going out of this house to-morrow, nor the next day, either."

" It is because she thinks these things are a trouble to me," thought Philip, silenced, while all the time, it's a pleasure to me to hope to serve her in such small ways as I can.

Hester had taken up to Dora's room, a letter and a packet.   She had put them into her hand and retired without a word.   But she did not go further than her own chamber.   Night after night she waited there. If there were good news, Dora would come and tell her. If not, she presently went down, and got the supper. Expectation was no longer breathless. Hope had quieted down into patience.

But hark! Dora had never paced her room like this before. And now her hand was upon the door. Hester flew to her's.

"It is taken at last," she cried ; "they've sent me the proof and a post-office-order. Come and look ! "

Hester had won the sacred confidence of young ambition and aspiration. The strong reserve of her silent sympathy had proved itself to be trusted. Beautiful curves were rounding off her straight line of duty. She did not notice that then. The beginner is rarely conscious of his first advance. But nevertheless she took the blessedness of it to her heart and shut it in there as we may fold away a dried flower, gathered on a happy day. It will be pleasant to look at in wintry weather.

"Let me read the poem," she said; may I read it aloud, Dora ? "

"If you like," she said, smiling. And she read.

DIVERGING PATHS.

"I can't go with you farther, Willie,
For an old man soon grows weary
Though your sunlit path looks tempting
And my backward one but dreary.
We don't know what awaits you at the other side the wave
But don't forget your English home, and your mother's English
grave.

"God blesses honest labor, Willie,
   He has blessed my work to me :
   Though the cottage roof is leaky,
   And my best clothes what you see.
You are almost smiling, Willie, an' I judge you think it strange
If your father had his life again, he would not wish a change.

"When I wed your mother, Willie,
   Ah, how fast the seasons roll !
   It was summer on the meadow,
   And 'twas summer in my soul,
But God for wealth gave need, and for pleasure He gave woe,
But he gave us also, Willie, hearts that answered, " Better so."

"God knows I nearly failed, Willie,
   For we are not always strong ;
   But your mother only kissed me
   When I said that things went wrong
Just because God spared her. One by one her babes he reft,
You remember when she died, Willie, only you and I were left.

"If you grow a rich man, Willie,
   Never scorn your early home,
   And you need not miss your mother
   Though to farthest land you roam.
You're the only one, my Willie, little like her grave to share,
But her soul is safe in Heaven and Heaven is everywhere.

"God forbid I daunt you, Willie,
   When He gives us strength and health
   Sure He ne'er forbids us use them
   To gain honest place and wealth.
An' He gives bright hope at starting, only when it comes to pale,
Pray that your heart receive instead the faith which does not fail.

> " Now, God bless an' guide you, Willie,
> I'm tired out—you see I'm old,
> And I'll go home the churchyard way,
> It's nearest—though it's cold
> I'm thinking, lad, in little while your mother's grave I'll share,
> An' then you'll have us both again for Heaven is everywhere."

"Why, Dora," cried Hester ; " of course that is the best thing you have ever written ! It's not a fancy, it's a fact ! you are right in saying everybody knows, and feels all that. But then that's just the beauty of it. We shall all be proud of you, Dora, I am ever so proud of you, already."

And then she left her. Dora did not see anybody else that night. She heard Sibyl come to her room, but she did not go to tell her glad secrets to her. We want to share everything with somebody, but so long as we have one true heart who knows of our treasures, we are chary lest any rougher hand should burst away their bloom.

Sometimes "Sibyl's," may remain confident to the end ; but only for lack of " Hester's." Work generally finds its way to the fittest workman, if he is only to be had.

Next morning Dora rose with the first sunbeam. She was glad to rise and open the window. There had been a shower at midnight, and the quiet street and the trees beyond, looked refreshed and cool. There is a strange and solemn charm in the dawn over London. Dora felt the spell. The girl's soul was drawn out of herself, and nearer to God than it had ever been before. Somehow, she never knew how there arose before her mind, a vision of a Divine Youth sadly asking his grieved parents, "Wist ye not that I must be about my Father's business?" And it came to her like a revelation—all the throbbing aspirations, which seemed only beating themselves to death against the bars of a rebellious human nature; and all the weary marchings towards lofty virtue through steep and narrow paths that always ended in some "No Thoroughfare" of innate depravity, were suddenly lifted into a higher region of light and liberty, by that glory of the Godhead, shining through a veil of flesh, showing what manhood might have been, and atoning for what manhood could never be—and the young poet in the glory of her new-born hopes, bowed her head and prayed: "Father, for Thy work—not mine own—help and strengthen me!"

And the dawn deepened into crimson daylight.

CHAPTER XVI.

KNIGHT-ERRANTRY IN 1800.

SIBYL'S advertisment appeared in the Times at last. But her first pupils were obtained by Philip's tact. Lunching with a gentleman for whom he was arranging some out-houses, he overheard that the family required a Music Mistress, and promptly spoke a good word for his late partner's daughter. Sibyl did not accept the appointment at all enthusiastically, she asked every question that was calculated to develop its disadvantages until Philip felt almost ashamed of himself for suggesting it, and she quietly kept to herself what she considered a point so favorable as to outweigh everything else— that the family lived on the south side of Hyde Park, and that her way to and fro, would lie through her beloved West End. She finally agreed to undertake the duty with the satirical remark, " that chivalry had phase peculiar to every age, and that the last was to find work for the lady-love."

But there was no such modern chivalry ; for Hester,

Indirectly she raised the subject of her future once or twice in conversation with her future brother-in-law, but afterwards regretted doing so. According to his views, there was no occupation for well-bred women but teaching—surely every woman could teach something, from graceful arts like his Sibyl's, to the primer and pot-hooks of the nursery governess. There can be nothing more womanly than teaching, he declared. Every true woman has maternal instincts and it gratifies them. It is the noblest work in the world and worthy of woman. Women need never want any other work while they have that."

"I suppose the ministry is the highest calling for men," Hester murmured, rebelliously. "But I doubt whether the min'stry would gain as much as other walks of life would lose, if all men were forced to be ministers!"

"Women are meant to be wives and mothers," Philip went on. "They are meant for the duties of the hearth, and the shelter of home."

"Who means them?" interrupted Hester, quietly.

"God himself," said Philip, with solemn certainty.

"Then you mean that God does not have His own way in the world," Hester retorted; "For there are women who would have neither hearths nor homes unless they earned them for themselves, out in the world."

"Women are made for dependence." Philip proceeded, never meeting her retorts full in the face, but travelling on safely beside them ; " They are made

ʼto lean on man. Their strength is their weakness. Woman's rights indeed ! a woman's right is her right to the love and cherishing of one man ; give her that and her whole nature is satisfied and she is happy."

Alas ! when our best weapons are so sharp that we dare not use them lest they wound too deeply ! Hester longed to say, if this were so, she wondered Sibyl was not better tempered and more restful. But she kept silence and while she paused, Philip resumed his eloquence.

"What does the good old-fashioned poet say ?

A woman's noblest station is retreat.

She is made for it. Is her tender and sensitive nature to be torn and worn on on the rough wheel of the world ?"

"A woman will hardly find anything in the world worse than a bad husband, Mr. Lewis," said Anthony Fiske, reflectively. Mr. Fiske had left the house a few days after Mr. Capel's funeral, but he had taken lodgings close at hand and was a constant visitor.

"And I can't see that ʽ a woman's noblest station is starvation in a garret ! ʼ cried Hester ; "no, nor yet living upon other people who don't find her existence to be either a necessity or a luxury."

"Of course you think women's intellect is the same as men's ;" Philip resumed, with supreme satire ; "You would like them to be physicians and lawyers and merchants, I suppose."

"It does not matter what I should like," said Hester. "They can't be such ; one or two very clever women may be just able enough to kill themselves in

9

striving to do what ordinary men do, easily. But I do say that men have no right to dictate to women what they shall be or do."

"A woman's strength is in her heart," Philip pursued, grandly. "Men do not want clever women to contradict and argue with them ; they want women to love them."

"Have men so low an estimate of themselves, that they think they can only win the affection of fools ? " asked Hester, scornfully.

"If I wanted a wife to love me," said Anthony Fiske ; "I'd marry as wise a woman as I could find. But then, of course she wouldn't have me. That's where it is. There are some women who could be the salvation of some men. But they are the very ones who won't have anything to say to the men that want saving. I know this is outside the discussion, but I couldn't help saying it, because I've so often turned it over in my mind."

"A woman is just a woman," said Philip, dogmatically. "Her highest ambition is to have a home of her own. Every action of her life is set towards that aim. Show me a woman who is not looking out for a husband, and I tell you she is either an abnormal creature, with no womanly instincts, or else she is a crushed being with all the springs of hope and joy dried up within her. In the discipline of marriage the woman is developed into the angel."

"The Bible does not say that marriage is the straightest road to heaven," murmured Hetty.

"All women are not seeking husbands," said Dora, looking up from her books and joining in the conversation. "Why, the very idea takes away all the bloom and beauty from the gifts of a woman's love!"

"And it would make it horrible to be an old bachelor," observed Mr. Fiske comically; "somebody so worthless as to be overlooked even in the universal search!"

"A crushed being, with all the springs of hope and joy dried up within her," repeated Hester, thoughtfully; "and that is your description of a woman who, having loved truly, and lost, will not put a common pebble where she once wore a diamond. That is your kindest name for the women whose hearts have gone before them to heaven. Mr. Fiske, I suppose this description applies to your Richard Wriksworth's little puss, and other single women, who have never seen the man they could love, or have seen him too late, or with some barrier between them; and so looking for no earthly change are cheerfully content to live the life that Christ lived. They are all 'crushed beings' with the springs of hope and joy dried up within them."

"You needn't defend old maids so fiercely, Hetty," said Sibyl, laughing; "don't make common cause with them just yet, nobody knows what may happen."

"The great body of women are quietly contented with this holy and happy lot," remarked Philip. "Their religion and their domesticity, go hand in

hand.   If a woman surrenders the one, the other fol-
lows.   The woman who begins to think that the life
of her mothers is not sufficient for her, will presently
question the creed of her fathers.   The faith that satisfied great theologians and philosophers will not be
spared by her inquiring mind."

"What a pity the world ever moved on at all!"
said Hester, excited to catch so good a throw at her
opponent.   "What a pity, we sweet gentle women
dare to differ from Luther, when he condemned a con-
sumptive baby as a thing bewitched of the devil!"

There is scarcely an error or heresy into which such
rigid following of precedents, might not guide us.

"Well! let a woman surrender religion, and she will
find that it alone secured her from becoming a slave
and the prey of wicked men," said Philip, composedly.
"Women are instinctively religious, and in her own
interests let her keep that instinct."

"I don't believe women need religion a whit more
than men," returned Hester, fiercely.   "It does not
say so in the Bible, and the thing is often called religion in women is not so good or so near the reality as
the common honor of men.   I have known women
with all the outward developments of this instinct, who
have been regular Sunday school teachers, and district-
visitors and church-goers, but who would dock half-
pence from their tradespeoples' bills, to swell their
charity lists ; who would open desks to read others'
letters that should have been held as sacred as their
lives ; who would underpay the women they employed

to make knick-knacks for a fancy bazar, and then allow the said knick-knacks to pass as the product of their own ingenious industry. This is the morality that sprouts from the mere 'religious instinct' which is nothing more than a tendency to go to church as men go to a music-hall, to fill up an idle hour. And it seems to me, that to uphold religion on the ground of personal expediency may be very natural, but is scarcely commendable. If that is the only reason why women should cling to it, the least selfish natures will resign it first."

" Hush Hester, dear," said Lizzie, gently.

" It is not I who am saying so of religion," cried Hester. "It is only the way in which Philip puts it that forces my answers to seem as if I did not think marriage the happiest lot of man or woman, and re-ligion just the one thing that makes life endurable," and Hester paused, as if she scarcely realized the last truth she had uttered. Then she went on, " But I do utterly deny that it is anybody's worldly interest to be religious. I utterly deny that real religion ever walks in silver slippers. God often pays his servants well. But the devil appears to pay better ; I know it is only in appearance, because God's payments are only on account, and his are in advance."

" But God alone gives the peace that passes under-standing," whispered Miss Capel.

" True, Lizzie," she answered ; " I know good peo-ple are happier than bad ones. They get the full good out of everything; a crust and an appetite are

better than venison and none. But then it is the same
with men as with women. You never find these distinctions in the Bible. We are all fellow-creatures
there, with a great deal more in common than in particular."

"These questions were not raised in Bible days,"
said Philip; composedly. "It is just a mania that
has seized the present age, and will die harmlessly
in the natural order of things."

"It is a question as old as the hills," returned
Hester. "Though it is one of those things, which as
Sybil says of chivalry has a phase peculiar to every
age. Isaiah pays no tender compliments to the careless woman, 'and the women that are at ease.' And
if all women were equal to the model in the last chapter of Proverbs, we should not have so many pamph-
lets and speeches about us."

"But you see they are not," said Philip, compla-
cently ; "that is all the difference."

"Just the same as very few of the men are like the
one in the fifteenth Psalm, but it is what we are meant
to try after," returned Hester.

"The wise woman depicted was a wife, remember," rejoined Philip, in positive triumph.

"I know it;" "but she would have earned a good
income, and have been an important person, if she
had been an old maid. She was a good business
woman and did not sit still with folded hands, to receive honor from her husband, but reflected it back
again so that he was known in the gates. He in his

turn, evidently left her independence in her own good keeping, ' for she considereth a field and buyeth it— with the fruit of her hands she planteth a vineyard.' Her chief attributes were not tenderness and delicacy, ' but strength and honor were her clothing;' and although 'she opened her mouth with wisdom,' Solomon did not think it incongruous to add, that, ' in her tongue was the law of kindness; ' nor does it seem that her husband and children were dissatisfied with their relationship, since the one 'praiseth her,' and the 'others rose up and called her blessed,' and what you, Philip, must think very singular, God himself signed her character, ' as a woman that feareth the Lord.' ''

And Hester thought her argument very unanswerable till Philip said, with aggravating composure.

" Well, if it is as you read it, and women are so well able to take care of themselves, not to add, of us into the bargain ; of course it is unnecessary that we should step into the gutter to let them pass dry shod ; or stand that they may sit ; or grant any of the late prerogatives that we so gladly yield to what we have been taught to regard as the softer and weaker sex."

Hester drew a long, almost sobbing breath : " We don't think we can take care of ourselves in some ways without you, any more than you can take care of yourselves in other ways without us. But we do say that you have no right to make us puppets whereon merely to exercise your gallantry. I don't see why a beau should not be as willing to make life smooth and pleas-

ant for an industrious woman going about her business, as for an idle dame, occupied solely with her
pleasure. I don't see why a woman must make
herself less than she is meant to be, to save the men
from making themselves less than they ought. I
think all men whose courtesy was not a positive insult,
will be courteous still—but if not—if we must choose
between giving up the inner path and the proffered
chair, or the noblest attributes of humanity, then by
all means let the first go!"

And there the arguments ended; having simply
strengthened both in their own opinions, which, as in
the case of so many opponents, were far less dissimilar
than they seemed. Between natures so unlike as
Philip's and Hester's, apparent harmony would have
been direct discord. There was no mutual ground
whereon the two could compare notes; scarcely a
single word had the same meaning to both of them;
and in each there was an under-current of personal
experience and feeling to which neither chose to give
utterance, though by so doing either could have won
the warmest sympathy of the antagonist. If Hester
had only known that notwithstanding all the dainty
euphemisms whereby Philip seemed inclined to turn
womanhood into a perishable piece of sugar-candy,
and which to her enlightened sense, answered to a
true description of the height and depth and breadth
of Sibyl's character; yet the other and truer half of
his ideal was genuinely embodied in his own mother,
who would willingly have slaved herself to death for

her boy's sake, but finding no such outward scope for her loving energies, had turned them inward, and spared and cared and borne the reproach of a mean and miserly housekeeper, and undergone a series of petty misunderstandings and slights, which, however ridiculous they might seem to eyes grown strong with wider views, were a perfectly real martyrdom to one whose world was her village tea-parties. And if Philip had only known the tremblings and pangs that throbbed and ached behind the brave front that Hester was turning to duty! If he could only have understood the high pure spirit that would gather all the scattered roses of its destined way, while it refused to own that it felt the thorns which its feet must tread down! If he had only known that she felt herself to be the lovely struggling woman of whom he talked so coolly, and that it was her duty to become the strong courageous woman to whom it pleased him to give such hard names. Sighs and tears win sympathy ; but oh, for the wise insight which can sympathize with the sighs that are breathed inwardly and the tears that are never seen ! Hester did not wish to deny womanly weakness, yet she indignantly felt that no woman should think it an affliction to have to be worth her place in the world, whatever place God might assign. But is the weaker horse heavily handicapped ? Is the feebler wrestler encouraged with hisses and stones? Or if this be man's way, is it God's? Although all Philip's rhetoric failed to shake Hester's opinions, and indeed only strengthened her in their advocacy,

9*

yet her mind was too open, too thoughtfully impartial for her to pass over her, wholly without influence. His words meant more to her that heard, than to him that spoke. There was a convenient inconsistency between Philip's mental processes and their practical result. Instead of adapting his theories to facts, he adapted facts to his theories. He laid down strict and narrow laws, and whenever a stern reality set them utterly at naught, he instantly accepted it as one of those exceptions that are said to prove the rule. If Hester had said to him, broadly and plainly, "I have to provide for myself—am I to make up my mind that it is impossible so to do, or that even if I can, I must reconcile myself to a life of dissatisfaction and misery!" Then he would have been the first to say, "No, you are not lost in the great army of incapacity. There may be but little work going among women yet, but there are not enough women fit for what there is!" and he would have reconciled this with his usual train of thought ; by such elastic links as "You are different!" and "Circumstances alter cases."

But between these two, such explanation could never be—and so the way before Hester looked doubly as steep and as long as it was. Under so treacherous a surveying-glass, a weaker woman would have sat down discouraged. But Hester girded up her strength with a brave determination to be equal to all the trials of the unknown future.

CHAPTER XVII.

" IN ALL TIME OF OUR TRIBULATION."

THE summer wore away. It was a weird, and ghastly time to Hester.

The hours seemed so long and weary and yet the days appeared to run down so swiftly towards Michaelmas. Lizzie never spoke about the change that was coming upon them, except in a plain matter-of-fact way. Her old duties of work and saving, as long as they lasted, would quite absorb her time, who shall say. Whether she had so learned to cast her care upon God, that she could keep her thoughts in the same sphere with her busy hands, and trust that one gate would not close until another opened, without even any breathless watching for the first creak of the hinge? At any rate she was not one of those people who neglect to-day's work, lest they should have none to-morrow. If there were some silent anxieties in her mind, depend upon it they were like the patient interest of a child, who does not doubt that his father will bring in something good for the next meal, but only wonders what it will be.

Hester had no absorbing duties; her leisurely days fell upon her as a dead-weight ; like gold upon a capitalist shot in a beleaguered city. She felt bitter forebodings lest she should some day sorely need the moments that now wore away so heavily. She was discovering a new meaning in life, which is a word of many significations. She had always known that the family was what is termed "unprovided for" but hitherto the fact had only flashed into her mind, with a sort of ambitious delight when she had read of the triumphs of self-dependent women. But it is quite one matter to look at an object, and another to look from it. The lad who whilst listening to the recruiting-sergeant, who feels himself sure to become a great officer, once enlisted, is only too likely to forget that he has at least, a chance. Hester no longer thought of Mary Russell Mitford waiting in the empty twilight auction-rooms, to be told that a thousand voices were applauding her drama. She forgot Frances Burney, at that auspicious moment when her father laid his finger on the advertisement of "Evelina," and observed "that he must read that book." She forgot Angelica Kauffmann's academic honors. Nay, turning to a nearer and wider level, she no longer mused on the widow who lived but a few doors off—a merchant's widow, left with no legacy but her husband's debts' and five small children—who had gone up to her husband's place of business and attended her markets, and done all kinds of brave and unusual deeds, at first, because nobody should lose by having trusted her husband, and then, because she would like to do justice to his orphans, and lastly because she had grown used to it, and didn't see why she should not go on till she had made a little purse for her old age, and her eldest son was old enough to take her place. Hester even forgot to think of her dressmaker who kept the corner house, a single woman always picking some scapegrace relation out of trouble ; and yet thriving and happy through all. No, Hester now thought of the great army of daily governesses ; many of them so terribly glad to earn something, and yet comparatively so few like herself with positively nothing and nobody to fall back upon. She had known such, out of engagements for months together, and then away went her imagination, to some draughty upper-chamber where she saw herself stitching some weary seam, and dreaming of green fields, one glimpse of which, would " cost a meal." She began to observe women who went to and fro past their houses at stated times, to notice what dress they wore, and how they looked, and to wonder what each of them did !

Then with some strange memory of the text " in all labor there is profit," she set herself all sorts of great tasks. Work, sheer hand-labor, was a kind of comfort to her. If we are to have a new house-mate, we want to grow a little acquainted with him before-hand. And Hester wanted to know how it felt to sit for hours and hours at one monotonous task. She chanced to hear Lizzie say that they must buy some flannel to prepare for winter petticoats, and she instantly suggested that yarn should be bought instead, and that she herself would knit them, as she had heard that such was held to be a thrifty practice in many Scotch country-houses.

The yarn was bought, the saving on the whole purchase was found to be only three or four shillings; but Hester was proud of that, and set to work with all her might. She rose early and worked from meal to meal till ten o'clock at night. Nobody knew the whole of her diligence, for she carried it on in secret, in her own room, where she was supposed to be reading, or otherwise amusing herself.

All through the hot July days, the fuzzy yarn passed through her fevered sensitive hands. She did two petticoats in a week, and triumphantly " cast off" the last stitch before tea-time on Saturday.

When she descended to the parlor, Sibyl was there, having just returned from her afternoon teaching. It had been a treacherous changeable morning; but Sibyl had refused to cumber herself with umbrella or waterproof, or to go in anything but her best dress, and crape-trimmed jacket. Consequently, she had been caught in a shower, and was now daintily dabbing her moist finery with her pocket-handkerchief.

"I am afraid it will never look as well again," said Lizzie.

"I only hope you won't catch cold yourself," observed Philip, standing by.

"Aren't you sorry, now, that you put it on?"

asked Dora, who had heard her reject her sisters' advice on the subject before she started.

But Sibyl seemed by no means inclined for regret just then. She was scarcely in a good temper ; yet lively and excited. No, I'm not, she retorted. " What are clothes for, but to wear? If you are always reserving your best for fear of accidents, they grow dowdy and old-fashioned before you have got any good out of them. And whenever you go shabby, somebody's sure to meet you."

" By that rule, if you go fine, nobody will meet you ; the finery is wasted, and the friend missed! " said Dora, mischievously.

" Oh, it need not be a friend," answered Sibyl, with a shade of contempt at Dora's youthful green- ness. " Friends don't notice so much, and if they do, it doesn't matter. I mean people that you know. Spiteful sort of acquaintances, particularly."

" But wouldn't you rather adorn yourself to please the eyes that love you, than to spite malice ? " asked Philip ; in that tone that signified certainty of at least, secret acquiescence.

For a moment Sibyl pouted dissent. Then adroitly turned off the question with a sentiment. " The eyes that love me, would fancy I adorned what- ever I wore." And a bewitching glance carried the pretty arrow straight to the soft side target of Philip's heart. She uttered the sweet soft compliment, not in the tone of sprightly raillery, which would have made it sincere—but with a semblance of grave sincerity that turned it into bitter satire and sickened Hester, who instantly requested Lizzie to give her a cup of tea, as quickly as she could, as she wanted to go out.

"It promises to be a lovely evening after the storm," observed Mr. Lewis, "shall we take the omnibus, and spend an hour or two in the Regent's Park, Sibyl?"

Sibyl hesitated. "O, my boots are soaked," she said (she had a dry pair in her room); "and I shall have to change this dress for the nasty old one. And I am very tired, and I have a good deal to do. I can't go to-night, really."

"I am ashamed of myself for being so thoughtless as to ask you," answered poor Philip.

Then Hester went away and prepared for her walk. Before she had finished dressing, she heard Sibyl go into her own room, and as Hester passed out, she saw through her sister's open door, that Sibyl was sitting at the window, her hair half loose about her shoulders, and her hands lying in her lap. Fearful lest she should call her, Hester hastened quietly away, for she had a particular purpose in her walk, and did not wish to be delayed.

Two or three years before, in the course of a summer's evening visit to Chelsea Hospital, she remembered seeing a shop in the King's Road, where knitted garments were displayed. She and Lizzie had taken particular notice of them at the time, but in those days they had not noticed the prices, knowing they had no money for random purchases, and never thinking of any need for sale. But it struck her now, that she should like to know the money-value of her week's hard labor.

It was a long long walk to take for such an object. But her mind was the calmer for any strong exertion, and Hester, as yet, knew nothing of " re-actions." There is an ignorance which is the first stage of wisdom. While stern necessity stands over us, like the centurion, bidding us " go," and " come," it is well that we should not think much of the consequences of commands for which we are not responsible, and which we must obey. When a lad has to choose a calling, if instead of at once taking that to which his tastes lead him, he resolves to read the medical opinions upon all professions and trades, determined to choose only that which is distinctly stated not to have its own peculiar short-cut to death ; then we may safely predicate that the King of Terrors will soon come to him in the shape of starvation, at the work-house door. There is a divine ignorance, as well as a divine defiance of " consequences." It is dangerous " to count the cost too carefully," when we have no opportunity to compare our arithmetical result, with the correct answer written in God's key to the problems of providence. If Jacob had not risen above his calculations in that forlorn assent—" If I be bereaved of my children, I am bereaved," would he have seen Joseph again ? No, unless youth has other thoughts to call it away from economical considerations of its own energies, mental power and physical health, it will find itself like the young man described by the old essayist, whose mother had been so fearful lest study or exercise should injure his eyesight, his lungs or his limbs, that he proved as helpless as he could have been, had he lost the use of all. Life will not trust us in any worthy post, until it has part of our very being in pledge.

Hester kept steadily on her road. But when she reached Piccadilly, she grew doubtful which was her nearest way, and not being very well acquainted with the intricacies of Knightsbridge, she resolved on the route which she knew—across the Green Park, and through Pimlico. Out of the hot dusty streets, the cool breeze of the Park was refreshing enough ; but she did not even feel a wish to loiter there—what was there in common between her, and the happy lovers seated in bliss together, with hands slily clasped under the treacherous screen of the feminine shawl ? Some of them might be poor enough. That fact was too patent for her to assume otherwise, but at least they were secure and settled in their own humble spheres. This she could assume with all the gloriously uncertain latitude allowed to assumptions. How could she suppose that one girl, who looked at her as she passed, with a face still blushing from her lover's praises, spared a thought from her delicious dream to wish that her jacket was as well-made as Hester's ? Or that another, in all the glory of a " respectable married woman," husband beside, and child in arms, glanced from her own shabby dress to Hester's trim mourning, and half-longed for the days when she was a milliner's show-woman, and had "eighteen shillings a week all to herself;" two silk dresses in wear at once, and no baby, nor back-ache!

Hester walked on; she had passed the middle of the park, and was nearing its southern margin when she became suddenly aware of somebody hurrying after her, and a gay voice just behind, cried, lightly, "whither away so fast, fair lady? I did not expect the pleasure of seeing you again to-day." And a tall gentleman sprang in front of her, looked smilingly down at her startled earnest face, and with an instantaneous change of tone and manner, raised his hat, apologizing for a very foolish mistake, and was gone; Hester scarcely knew in what direction. She had not even paused in her amazement; but yet she had taken in the face, figure and whole bearing of the man. A tall young man, aristocratically ugly, with a chesnut beard, and lilies of the valley in his button-hole. Such a thing had never happened to Hester before. Was there something by which men knew when women were in sore trouble, and chose that moment for overture or insult? Forgive her the morbid thoughts —her poor brain was sadly beaten, and she was weary already. It was gone in an instant, as she remembered the quick subtle change in his style of address, when he found that he had taken her for somebody very different from what he found her. No, it was nothing—nothing at all, but what he said; "a very foolish mistake." But yet it left a sense of unprotec-

tion in the midst of a cruel mocking world, which was
an added drop of bitterness in the cup of gall she was
drinking.

At last Hester reached the end of her journey; she
found the shop not shut, and though most of the window was devoted to goods more suited to the season,
still there were a few petticoats just like those she had
been making. Alas. alas, the price-tickets told her—
that leaving the very narrowest margin of profit for the
shop-keeper, and supposing that yarn was very much
cheaper when bought for "the trade"—her weeks'
industry would not have brought in five shillings'
profit. Something hot flushed up to Hester's eyes,
but no tears came, as she stood motionless, among the
bustling group that paused to admire the gay display.
Should she ever care to look at shops again ? When
one reads an old-fashioned story, and enjoys it just as a
story, till one comes to a grim moral at the end, one
can never reperuse the tale without hearing the moral
all through. Ever after one has seen below, one's
eyes refuse to stop at the mere surface.

She walked slowly down the road, not in the direction of home. Then turned back. Five shillings
was very, very little. But if life was hard as this, she
must not miss the opportunity of laying in a little
store, offered by the few weeks still to be spent in the
now burdensome leisure of her old home. This shop-
keeper might have work to give. Hester was as yet
quite ignorant of such petty details as "references,"
and "experience." She would go in and ask if they

could employ her, or if they would at least take down her name for the first vacancy. But she quailed, when she saw the brilliantly lit shop, and an affluent looking pair of customers purchasing Balbriggan hosiery. There was a young man lingering at the door too, who did not look like a mere shopman, and though he was quite a lad, not more than nineteen or twenty, yet to Hester's nervous excitement, even he, was formidable. She walked down the road again—resolving she would go in when the shop was clear of customers. On her next return she found it so. Then with a heroic exertion of will, which to the inexperienced must seem altogether disproportioned to the occasion, she entered. The departed purchasers had closed the door behind them. It had a bell fastened to it, which rang as if to herald the approach of an order for not less than five pounds' worth of goods. Two shopmen and one shopwoman made motions of obsequious welcome from their respective posts. Hester made a desperate movement towards the girl. What she said, she never knew; but she said it so hurriedly, that she was forced to repeat it. And then? why then, the obedient smile died on the shop-girl's face, and she drew herself up, and said, coolly :

"O dear, no. We procure all our work through regular agencies like other respectable establishments."

"What is it, Miss Smith ?" interposed one of the shopmen.

shopmen.

"The young person wants to find employment.

that's all," returned the girl, retiring from the counter.

Hester looked forlornly at the man as he came forward, as if she hoped against hope for better news from him. He was a good-natured, common-looking man, with an immense chain and seals—the sort of man who can speak lightly enough of distress behind its back, but cannot help feeling sympathetic while he meets its eyes.

" You see, miss," said he; " we take our embroidery from the Madeira nunneries, and our knitting from the Shetlanders, who are always in such distress when their fisheries fail as they do, pretty often. Ladies always ask for Madeira work and Shetland goods. But, lor, miss, you don't lose much, for it's awful bad pay. You couldn't get anything worse."

He meant no harm by his familiarity—rather the reverse. Hester remembered his words afterwards, as a coarsely-distilled drop of human kindness. She uttered her apology and thanks heartily, and turned away. The youth who had been standing in the threshold, opened the door for her, and let her out with a bow. The shopman did not like to see courtesy so wasted by his grave young master, who had just taken the place of a suddenly deceased father, and had discontinued Academic preparations, for a different career, to do an eldest son's duty to a widowed mother, and a crowd of younger children.

" She was only a gal wanting work, Mr. Melvill," he said.

"What of that?" asked the young principal, gravely.   And the shopman was abashed.

"Are there many such come here?" inquired the young man, presently.

"No—oh, no, sir.   All the years I've been here, sir, I've known but two or three.   Those that do, must be dreadful green—hem!—very inexperienced sir."

"It is very sad, said the young master," as if thinking aloud.

"O, I don't suppose they're in want of a living, sir. Only pocket-money and so forth, most likely, sir."

Mr. Melvill made no reply, till he said, suddenly. "If it ever happen again, Webb, I will answer them myself.   Please to remember that."   And he went off to the counting-house.

"Well, I never!" ejaculated the shopwoman.

"When the master knows a little more, he won't take upon himself trouble that he needn't," said the shopman.

Hester walked on again.   She did not turn in the direction of home.   For the first few minutes she did not notice where she was going, and when her consciousness came clearly back, she found herself near a long rambling old street that she remembered in former summer rambles.   It led down to the river.

The houses were poor and sordid, and sluttish women were hanging about the doors, and ill-kept children quarrelling in the gutter.   Gradually it became more respectable in appearance—the houses with their short white curtains and neatly-trimmed evergreens looked like the homes of decent working-people. Hester, as she went along, wondered to herself how they got their living! She almost wished that she might rap at the pretty little green doors and inquire. But suddenly, the houses were of an utterly different character. Tall brick structures with many small-paned windows, and wide thin old steps. Little bits of grotesque carving above the door, and fancifully devised fan-lights. Homes, once of rank and fashion and still of comfort and affluence. Plates announcing well-established professions, adorned the old doors whereon footmen had once thundered, while the link-holders remained to tell of many a night of splendid revelry. Hester was on one of the classic grounds of London. Coming through Manor street she had reached Cheyne Walk.

The sun had not been set too long for a glory still to linger over the river and the opposite shore. Hester stood by the rude old paling, and looked down at the boats moored below. The boatmen were moving to and fro, laughing and joking with each other. In one barge, sat a young woman darning a child's stocking, the baby itself asleep on a cushion of shawls near her. Two boys came along beside Hester, and leaned over the balustrade, one was munching a hunch of bread, and the other took to the amusement of throwing pebbles into the river. They were errand-boys, just released from their day's labor.

"I'm to have my holiday in August," said he of

the pebbles. "I'm going down by the boat to my uncle's at Yarmouth; ain't it jolly?"

"I don't have no holidays but at Whitsom," said the other; "but I don't care. I'm to have two shillings a week more after Michaelmas. Well, I ought to be worth it. I be kept my place two year, and I'm big and strong now;" and they moved away.

Hester's eyes strained painfully over the river. It was a lonely world, and it seemed a good place for everybody—except one like herself! Gloomy images crossed her mind. She remembered having heard some lecturer allude "to the necessary victims that must be crushed under the Juggernaut-car of civilization." Bitterly arose the cruel phase, "superfluous women." Underneath all its beauty, the earth seemed of iron, and all the glowing sky as but burnished brass. And God Himself—how could He remember her!

The boy with the bread had dropped some crumbs. Hester saw them, and with the strange arithmetical tendency of an over-wrought mind was mechanically counting them. Five, six, seven. Down came a sparrow, and carried off one, straight up among the trees and presently came again—she was sure it was the same one—with another, and they both pecked and chirped together, like a married couple making purchases. Who sent the bird to the crumb? Who did not forget the sparrow? And yet—and yet—there were storms which left dead birds strewn upon the ground, and depend on it, in many a chimney and architrave little feathered skeletons withered away to nothingness. With a great heaving sob she realized it—it was His will. Christ did not say, no sparrow ever fell to the ground, but that not one should fall without the Father. "Fear ye not therefore, are ye not of more value than many sparrows?" It was Christ's own inference that the fall lost its terror, if the Father knew it. And Hester owned it, with the tears streaming down her face. She could not take it joyfully; could not take it, feeling sure that every bitter bud would burst to beauteous blossom. But she could say, "Though He slay me, yet will I trust Him," even without the aid of that precious secret sense that God's slaying is His benediction. She accepted his will. She did not yet understand his love. She was not so far advanced. St. Paul tells us that "tribulation worketh patience, and patience experience, and experience hope."

And then she went home. Had she lost her evening, and spent her strength for naught? No, she had gained more than she knew, and she felt she had gained something. It would never be so hard to ask for work again. This fact struck her so forcibly as to make her smile ; she had got over one of the times that she was appointed to ask in vain.

But Hester did not know that these painful experiences acting on the peculiar intensifying nature were giving her a concentrated depth of wisdom, breadth of sympathy and quickness of insight, which ordinary natures set in comfortable lives can barely touch by the season of white hairs and failing energies.

And now, all the fashionable and well-to do had vanished from the streets, and there was a brisk ready-money trade going forward in the shops, and the light-hearted working-people seemed to find more interest and fun in their purchase of six-penny necessaries, than do many of those who have all climates under contribution for their luxuries. The variety possible, might only be between a " cottage loaf " and " household bread ; " the wit nothing more than the butcher's broad joke. But one variety or one witticism will serve human nature quite as well as another. Hester recalled an adage she had seen somewhere.

> " A good many people lose sight of enjoyment,
> By trying to catch it to make it employment."

Happiness with all its outward signs of genuine excitement and mirth, is the cheapest thing in the world. Only man is like the savage natives of countries where gold is common, who will barter rich treasures for some flaunting finery, or a cracked looking-glass. Happiness may be of very common materials, the secret lies in the skill which makes them up.

By the time she reached home, Hester wondered at her own cheerful calmness. She was very tired—quite exhausted—so that perhaps the agony was rather blunted than removed. But she did not think of that, then; and besides God sends His blessings in various ways, and sometimes there must be an opiate to calm us, before we can be strong enough for a remedy to cure us.

Dora and Mr. Lewis were alone in the drawing-room, and her inquiry after her sisters, elicited Philip's reply that Sibyl was still busy up stairs and Elizabeth was in the kitchen. Hester sought her elder sister, who was engaged with some pastry for to-morrow.

"Why, wherever have you been ?" Lizzie asked.

"All the way to Cheyne walk—and I saw such a beautiful sunset," Hester replied.

" It is a pity you did not start sooner—it must have been dark nearly all the way home," observed Elizabeth.

"O, I am not frightened. There is nothing to be frightened at, Lizzie. The streets are quite bright and lively with the marketing folks. And for the matter of being noticed, if you walk straight ahead, and don't stare about, nobody is likely to see whether you are a girl or an old woman. If you are noticed, what does it matter? And it's as likely to be in the day time, too. For instance, this evening as I was crossing the Green park while it was broad sunlight, a gentleman came up to me and said, ' Holloa, fair lady, I didn't expect to see you again to day!' He said he'd made a mistake and begged my pardon. If he had, what did it signify? If he hadn't, he only made himself a simpleton. I was none the worse."

" What was he like ?" asked Lizzie.

" Tall and rather fair—what Popps would call ' a swell !' Much too fine a gentleman to be any friend of mine," she added, archly.

And so they chatted on. What did it matter that Mrs. Edwardes was washing up dishes in the scullery, and could hear every word?

CHAPTER XVIII.

SPILT SALT.

ON Monday morning, Hester, as usual, took in the letters. One from Ribbock for Philip, and one for Sibyl. She looked twice at this last, because the handwriting struck her as sadly like her own. However when she looked again, it seemed dissimilar enough. She put them into the dining-room, and went on to the kitchen, whence came a round of singing.

"You seem lively this morning, Popps," said she.

Popps laughed; "Well, miss," she answered, "thare's enough grumpin always agoing along in the world. So when a body feels a bit inclined to sing, I say its her bounden duty to sing."

"Whether she can or not!" laughed Hester.

"Never fear," returned Popps; "there's Miss Lizzie always a-saying she's got no ear nor voice and all that—yet haven't I often heard her a-crooning to herself, real beautiful, all out of her own head. Miss Lizzie's only a-savin her voice for heaven. That always will come into my head when I hear the very parsons a-talking about singing bein' the only gift that we are sure we shall practice above. I ain't sure where the Bible says that, are you, Miss Hetty? only some folks will take a great deal for granted. But I'm certain sure that there's a many who will sing less above for their singing below. There was Polly Kite, as used to be in your sister's class along with me. She'd a voice, if you please. And she went into the singing-class. Polly was seriously disposed then. But others wasn't. When a minister sets up a singing-class, may be he'll have to shut his eyes a bit while he's listening to the fine voices. The devil's at many a prayer-meeting, as well as many a singing-lesson, I know. But then he has to behave hisself, and at t'other he has a bit of fun on the way home. And ye can't be out twice a-chapeling in the week, and Polly dropped the service when she joined the singing. Then Polly took to going to a church that had a good organ, and warn't too particular who was in the choir. There was somebody there too, that, to do our minister justice, he'd turned out o' singing-class after tryin' him over and over again—cause why, he was the only tenor they had. And at last, Polly wasn't no good at all ; and now she sings at publics. I can't sing properly, Miss Hetty, and may be, it seems as if I said this out o' spite ; but when we hear those that happen to know their notes, has such a lot o' fine talk about it—it puts me a-mind of a shopman chantin' a gown, 'cos he don't want you to turn up the other side, where it's a bit faded.

Popps had spoken very fast, as people often do, when they really have something else to say—a natural piece of Baconian policy. After a moment's pause, she asked, quickly :

"May I just speak to you, Miss Hetty?"

"I'm sure you needn't ask," said Hester.

"I don't like to mention it to Miss Lizzie," Popps began in a flurry. "I knows what it'll be for her to leave this. She takes it like a sort of dream, yet. Them dreams when you knows you're a-dreaming and has got to wake, but wouldn't while you can help it. It won't be so bad when it comes, I 'spose. But any how, that'll be God's business. It's queer it is, you don't get more tired o' things the longer you have 'em. I almost wanted a change myself after I'd bin in my place a year, I did. After a while you settles. It'll only be a nice change for *you*, Miss Hetty. Change is good for plants and people. It'll be good for Miss Lizzie too, I'll be bound—only it's no good to keep talking about it beforehand. If you're going to have a rotten tooth out, you'll be all the better when it's done ; but what's the good o' looking at the dentist's tools ? So what I want to ask is, where do you think o' goin' Miss?

"Mr. Fiske has been recommending apartments in some of the quiet little streets near Percy Crescent," Hester answered, with a great lump in her throat ; "but Mr. Lewis wishes us to go westward not to give my sister Sibyl such long journeys. It will be only apartments somewhere, Popps."

"But I'll go with you," Popps suggested, fearfully.

Hester was silent for a moment, nobody finds it so hard to speak about poverty, as those who have long known it very closely, but never before needed to give it a name. Then it struck her that Popps had a claim on the truth. After her long and faithful service, it was too bad to keep her just as long as it suited themselves, while she might be losing chances of more permanent provision. She might be ready to stay, because she knew they were kind, and believing in a prosperity that did not exist, would have a homely faith that they would "see right." So Hester spoke out.

"I am afraid not, Popps. You see I don't suppose we shall keep more than three rooms. There will not be much to do.

"Is not Miss Dora to stay with you Miss?" Popps asked, in a smothered voice.

"Yes, at least at present. But we shall have a little bed made up for her in our room. That will be easily done. It would not be worth while to keep another bedroom. In fact it is just this—Popps—we have nothing but ourselves to depend on, and must live on as little as possible, till we see how matters turn out." Hester finished, bravely enough.

Popps began to cry. "I'd stay with you, anyhow, Miss. I shouldn't want no wages, and I eat more bread than meat, and you couldn't be doin' the housework if you was a-teachin, an' if it aint a rude thing to say, Miss Hetty I could sleep on the floor in the

10*

other corner of your bedroom. Don't turn me away. Please don't!"

Hester felt something moist on her own face. "We dont want to turn you away," she said. "Don't say that. You know better. You are a good girl. I know you have reason to be grateful to my sister Lizzie, but it is not every one who is! Only you must think of yourself, too. The less you want to think of yourself, the more we must think for you. We can't let you ruin yourself for us."

"'Tain't no such thing at all," sobbed Popps. "It's real selfishness of mine, that's what it is. I couldn't bear another missis, they're so masterful! And here am I a-doin nothin, but think o' myself, a-goin' and gettin' married, an' just wanting a comfortable place to finish up to my wedding-day, where I'd get time to make my bits o' clothes, and may be a little help in cutting of 'em out. I'm thinkin' o' nothing but myself, Miss Hetty; so don't you go for to think better of me than I is."

Hester drew a long breath. Accustomed to the "hopes deferred," of the lengthy engagements too common among "genteel people," she had never thought of so speedy consummation of Popps' courtship. For a moment, it diverted her thoughts, and she asked:

"When do you expect to marry, Popps?"

"Why that's where it is," Popps answered, coming nearer, in the excitement of reviving hope. "It wasn't to be till next summer or spring at nearest;

but now Tom wants it in January. He's got to be foreman at his place, only last week;" she went on proudly, "and that makes a difference o' money that will soon mount up. He's begun storing bits o' furniture, and making 'em an' so forth some little while, an' his mother she nags, and says they crowd up and make mucky; just because she won't make herself agreeable tó the thought o' me. Just as if she thougbt her talk might stop it, instead of making it come on all the faster! Oh, I'd give anything to stay with you, Miss Hester, and you'd want somebody at the moving, for movings must be awful work!"

"Of course, my sister will decide," Hester replied; not without a secret sigh at the fear lest stern necessity might force herself to set aside her sister's kindly influences. "But I fear we must give you up, Popps, even for that little time."

And she went up stairs. The change had fairly set in. Of course she had known it would. But the most definite future, is not the present. Hope and fear alike recognize that. But now the first axe was laid at the root of the old roof-tree. Hester had left Popps crying, but she herself felt as if she would never cry again.

She went on to her old bedroom. Sibyl was sitting there—a most unusual thing; but Hester did not notice that, since everything would be unusual henceforth and forever more.

Sibyl was reclining in an old easy-chair. Hester was never in the habit of taking much observation of her sister, or she would have seen that her face was pale and hollow, like that of one who has passed a restless night.　Presently Sibyl drew a long long sigh. But finding that did not elicit any remark from Hester, she asked :

"Did you hear the rats all night ? "

"No, I did not," Hester answered—"Yes. I think I did, though.　But I was only awake a minute."

Another sigh.　"They kept on all night up and down the walls.　It was a most peculiar noise. Scarcely like rats.　More like something else."

"What do you think ? " inquired Hester, ironically.

Sibyl did not answer the question, but said.　" It was just the same for a week or two before dear papa died."

" And how often besides ? " asked Hester.

" Dora has not looked very well for these last few days," Sibyl went on, still regardless of the question— "She is working too hard, the darling !　And I fear this change for Lizzie, she is so wedded to everything here.　Some hearts break very quietly.　Oh dear, dear, dear."

Hester began to experience a restless sensation.

" The salt was spilt over the table at supper last-night and I don't know who did it," Sibyl continued. " That is a bad omen (a prolonged sigh), I'm afraid something is going to happen, Hetty.　I used to hear the death-watch before papa's death too, and I actually heard it again last-night."

The prior suggestions about Lizzie, tortured Hetty into observing; " Perhaps it will be you this time ! "

" You never have any sympathy Hester," said Sibyl ; " you're always engrossed in your own affairs— never ready to feel with other people."

" I don't see why I should pick up people's fancy miseries, just when they want to throw them away ; and then I find I have them left to myself when their first owners have forgotten all about them," retorted Hester, fiercely. " You had better go down stairs to your breakfast, Sibyl. If you'd done so earlier, you would have found a letter."

" A letter for me ! "—and off flew Sibyl, at once oblivious of rats, and death-watches, and spilt salt. Hester did not follow her for some minutes, and when she did, the letter had disappeared, and Sibyl herself had nearly finished her breakfast, and left the table almost as soon as Hester went to it.

Sibyl spent the morning in her bedroom. Hester going about her household duties, caught one glimpse of her. She was busily renovating the hood of her waterproof—re-binding it and modelling it to a newer fashion. The sisters did not come in contact again, till Sibyl descended to the drawing-room, fully equipped for her afternoon journey.

She seemed in no hurry to depart, but lingered before the mirror, altering the set of her bonnet.

" I hate this mourning," she observed, it doesn't suit me a bit. How different I should look in white ! "

and she sauntered to the piano and rattled over a few chords.

'Hush," said Hester, " Dora is writing."

"Do I interrupt you, Dora?" Sibyl asked, still going on. "Dear me, at that rate I have lost my last occupation in the house—even playing to you, my dear!"

Dora good-naturedly laid down her pen, and rallied her cousin on her waterproof and umbrella! "You are determined not to have another souse to-day," said she. "Although the sun has never been behind a cloud once since dawn."

"I am learning caution by experience," she answered, and a strange and sudden darkness fell upon her face as she said the words.

"Where is Lizzie?" she asked.

"Gone out ;" answered Hester.

"Will she be long?" Sibyl inquired.

"She said she thought she would be home in time for tea." Hester answered.

"Oh," was Sibyl's only answer ; "good-bye, Dora. Good-bye, Hester."

"Good-bye," said Hester, standing on the landing. She waited there, as we are all so oddly apt to do, to hear the street door close. Generally Sibyl looked into the office as she passed, and said a few words to Philip. But to-day she went straight out.

And Hester went up and down the house, doing something there and something here. She utterly scorned Sibyl's vulgar superstitions ; the coward's wretched substitute for religion. Yet they came upon her like the baleful air from a tomb. They made the atmosphere inimical to all spiritual bloom. She sought to have despised them, to have put them aside as unworthy a moment's thought. And so she did. Yet God knew the secrets of humanity, when by the mouth of Ezekiel, He pronounced the doom of witches, "Because with lies ye have made the heart of the righteous sad, whom I have not made sad."

CHAPTER XIX.

TOO LATE.

ALL that afternoon, a young lady sat in one of the small picture-galleries near Pall Mall. She had paid a shilling for admission, and had left a waterproof and an umbrella with the cloak-keeper, but when the money-taker suggested a catalogue, she answered that it did not matter.

The season over, and London growing empty, she had found nobody in the room when she entered, but the secretary, in readiness to answer inquiries about prices.

At first, she made a pretence of looking at some of the larger paintings, but once sitting down opposite a life-size picture of a gaily dressed mediæval gentleman chatting with a pretty woman in a goldsmith's shop, she did not stir again. The secretary looked at her once or twice, and being a kindly old gentleman, by no means oblivious of the little by-play that often went on beneath his eye, concluded that she was waiting for her lover.

But the afternoon wore on, and no lover came,

though several parties of sight-seers passed in and out. The young lady only roused herself a little whenever an elegant toilet entered. She was taking so minute an observation of one such, a graceful Parisian robe of delicately ruched muslin, over a green-silk petticoat, that she did not hear a fussy old gentleman inform his gawky daughter that this life-size picture before her, represented "the first interview of Edward IV. and Jane Shore." But at last, five o'clock struck, and she rose listlessly and sauntered out to the street.

She turned westward, and descending the steps from Carlton Terrace, walked slowly up the Mall, and crossed to Pimlico, stopping to look into every shop that afforded the least pretext for whiling away a moment. So she went on slowly to the Victoria station, new then, and very bewildering to one who had never travelled from it before. She asked a porter where she could take a ticket for Brighton, and followed the direction he gave, but instead of going to the booking-office, found the waiting-room nearest to it, and went in, and looked at herself in the mirror, and flecked the dust from her face and bonnet with her handkerchief. There was a girl suffering from toothache in the waiting room, and also an old woman with a band-box tied up in a blue spotted handkerchief, who was pouring forth the profuse sympathy, in the shape of an elaborate list of recipes, strung together with such emphatic comment as—" You try that, my dear—I never knew it to fail. It's a good thing to put a toasted fig between the gum and the cheek. I've tried that, and it's easy and pleasant, and draws off the pain before you can say, Jack Robinson. You try that my dear, you won't regret it. And it's a good thing to take the steam of warm water into your mouth out of a funnel, or a jug or anything you can get for that matter, my dear. Don't think it's too simple to be a cure, my dear, but try it and it will pay you for your trouble. Highty—tighty, but she's a stuck-up looking piece of goods;" as the new comer vouchsafed·a scornful glance at the pair, and went out to take a survey of the platform—" she reads her novels, and plays I'll warrant, and grizzles and frizzles over what never was, or will be ; but she'd think it beneath her to offer a honest cure for the reallest pain that ever was in the world, that she would. She'll know what it is someday, perhaps or worse. And serve her right ! "

Sibyl sat down outside. The waiting-room was too close for her—there are times when we become peculiarly sensitive to closeness, when the very soul seems to gasp for breath, some enterprising trader had set up a row of advertisements all alike, aiming to catch the public attention by their repetition, and as her eye went from one to the other, she half unconsciously repeated the old charm, slightly varied—" will he marry me ? will he not ? will he marry me ? " That brought her to the end of the line, and she was fairly glad that the miserable oracle was in her favor.

Does a man, slipping over a precipice realize that in a moment he will be in a crushed mass on the stones below ? Does he not rather in the very act of falling, stretch out his hand for some pretty flower with an odd flashing thought that it will be a beautiful memento of his escape? How soon does the rider yielding himself to the wild energy of the chase comprehend that his steed has suddenly over-mastered him, and is bearing him on against his will? scarcely till earth and sky seem to flash into a million of rockets and the horse is away and the rider is—dead!

At last, a porter came along with a truck full of luggage. Dainty aristocratic luggage, each case of the best make and newest fashion. Behind walked a tall gentleman, with a soft travelling cap on his head, a tall fair gentleman, with a long sweeping chestnut beard, and a face stamped with the sins of a class rather than an individual. A calm polite selfish cynical face, not more than seven or eight-and-twenty, but cool and assured, with the quiet assurance gathered from all the Ancestral Sir Rolands' and Sir Arthurs' who had fibbed and seduced and fought and conquered, and had it all their own way, since the time of William the Norman. He was looking for somebody, that he was quite sure to find, and as if he did not very much care whether he did or no. He was early, for why should he wait for a train? yet not late, lest he should be humbled by the fact that the train would not wait for him.

As he advanced, the young lady arose and he came forward and greeted her with a degree of impressment that seemed a great exertion to him.

" I hope you have not been waiting very long ? " he said.

" Yes I have," she answered ; " you know I had to leave home at the usual time." There was a strange tremor in her voice, as if it meant more to her than it seemed to him ; as if a little pathos was fluttering behind the smooth girlish face, so hard in all its bloom and softness.

"Oh yes, to be sure," he replied ; " poor little Sylph, she must be nearly tired out ; never mind, here are the tickets for our journey, and first-class carriages are a very comfortable mode of transit to Paradise, eh ? For it is to be Paradise, you know."

The girl looked more than half-doubtful. If there had been somebody at hand with one persuasive word, one warning look ! But then that can never be. At all great crises of our lives, we are left to our guardian-angels. And if we have not been in the habit of heeding them we scarcely know their voices then !

" She is quite soiled and moiled and fagged," he went on in the petting manner we use to a child or an animal ; " soiled and moiled and fagged ; never mind, she will never be soiled or moiled or fagged anymore."

The doubtful look died away. This is what she wanted.

" She does not guess what I have in my breast-pocket—or my heart," he continued.

She looked up interested and curious, " will she guess ?—can she guess ? " he asked, drawing out some tiny thing and hiding it in his palm.

Her face flushed just a little—" Is it the wedding-ring?" she whispered.

" Good girl. It is. Now take off your glove—nobody is looking and what does it signify if they are? Put it on. Now she is my wife, as much as if twenty parsons had married us, is she not?"

She murmured something, which he understood rather than heard. " Do you doubt, Sibyl?" he asked, and there was a sternness in the soft voice like a dagger sheathed in silk.

"O no, no," she answered, hastily. There was a covert smile on the calm face lifted high above her bowed head. He understood her. It was but a tournament between the two. She was playing for his fortune and his prospective coronet and all the ease and luxury involved therein. He was playing—for a new toy to divert the ennui of patrician idleness. The stake might be all hers, and her all, and the odds ten to one against her. But as it was her own will, he did not feel that such contest was unfair, nor did his lazy chivalry call upon him to save her from herself. He had spoken sweetly, and she had answered softly. He did not bring any sentiment into the affair, why should he?—she brought none. He knew whatever other odds there might be, their hearts stood even. He was a vain man, but not vain enough to fancy that he himself was the prize that was worth such risks to secure. There were circles where he was proud of his graceful stature and aristocratic face and winning manners. But here his rank and wealth were his strong points. There was no appeal to the nobler instincts which were not so utterly dead in the young aristocrat, that he did not flatter himself upon possessing them. A seducer? He would have smiled serenely at such a plain word—coarse people with broad judgments might so write him, he did not feel himself to be such. He had never encouraged a silly girl of inferior grade to fall in love with him. He fully believed that if such a thing had happened he would have taken no advantage of the mistake. But this girl was no more in love than he was. Each had an end in view, to obtain which they must play the hypocrite. "If I did not, somebody else would;" he thought, and handed her into a first-class carriage.

"What do you think?" said he, on Saturday evening, I spoke to a young lady in the Park mistaking her for you. Her dress was exactly like yours; she must have been your sister."

" Hester, I suppose, but (piqued) I am sure she has quite a different figure."

" I wonder how I made the mistake, for I could see instantly, that she is quite different from you, entirely different."

He always prided himself upon uttering an irony, like a compliment.

The train stopped for some minutes at London Bridge. It would not stop again until they were far on their journey to Brighton; somebody in the next carriage had a concertina and was playing one of Mendelsshon's 'Songs without words.' The girl knew it. It brought up the old chintz-covered drawing-room, the little dark-eyed cousin on the sofa, the two sisters at their work. By this time they must be wondering where she was. Popps would be setting the supper, and asking if Miss Sibyl wasn't coming home. It had been very comfortable, after all. But then it was not going to be comfortable any more, even if she had stayed. It had all turned into daily teaching, and cheap clothes and dreadfulness! whereas now she had a chance—Oh, sitting there, she suddenly felt what a mere chance it was! It appalled her. Her heart failed not at the memory of home, not under the sense of sin, not with tender remorse for the love left behind, but at the risk to her own sheer selfishness, she half started up. But the relentness train moved.

"You are not very brilliant this evening, Mademoiselle," said her companion ; " well you are tired, rest yourself, and leave the duty of my entertainment to myself for once," and he produced an evening newspaper, and was soon lost in the mysteries of the sporting article.

Presently she rose and stood in the doorway. The city lay in a dun mass beneath the sunset sky. Rather a stormy sky, with lines of dark clouds across the golden glory. There would be rain very soon, she stayed watching, till the houses divided into broken groups of stunted villas and the flat fields gave place to the undulating sunny hills. Then she sat down.

The doubt had died into a defiant desperation, she must go on to the end. It was too late to turn back !

Too late ! Too late !

CHAPTER XX.

LEFT LETTERS.

 " I WONDER what has become of Sybil?" asked Lizzie. The clock struck eight as she entered the drawing-room where Hester, Dora, and Mr. Lewis were sitting.

" I suppose her pupils have taken her somewhere," Hester answered. " You remember she was kept late one evening last week."

" It is too late for her to come through the streets alone," said Philip. " I shall go and fetch her. If we miss each other, Hetty, will you tell her where I am gone, and that I shall return as soon as possible?"

" Very well," Hester replied. Hetty was acquiring a habit of only speaking in answers, and of making even those as short and plain as possible. She never chatted now, not even with Lizzie. There are some people, who, when they first come upon a great trial, must lock it up and even hide the key. Well and good. When the day of opening arrives, they will find in its stead a great treasure of experience and wisdom, with which they may enrich others without impoverishing themselves, since such capital can never be lent without receiving interest at the rate of cent. per cent. Only alas! sometimes, they forget ever to open. And experience and wisdom, great treasures as they are, are not the heavenly treasure which neither moth nor rust can corrupt. And a day of opening must come at last, when a hand not their own, shall unwrap the shroud of silence, and behold the experience and wisdom rotted and withered into misanthropy and selfishness! And lo, they shall learn these were not their own, after all! and a voice shall ask, "Wherefore then gavest not thou my money into the bank, that at my coming I might have required mine own with usury?" There is a time to keep silence and a time to speak; "He that withholdeth corn the people shall curse him;" but since people need wisdom too sorely to know their need, God himself shall curse him that withholdeth that. "To whom much is given, much shall be required," and God counts his special disciplines as very much indeed. If the idle words we speak shall bring us to judgment, is there no penalty when we refrain from speaking good words? Verily "if Thou Lord, shouldest mark iniquities, O Lord, who shall stand?"—but Thou Thyself, "hath clothed us with the garments of salvation and covered us with the robe of righteousness."

So when Philip was gone, and Lizzie had passed on to some other domestic task, there was no sound in the drawing-room except the scratching of Dora's pen, Hester was diligently reading Jeremy Taylor's "Holy Living," in the article on "Contentment," turning over page after page, scarcely remembering the clauses of the argument, yet imbibing the sublime cheerfulness of the simple Christian philosopher. She was just nearing the end of the subject, having turned over the few remaining pages, and calculated that she should have time to finish it before Philip and Sibyl could possibly return, when a cab came tearing up the road, and in less than a second the door-bell rang an alarm peal. Hetty flew into the hall. She could not have told what she had expected—but it was certainly not to see Philip alone, with wild eyes flaring in a face of ghastly pallor.

"She's never been there to day!" he cried. "O God! Oh, Hester!" and sat down blank and benumbed.

Lizzie and Dora and Popps, and the charwoman were all on the spot in a moment. But Hester paid the cabman directly. It struck her that he would charge for waiting. He asked her to consider that the gentleman had been driven "werry fast," and she gave him an extra six-pence, and dismissed him.

"Something has happened to her," sobbed Lizzie.

"Oh, Mr. Lewis, if you had thought to stop and ask the people at St. George's Hospital! But how could you think, poor fellow?"

"They wondered we were not alarmed before,"

said Philip, half-stupidly ; " they wondered we should suppose they had kept her."

"Why they kept her only last week !" exclaimed Dora ; " did not you remind them of that, Mr. Lewis ? Did you forget it ? "

Philip shook his head. He had remembered only too bitterly. But in some forlorn hope that would live on in his great dumb tenderness, he had hidden the treachery from strange eyes, and in the first agony of his return it had receded into the background of his own mind. But now it started forward afresh, in all its damning deformity. And he looked helplessly around from one face to another, and become aware amid all the trouble and grief, each felt a separate pang of pity for him who must drink the bitterest dreg of this fresh well of Marah. And he seemed suddenly to feel Sibyl's gloved hand on his arm, and to see the blooming beauteous face raised to his own. Oh, it had always seemed such a sweet face to him ! And there was a heavy lump in his throat that wouldn't go down. And he bowed his head in his hands, and great sobs came, and scalding tears fell hard and fast between his fingers. There are some sorrows which manliness cannot bear manfully.

They were all frightened. Lizzie and Popps were crying themselves. Dora looked white and cold. Hester turned to the charwoman. A thought had flashed into her mind, and strangely enough, she seemed to read a response in Mrs. Edwardes ashen face.

"Don't break down yet, Philip," she said ; as gently as ever she could, for it is not easy to speak gently when tears are rushing forward, only repressible by iron bars of sharpness and austerity. But the Christian name which she had rarely used, made amend for a queer rasp which she could not quite banish from her voice. There are times when a Christian name is like a caress. It puts the two so close together. There may be some mistake. It may be all explainable. We must find out everything as soon as we can. I think I had better go to her room, and see if we can find anything there. Don't you think so Philip ? "

The direct appeal, superfluous as it seemed did Philip good. It diverted emotion into action, and he also felt the soothing influence of a sympathy which did not forget his strongest right in the lost one.

"Yes, go," he said, half lifting his wet, convulsed face. Hester never forgot it. God forgive her for whatever might be harsh and hasty, but had Sibyl stood before her at that moment, she might have heard some old-fashioned Saxon and scriptural language.

She went up stairs leaving the rest standing just as they were. But Mrs. Edwardes followed her, but did not overtake her till she reached the highest landing, and then stood behind. Sibyl's door was closed—and locked !

"Oh can she be inside ! " cried the charwoman, so earnestly that it started Hester, who had shrewdly

and silently guessed a very different explanation—that
her sister had wished to keep out all observation,
until such time as suspicion should be fairly aroused,
and she could have gained a start. Did such a
thought show an unkindly or evil mind ? Surely not.
If a man who missed some property knew an accom-
plished thief had been in his room, would it be very
uncharitable if he had certain suspicions. And Hester had her own estimate of Sibyl's character founded
on the close acquaintanceship of more than twenty
years.

"No—no, she is not there," answered Hester,
"but we must fetch somebody to break open the
door."

"I can do it, I can do it," said Mrs. Edwardes,
"don't let us lose one moment." And before Hester
could declare that she was unable for the task, it was
done. Done, as it seemed, without an effort. Mrs.
Edwardes must have been a strong woman, for strength
is strength, whether it be in the muscles or the will !

There was a sign of confusion in the empty chamber. Only by the moonlight, Hester could see a
drawer standing open, and from it, her quick eye missed a little painted case where Sybil kept her ornaments.
Without waiting for any direction, Mrs. Edwardes
took a candle from the mantle, and lit it.

"Here's a letter," said the charwoman, picking one
from the rug.

Hester took it. It was in the envelope whose su-
perscription she had thought so like her own.

"That came this morning," she observed, pondering.

"Read it, Miss Hester," urged Mrs. Edwardes. Hester shook her head, decisively. "If it must be opened, Mr. Lewis must do it," she said.

"She would not have left it lying about, if she had cared for it," said the charwoman, wailingly.

But Hester kept it folded in her hand. And they both looked around the room again. It came oddly to Hester's memory, that she had once or twice surprised her sister bending over the drawer of the toilet-mirror, and that Sybil had shut it with a startled jerk. It might seem unlikely that anything possessing an unlawful interest should be deposited in a place without a lock. But the habits of the family were such that none of them would think of opening any such depository of the others' possessions, unless they had the right of mutual use. Lizzie and Hester, had all things in common, and had they wished to keep a secret from each other, must have taken certain precautions; but nobody had occasion to interfere in Sybil's apartment. And so strong was Hester's sense of implied trust, that the color flew into her face, now that she felt it was her bounden duty to make search.

It was a disorderly little drawer, filled with broken combs, and scraps of torn paper, but just one corner was kept clear for a photogragh. It was the portrait of an officer in uniform, with a fair, haughty face, and long whiskers. For half a second, Hester asked herself, where she knew that countenance. Then she remembered the stranger who had spoken to her, in the park, only the Saturday before.

" 'Tis he, cried Mrs. Edwardes, looking over his shoulder.

" Who ? " asked Hester, fiercely facing her companion, with a sudden and sharp distrust expressing itself in every feature.

" He—who—I mean somebody she has gone away with," groaned the woman, sitting down on the edge of the bed. " Oh, God in Heaven !—God in Heaven !"

Hester caught sight of a paper beneath a toilet-bottle. It was simply a sheet of note paper, not even folded, and there was writing on it—Sybil's writing, large, light, and straggling. Hester's breath stopped just a moment, she forgot the lie concerning her delay the week before, she forgot the missing jewel-case, and the mysterious portrait in the drawer, and she had a queer memory of years before, when she and Sibyl used to go to school together hand in hand; and of a doll that Sibyl once gave her (she coaxed a new one from her father the next week on that very pretext). There was a beating in her ears, and a mist before her eyes, but they passed and she read :

" I have gone away of my own accord. Perhaps you will hear from me in a very few days. But if not, *take no trouble about me.* Anyhow I shall be better off than I *deserve.* I hope Mr. Lewis will soon *forget* me, I was not *worthy* of him, and I hope he will find somebody who is. Thank you all for the *much* kindness you have *wasted* on me. Perhaps it will not be

QUITE wasted after all.   You will all think I have no
feelings.   Well! think anything you like, which will
make you feel me to be a good riddance, *and prevent
you from fretting.*   I shall remember *you,* even if the
worst comes to the worst.   And now, good-bye all.
I suppose *I* must not write, *God bless you.*   Only

> ' Fare thee well, and if *forever*,
>   Then *forever*, fare thee well.' "

Hester almost crushed the paper up in her hand,
and there was something in her face which made Mrs.
Edwardes start up and catch her dress imploringly,
saying incoherently :

 "Don't, don't—at least think as kindly of her as
you can.   You can never know all of it.   There are
wheels within wheels.   It's only God's grace, my dear
—if there is a God—and I know there is.   And as for
hell—if you only knew what it is, you could pity her,
Miss Hester."

Hester freed her dress with an impatient pull.
" I prefer to keep my pity for those she has disap-
pointed and shamed," she said, sternly ; and I find
none over.   "Let us go down stairs ; something may
be done to-night, perhaps."

She found the others, forlornly waiting where she
had left them.   Only Popps had stolen away to the
kitchen to answer a ring which she knew to be Tom's.
Nobody questioned Hester as she came down stairs.
But Philip raised his head in expectation.

" Nothing has happened to her," Hester said,
quietly, going close to him, but keeping her three

wretched findings in her own hand. "She has left a note behind her. She has gone away of her own accord."

"But doesn't she say why—or where?" he cried, starting up ; "can't you find a clue?"

"Sit down, Philip," said Hester, with her hand on his arm. "I have also a letter which came to her this morning, that may be of service. I have not read it yet. I meant that you should read it first. But you must not, now. She is nothing to you, any-more. God help you, Philip, dear. And he will—somehow!"

Philip stood dumb for a minute. Then he burst out : "I can't believe it. You were always harsh to her, and you've put a wrong construction on her words. Let me see her note, myself! I will! I must!"

Hester laid it on the table. His eye swept up and down the scrawling lines with frantic rapidity. Then he laughed—lightly, terribly. "There's nothing there," he said, defiantly. "Is that all? Have you no more fine evidence against your sister?"

She had the protrait in her hand, and its strangely coincident history on her lip, but she had mercy on his madness and misery. She slipped the photograph into her pocket, and let his wild questions pass unan-swered ; only bringing forward the other letter, with the simple comment : "Perhaps this may be some-thing, and handed it to Lizzie, so that the sister and

11*

the lover might read it together, while Mrs. Edwardes slunk away to the kitchen.

The letter had neither date nor address, and the handwriting was strong and marked, but with indications of that haste which arises not from pressure of time, but from rapid mental movement. It was headed " To Miss Sibyl Capel," and began :

" DEAR YOUNG LADY :

" If you know partly who it is that writes to you, you would be very annoyed and angry, but if you knew altogether who it is, it would be a far stronger warning than that which I pray to give you. But I can't tell you this, and yet without it, I don't know how to make my warning strong enough ! There is somebody who you think loves you. But there is a love which is like that of the hawk for the sparrow which it devours. Or rather like the serpent for the dove which it fascinates to destruction. His honied words are so sweet, his compliments so graceful ! Why ! honest criticism from a true lover should be more pleasing to your ears. If you were like your sisters, you would feel this without being told. A true woman knows a false man by instinct—at least I think so—I don't know—for I was not one myself ! I know the road you are on. I know the end of it. I ought to be the last one to reproach you ! God knows, the very last ! I only do it, in love. There is a reproach that spurs virtue. You will say ' this is a raving mad woman.' Perhaps I am. Do you wish to be the same ? I dont want to justify myself. I couldn't if I did. But still you haven't the excuses that I fancied I had. I can't think what is wanted to make your life happy. The devil can't find despair in you, and that is the instrument upon which he can best play his favorite airs. It seems to me that you can want nothing. You have love and health, and a busy life before you. You don't know what it is when life is solitary confinement, your soul sickened with its own dead hopes fastened round it. But better dead hopes in all their corruption, than a living sin, gnawing, gnawing! I don't want to make you unhappy with my words. Things may be different from what I think. That is the worst of it, we cannot advise or warn or chide, except doctors trying to cure a disease they do not know! But just reflect on this —Live so that if the day come, when you have a daughter of your own, you will not have to speak to her of yourself as I have spoke of myself to you this day. And now, God help you, and keep another sin from my door!

"There!" cried Philip ; "there is some miserable creature mixed up in it ; jealous one can easily see, and I daresay without any cause! Nobody knows what may have happened with such a vindictive maniac as that. And yet Sibyl ought to have shown me this letter. I don't know, either. It was more natural for innocence to treat such insult with silent contempt!"

"I shall go to Mr. Fiske," said Hester. "Perhaps he will think of something we can do."

"I must do it—I will!" exclaimed Philip. "I trust her implicitly, and I will not behave as if I doubt her the moment a little mystery arises."

Hester paused ; she knew her sister, and she knew Philip ; and he knew also the secret she was keeping from him. She could not tell it yet. Let him grow used to misery first. Give him time for fear to creep in. Blame her not, because the glorious blossom of so perfect a faith, planted in such stony ground, seemed too fair for her hand to root up. And yet she could not let him humble himself still lower before this base clay idol—could not let the honest lover seek and pursue the false woman, fled with her paramour. But how could she put him off? Where woman's feelings are keen, her wit is quick.

"Stay here, Philip," she pleaded. "I am only going to ask for advice, not for tidings. They are far more likely to come here while I am away. You had better stay on the spot, than leave Dora, and poor Lizzie alone."

"Oh yes, do stay with us," urged Lizzie; though whether she took the cue in its whole meaning, who shall say?

Hester ran off for her bonnet and cloak, but she went down to the kitchen a moment before she started. In remembrance of the anonymous letter, she wished to give Popps a charge to take particular notice if any stranger loitered about the house.

Popps and Tom Moxon were standing in front of the fire, whispering. The young man started back, abashed at his own presence in such hour of trouble. Hester gave her instructions to the girl, and then glancing around the gloomy apartment, dimly lit by one tallow candle, asked if Mrs. Edwardes was gone.

"She's only gone out for a minute, she said, Miss,"

Popps replied. " I don't know what for, I thought maybe you'd sent her yourself."

" No, I did not." Hester replied. " But when she comes back, keep her here for the night. Tell her we may want her." But another reason, though very indefinite, floated in Hester's mind.

Dora was in the hall, with the street door open. " It's such a dreadful night, Hetty," she said. " The rain has just begun to pour down in torrents, and the wind is blowing frightfully. Hetty, I can't bear to see you thus. Let me go with you."

" Don't talk nonsense, dearie," she said, brightly. " You on this rough stormy night! The very idea! It won't hurt me. I'm neither butter nor sugar, neither soft nor sweet? But I know what you mean, darling," she added, " and it's nice to have you say so, only don't trouble yourself about me, it's all in the way of one's life, you know!

And tho' her umbrella was almost dripping before she reached the bottom of the steps, yet there she turned round to throw back another nod to Dora, standing in the bright framework of the gas-lit hall. Her face turned to the dark street, she could not catch the comfort of the love beaming from it, but she cried a warning " go in, go in," and then scudded away through the storm. " That's Miss Hetty, off," said Popps to Tom, as they heard Dora close the door, and return to the parlor " if she's a-going to kill herself over Miss Sibyl, it's a sending of good money after bad, that's all. And why couldn't you ask if you would be any use, Tom, instead of standing struck like a gawky?"

"I didn't know whether it would be right," Tom answered; "I'm only a working-man."

Popps snuffled. "Don't talk about pride, Tom," said she; "there never was nobody so stuck up as you are. What would you say if there was a duke always a-stopping himself and saying, "I'm a duke?" It's the same thing, Tom. You make your tool-basket as big a nuisance as old Mrs. Ganders' crest, that she would always embroider on her six-penny handkerchiefs, when she was as blind as a bat, and did it so that you couldn't see what it was, and might take it for anything you liked, which perhaps did as well!"

"You don't seem to take your young lady's departure much to heart, Bess," said Tom.

"Well, I can't help it," she returned. "That's just what Mrs. Edwardes said to me; says I back. "She wasn't my young lady. You can't expect a whole family made to your taste. You likes some, and the rest you puts up with." Says I too, "If I knew where she was a-gone to, I'd go and catch her back for them as wants her, which isn't me, mind." Says Mrs. Edwardes, "I can't think how you can be so spiteful to an amiable young lady." Says I again. "There's some amiable people as makes it precious hard for other folks to be amiable. And it's often the sour things that keep others sweet." Says I, "You wouldn't care much for fish the second day, without vinegar, Mrs. Edwardes." And to that she answers nothing, but puts on her shawl and goes out in all the torrents of rain. There's a-many people who can't see a truth till you shove it right under their nose, and who can be always doin' that, though please God, I will, whenever I get a chance! And now you'll go home, Tom, for I've been hindered in my work, and the house isn't going to look as if the world had come to an end, because she has took herself off. So we'll say, good-night."

And so Tom went out. Mrs. Edwardes passed in, dripping and breathless.

CHAPTER XXI.

DARKNESS.

T was indeed a wild and miserable night.
The people had done their marketing so
quickly that even the flaring shops of the
Gray's Inn Road stood desolate, the attend-
ants withdrawn inside, and the doorsteps only haunted
here and there. by some forlorn woman, whose earthly
cares centered in the comparative relationship of
ounces and pence. Hester sped on, unheeding and
unheeded—except by one idle butcher-lad, who said
he was sorry to see her out by herself—until she
crossed the wide dirty road, and struck into one of
the quiet hilly streets on the east. She slackened
her pace just a little, for she was almost breathless,
and the darkness and solitude seemed friendly instead
of fearful. .But the street was not so lonely as it
seemed. A woman rose up from a dark portico, and
begged Hester "for the love of God, to give a thought
to some who had no roof over their heads. Her
husband and child were there," she said, indicating
the gloomy recess. "He had come out of hospital

only a week ago, after a long illness, and she had to sell every stick they had, and he had been on the tramp for work ever since and could get nothing, and their landlord had put them into the street at last." At first, Hester hurried on. The woman did not follow with "my lady's, and May Heaven forever bless you!" of a practiced beggar. Hester pondered. Surely the six-pence in her pocket was her own yet. A week or two more, and their poverty might be so definite, that she would not have the honest right to spare even a penny. She would give this once— perhaps it might be for the last time. She turned back. The woman was standing under a lamp-post. "Oh, miss," she said, as Hester fumbled for her purse; "it's very kind of you to pity us. for you can't have much idea how hard life goes with some folks."

Hester went on again, until she reached Mr. Fiske's abode, which she found without much difficulty, having been duly informed by that gentleman, that he lodged "in a private house, between a tavern and a chemist's." Hester knocked, and then rang all the three bells in rotation, which process at last produced the maid of all work in the last stage of blacking— bottle—and—patent—dubbing.

"Mr. Fiske?" echoed this attendant; "are you from any body as has been before? cos, I've told him all about that there, and three pair o' stairs over again for nothing, is no joke, of a Saturday night."

Hester explained that nobody had been before on

her business, and that it was very urgent, and that she wished to see Mr. Fiske himself, if it were possible.

"Well, I'll see," responded the reluctant damsel; "but I shouldn't think you'll be able to go in his room, for he always keeps it like a pig-stye with papers and rubbish, and sets a-writin' in his short sleeves. But you can wait in the passage, if you like, only there's been a lot o' paraffin oil spilt—somewheres about here—something else for me to clean up, but there's always something else, so that ain't anything new—only, you'd better look out after your tails."

Hester meekly drew her skirts about her, and directed the girl to inform Mr. Fiske that it was a Miss Capel who wished to see him, and that she was very sorry to disturb him at such an hour, but—

"Oh you needn't mind that, Miss," the girl answered; "day and night is much the same to him—the way he mucks the candles settin' up, and then laying in bed in the morning, a-turning all my work topsy-turvey;" and so she left Hester to wait in the dark.

Hetty could hear her shuffling step mounting on and on, till she passed the region of stair-carpet and clumped on over bare boards, and shook open a rheumatic door, and grumbled out something which Hetty lost, though she did not lose the high clear voice that answered, eagerly:

"A lady—a Miss Capel—Capel, do you mean?" Are you sure it is herself? Not a servant? Dear, dear, this tie will never get right. What sort of a lady is she? What age? And what a dreadful thing for her to be out; Where is she! What.is she doing? standing in the passage—oh dear, dear! And she can't come up here. There's not a chair empty. Ask her into the parlor, like a good girl, and I'll make it all right with your mistress. Tell her I'll be with her in the twinkling of an eye—if this tie would only fasten! Go away,—I'll get on better when you are not staring."

With a poor attempt at civility, the ungracious damsel conducted Hetty into a small stuffy room, strongly odorous of tobacco, where, when her fourth attempt at match-lighting was successful, the candle displayed some very remarkable china on the mantel, and two crayon heads in gilt frames, sufficient to scare all the bachelor-lodgers from any attempt to allure such beauty to displace even their old land lady. In the dark, Hetty had drearily dropped down upon a dingy, starved sofa, but the old mental activity would have its way, and she rose to look at these works of art. Under one, was written in pale Italian hand : " Julia Figgins Christmas vacation, 1850," and at the other corner, a flourishing mercantile hand had added: " Her Last—died New Year's Day 1851." This hireling house was somebody's home after all. Love and sorrow had consecrated it—their own sweet selves; albeit, perhaps disguised in queer affected motley. For the first time in that horrible evening, tears started to Hester's eyes. No darkness felt dangerous, no cold bitings if God and human nature

could live on in them. For the change of which
Hetty had the sorest dread, was of some withering
change in herself, till perhaps she should fawn and
flatter for a shilling, and scheme and fit for a daintier
meal, or a softer garment, when the gardener waters a
flower perhaps it thinks "Now I am done for, to-
morrow I shall be but dead leaves," and lo !—at dawn
the bud is become a beauteous blossom ; meet for the
Master's gathering.

"Miss Capel,—my dear madam," said an airy
voice outside, and in came Anthony Fiske, quite trim
and neat enough to be oddly at variance with the
bespattered flat candlestick that he carried in his
hand. "Oh, Miss Hester !" and Hetty was dimly
aware of a fall in the tuneful tones. "Pray sit down.
It's a shocking evening, isn't it ? And so I'm afraid
there must be something very wrong to bring you
out."

"Yes, there is," Hester answered, gulping down a
dreadful lump that seemed to stop her words. "Sibyl
has left home, and gone we don't know where."

"Ah yes, yes," said Anthony Fiske, drawing up a
chair, with all the air of a confidential adviser, for he
could act most parts in life, but could never get ade-
quate scenery. "Yes, yes. And do you know that I
was just coming round to you. Just doing my toilet.
(Bah, this is the chair with the broken leg !) I have
just had a curious letter. I was sitting over my man-
uscripts, Miss Hetty, when the servant brought it to
me. Such an odd letter, and such a queer message.

The servant said the bearer told her to give me that, and I must attend to it for the love of God. I'll just show it to you;" and he produced a rudely folded piece of whitey-brown paper, whereon was chalked in large wild characters :

"*Sibyl Capel has inherited the curse, ask for Captain Verdon in Clarges Street. Ask at every hotel till you get the right one.*"

"There was an anonymous letter left in Sibyl's bedroom, said Hester, and whoever wrote this, wrote that. Wouldn't the servant know what the bearer was like?"

"Bless you, no! She takes no notice. Only last week she called an old woman a girl, because she wore a hat. Those are the appearances she judges by. And what does it matter about the bearer, Miss Hetty. Let us do what she tells us."

"What right reason can we have to take so much interest and yet keep back her name?" pondered Hester.

Anthony shrugged his shoulders, but did not meet Hetty's eyes. The motives that rule the world are often those that don't appear," said he. " I've noticed a good deal—having nothing of my own to notice, Miss Hetty. And I conclude I'll go to Clarges street. You never heard anything about a Captain Verdon, did you, my dear?"

"No," said Hester, "but I have found an officer's portrait."

"That is he, depend upon it. Now, my dear,

they'll expect you at home. I'll take you there, and leave you. To think of a young lady being out all alone in these dull streets at this hour! It's very shocking. Not that I think it matters much," he added confidently—"except for the sound of it!"

"I must go home first, indeed, sir," said Hetty; "because I promised so. But then I'll go on with you, please."

"My dear Miss Hester, it will be most unnecessary. I can find out whatever is to be found."

"But if you find her?" said Hetty, looking up with great brown eyes, pathetic with a burthen of duty, and of pitiful womanly tenderness which yet had no love to lighten it. Anthony Fiske looked at her and understood.

"We ought to have a cab," he said, buttoning up his coat.

"Oh, it isn't raining now," Hester replied, hastily, with an ever present consciousness of the iron grasp of need; "still, if you would prefer one,"——she added, remembering that she had no right to save from the comforts of others.

"No, no; I'm only too glad to feel the fresh air," he answered, opening the door and letting a current rush into the stuffy little passage. "There isn't a finer tonic than night air after a shower, my dear. The air is like a laboring man when he has washed himself, and is not going to begin again till to-morrow. But folks who have lots of fine clothes they want to show off in the sunshine, are not likely to find that out. Such, can't think how those live who don't get a three months' tour in the autumn, and a winter resort when they are poorly. They can't understand that nature keeps the same articles, done up in plain packets, and that they only pay extra for the gilding. The people who are the worst off, are those that can't buy the dear article, and won't touch the cheap one. Like old decayed gentlewomen who can't buy silks and satins like they used, but will still stick to their stiff old stays, and feel the old familiar pinch without the old pride to make it bearable. But perhaps they enjoy the pinch. Some people like pickles. There's food in life to suit all tastes. Those that have come down, can glorify themselves by thinking what they have been. Those that have never come up, can fancy what they will be. Only you can spoil the sweetest cup if you flavor it with salt tears. Or if you upset it at the beginning—but nobody's to blame but yourself, yet even then, it's wonderful how many people will offer you a sip out of theirs. Seems to me that nobody, never mind what a fool he may have been, need to be miserable in this world, unless he absolutely prefers it ; and then as I suppose, he finds happiness in that. Perhaps anybody has a right to keep the foulest odor bottled up for his own private sniffling. But the worst of it is, I never knew a man who enjoyed his own misery, who was selfish enough to keep it to himself. He is always for giving somebody else a taste. There ought to be some Inspector of such public nuisances to take these matters up and pour the decoction down

the owner's own throat, and set him to break stones
till the poison has worked itself safely off through the
pores of his skin. This is your street; see how I've
rattled on. Of course you've not been attending, I
did not expect you would. But it keeps the thoughts
from hammering each other up too hard. Can't
change 'em, but turns 'em round, like a mill, and flings
'em about, and while you're gathering them together
again, you'll maybe pick up something better as well.
Here is your house. Don't stay long. Every moment
is of the utmost importance." Hester rang the bell
so gently, that Philip, flung on his bed, grinding his
teeth among the pillows, did not hear it. Only Liz
zie answered the summons. She had placed some
wine and bread in readiness on the hall table. Hester
did not touch it, but Anthony snatched some hasty
refreshment, while she explained that they had a slight
clue, and that they must not be expected again until
they appeared. They spoke in whispers and were off
in five minutes.

"I have a very valuable manuscript that I promised to complete for a friend by noon on Monday,"
said Mr. Fiske. " I can keep my promise by putting
it in other hands. So we must just turn down
Chancery Lane, and then we will take a Piccadilly
omnibus at Temple Bar."

They paused before a private house with a strong
light burning behind its blinded parlor-windows.
Mr. Fiske left Hetty in the entry, and went in. The
door was only half screened, and she could see about

half a dozen young men busily writing at long desks. They took the bundle of paper from Mr. Fiske with only a few words. But as he moved towards the door, the clerk called out, "Where did you say it was to be left sir?" and Anthony replied:

"At Mr. Clinchman's, Lincoln's Inn Fields, before twelve o' clock, Monday."

" The fact is," said Anthony, as they again walked off, " I've renewed acquaintance with my old office-chum, Arthur Clinchman. And as it happened, I wanted work to do, and he wanted work to be done. So we matched each other, like knife and fork. Only one can do without a fork, if one's pushed to it— and so could he do without me!"

" But you could not have finished all that on Monday morning, could you?" asked Hetty, glad of a momentary escape from herself.

"I should have worked to-morrow," said Mr. Fiske, shamefacedly glancing at the pure face that turned away even from secular reading on the Sabbath, and kept its own simple store of 'Sunday books.' " I know it is not right. That's the worst of it. Once get out of the right groove, and you seem to have no choice except between two evils. But here's the Piccadilly omnibus."

It seemed such a weary, weary ride. The vehicle went so slowly and stopped so often, that Hester longed to jump out and trust to her own feet. They came to their journey's end at last, and passed up Clarges street among lounging waiters and cabmen,

12

until they reached a wide gaily lit door, where **Mr.** Fiske paused and inquired for Captain Verdon. The page knew he had stayed there, but thought he was away, and summoned an elder attendant who would know all about it. This man was a white chokered, oily insolent fellow, who surveyed Anthony and Hester from top to toe, and condescended to inform them that 'Captain Verdon had left London that afternoon for Brighton ; had not left the name of any hotel there, but supposed that anybody that could pay the pier fee would be able to find him out in the visitor's book on Monday morning.'

It was poor Hester's first experience of that liveried service which is hired not to work, but to wait, and mainly to do, what every man, not helpless or idiotic, ought to do for himself. Among all the pain and despair, like one particular little screw in a general rack she felt a bitter sting of degradation, and a sense of outrage and insult that would thrill her again and again, years after, when the great despair was dead, and the sharp pain was numbed.

"We can do nothing till to-morrow," said Anthony, as he drew her away; "I must take you home, and you must have a quiet sleep, and may be, Miss Capel will let me rest on the kitchen-dresser, or the coals, or somewhere, so that I may be with you betimes in the morning, and take you off by the first train."

"Nothing till to-morrow!" Hester's face flushed hotly in the darkness, and the Woman Angel that keeps record of her earth-sisters, struck a name from her white scroll, and wrote it down in dust!

CHAPTER XXII.

DREAMS AND AWAKENINGS.

T was the first Sunday journey that Hester ever made in her life; for all these arrangements had always been in Elizabeth Capel's hands, rather than her father's.

They were down in Brighton before noon, and had time to make fruitless inquiries at the Railway station ere the churches began to pour out their congregations. Then Mr. Fiske hinted that he might prosecute the search somewhere more effectually alone, and Hester yielded and went away to sit by herself on the beach.

How far away last Sunday seemed? It was a new world since then; nay, since yesterday morning, Hester had longed for the sea-shore so often, little dreaming how she should come down to it. Family groups passed by, and looked curiously at her, sitting on the step of a bathing-machine, she did not look a Sunday figure—with a sleepless night recorded on her wrung face, and the dust and disturbance of her journey in her dress—she had tried to dress carefully, poor thing, so as to win, rather than to repel this miserable sister of hers. But her mourning garments were so common and plain, that especially after the third-class railway carriage, the experiment did not seem very successful.

The sea came rattling and rushing over the shingles, and a fresh blue sky cleared by last night's storm, shone bright over all; what did the sea care for the shells, that it carried out and dropped into its depths, or for the other shells that it threw ashore, and broke upon the shingle; what did the sun know about it? But God had said that he knew all about it, had sent the little sparrow to the stray crumb on Cheyne walk—and knew each of the little birds pecking among the stones—knew her too sitting on the dry steps of the bathing-machine—and she looked meekly back at the curious half-mocking people that looked at her, and hoped that God would put them in mind of this whenever their lives should pass into the rainy season.

Anthony Fiske rejoined her in an hour or two—still unsuccessful, only one hope seemed to remain for that day, to go and sit upon the pier, if haply, those they were longing for might come out to seek where the freshest sea-breezes were blowing.

Hester thought the very toll-keeper looked at them, and it were small wonder if he did. They had biscuits in their pockets to refresh themselves from time to time if need were; Anthony Fiske had provided these, and did not forget them, Hester could swallow—nothing.

"You must think me very unfeeling," said Anthony, munching.

"No," she answered; "it cannot be to you what it is to me."

He shook his head gently; "I should have been dead of starvation years ago if I had not learned to eat under any circumstances," he said. Suddenly looking up at the pier they saw a tall man, and a graceful woman walking towards them. Hester's face whitened as she recognized them, and quick as thought, Anthony drew her behind the screens of the pier head.

"This isn't the place to speak to her," he whispered ; "but we will follow them when they leave."

The two sauntered to and fro for a long long time. Oh, it was so bitter hard to sit there waiting ! to see the dainty white ruffs round Sibyl's neck and wrists and the carefully selected familiar ornaments which told of such dreadful coolness and premediation. How she laughed and jested and retorted ! with what pretty coquetry she looked up in that haughty patrician face which poor Hester remembered only too well, under the trees of the Green Park. Oh, the sunny sea that was sporting around them might be cruel enough in its rocky bays, or far, far off, amid the silence of great glaciers ; but its cruelty was kind beside this cruel false woman, who would break a heart sooner than wear cheap gloves, and sell her own soul for a dress that was pleasant to the touch ! Seduced ? Hester sitting there watching her own sister, could have laughed with scorn at the word, she thought to herself with a pitiful womanly wonder. Did he fancy Sibyl loved him, that young aristocrat; if he did then, Hester knew she was wiser than he; feeling that if the sea had come up at that instant and Sibyl could have secured her dresses and gloves without him, she would not have held out a finger to save him from the waves. "And yet, oh, sister, sister—the doll you gave me years ago is put away in silver paper, and we used to sing 'the happy land' together, and you were our father's darling! Poor father, but dead now, and our mother so long in Heaven—what will she say when she hears that we have lost you?"

At last they followed them home to a large dreary house, far out to the West. Anthony and Hester waited outside for nearly ten minutes; after they entered, then Hester applying alone, asked for the lady and gentleman who had just gone in and directed the servant to take up the name of Miss Capel. She heard the girl announce it. There was a moment's silence. Then a rustle of dress up stairs and the well-known bell-like voice, directing the attendant to show the young person to "my bedroom."

The servant beckoned Hester up, and indicated, "the first door on the right;" it was left a little ajar and flew open as Hester approached and shut it swiftly behind her. Sibyl was keeping a strict guard over the proprieties. The two sisters stood face to face—"Now don't make a noise;" were Sibyl's first words. "I don't want the people of the house to know anything, and they're sure to be listening. Sit down and don't be ridiculous."

"Oh, Sibyl, how could you do it?" sobbed Hester.

Sibyl laughed and held out her ringed left hand; "Married this morning," she said.

"What, to a Captain Verdon?" cried Hester.

Sibyl had not meant to admit the true name, but she rapidly cast up Hester's possibility of information and replied, "Well, what if it is so?"

"But why need you have gone away like this? such a disgrace and pain, Sibyl? what was to hinder you from telling us and leaving home as you should do—however private you wished the marriage to be?"

Sibyl ascertained that the door was quite fast. "He does not wish to have anything to do with my family," she said. "It is best so. I, knowing you all, know you would never draw well together. It is not likely."

"And Philip Lewis!" as with a flash all things returned to Hester's stunned memory, she added, fiercely; "Sibyl, you are a wicked woman!"

"We must all do what we think best for ourselves," said Sibyl coolly; "it is best for others too, in reality, what good would Lewis have found in a wife that did not care for him, I am sorry for him, but what is to be must be, and he has you to comfort him, Hester!"

Hester looked at the handsome face that met hers so boldly. There seemed some strange hard lines in it, the initial letter of something that the iron pen of

Truth was presently to write all over the fair features. Hester the stern, looked at her and in the front of all that triumphant glow of the lust of the eye, the lust of the flesh, and the pride of life, indignation somehow turned to pity.

"Oh, Sibyl, Sibyl! God forgive me if I am wrong —but I cannot help doubting; When were you married? Oh, Sibyl, come home with me, for just one day!"

"Don't be nonsensical," said her sister. "Pretty sisterly counsel, to leave my husband. I was married down here—some church in the back streets, I don't know its name because I'm a stranger, and of course Captain Verdon had it all ready arranged."

"But what reason for all this?" Hester pleaded again.

Sibyl cast down her eyes for a moment and then looked up again; she had a cruel weapon in her hand which would perhaps serve this time better than any other.

"You shouldn't ask," she retorted. "Perhaps it's a good thing for all of you to have got rid of me. I know I'm very thankful to be safely married. Can't you guess how thankful a woman must be sometimes?" Her face did not betray the gnawing that was in her soul at that moment. "Now don't be foolish; I've been of age long enough, and nobody has any right to control me—not even poor dear papa, if he were alive, you know; I'm married; let that content you. Whether I shall be happy or unhappy, is my

business, I don't expect much in that way at first, but
I don't forget that I have to be grateful to my husband"—she paused on those words, as if to leave their
whole depths of meaning clear in her sister's mind.
"It will only make it worse for me, if my family is
troublesome , I can appreciate your motives, dear
Hetty, but he will not. It will only hamper and burden him, and make him impatient and angry with me.
Leave me to fight my own battles, I am quite able ,
unless you tie my hands, I have no fear, that I shall
find him liberal and indulgent. His own family does
not know of his marriage yet, and they will make
bother enough—without my people helping them."

And she rose from the chair to imply that their
interview was ended.

Hester went up to her and kissed her. The caress
meant something, for it was years since it had been
common between them. Sibyl returned it coolly, and
instinctively re-arranged the collar which Hester had
ruffled.

"Did you come by yourself?" she asked.

"No, Mr. Fiske brought me," Hester answered.

Sibyl made an impatient gesture. "Take that
meddlesome idiot back with you, as soon as you can,"
she said ; "or there will be some trouble between me
and Verdon, it is not much ; you may write to me if
you like, but never come to me till I ask you. I am
married. Let that content you."

"But all the sin of it, Sibyl ; the sin, have you
thought of that?"

12*

"Haven't had time yet," Sibyl rejoined, lightly. "Don't begin crying. Hetty—you who were always so strong-minded ; go away now, like a good girl, give my love to them all at home."

And she almost pushed Hester from the room, shut the door behind her, and left her to find her way down stairs by herself.

"Take me home, take me home," said Hester, gaspingly, as she rejoined Mr. Fiske ; "she is married, and doesn't want anything to do with us. Oh, poor Sibyl, poor Sibyl !"

"Married, eh !" exclaimed Anthony. "Married, indeed ! Married to young Verdon ! when ?—But there's a train to London in half an hour, you want home and quiet now ! we can't do any more for her —Married, eh !" Yet Anthony let his incredulity, pass in the mask of astonishment, for the figure at his side hung heavily on his arm, and still went on moaning.

"Oh, poor Sibyl—poor Sibyl !"

It was strange. For then Hester held fast by a confused hope, that there was truth in her sister's asseverations and that Sibyl had really, though by a dark and polluted path obtained her idol—temple of indolent luxury. Her whole moral and mental nature too, was throbbing from this sharp collision with a disposition that threw back its forces, calm and unmoved as a rock in a storm. And life for herself and those she loved lay before her, desolate as a flat morass beneath a thunder sky. And yet the feeling that rose uppermost was still no just indignation, no bitter sense of wrong, they might rise again and would, but not now; nothing but pity—only pity!

Home again—home through the darkness and heat of a third-class carriage, home through the strange familiar streets leaning on Anthony's arm! Pale —voiceless.

And the moment she was back in the old house with the dear old faces crowding about her, her strength returned ; she must be the staff here, the very weight of the loving pressure upon her, restored her to her true vocation. More than ever when the letter that Lizzie instantly wrote to Brighton, presently came back through the Dead-letter office, marked on the back 'Gone on to the Continent, and left no address,' they knew what that meant. It cut off their forlorn hope, and made Hester shudder at the thought of her half-trustful parting from the sinner. Metaphorically she again girded her sword upon her thigh. There were sharper wounds than hers, since she had only family feelings, and high sense of honor—where dear Lizzie had sisterly affection, and poor Philip his slighted manly love. She must be brave for them ; she must speak stern truths in sharp words for them, she had felt happier while she sat still and sobbed for poor Sibyl ! But what would become of them all, if she did any more?

Does the north wind ever cut bitter and keen upon itself? Does it ever wish that God had put it in the south instead? Never mind, God made all things well, and if the north wind did not blow, what pestilence would rise from the south ?

Only God be with them all, those who are strong enough to be set to cut the gordian knot and to tear up the rank weeds that will entangle this world of ours ! The reaper may be fit for his hard work in the sun, but Oh, how weary he is by nightfall l And Oh, how rough and brown and rude he looks beside the sheltered folk, who eat the fruit of his labors.

But something happened on that Monday after Hester's return from Brighton, while the poor family could still wrap themselves in one poor last delusion, and Hetty dared still to drop a tear and to sigh "poor Sibyl !" No event ; only one of those curious things, which hint to us that there remain sciences not yet reduced to system and competitive examination. That Sunday night Hester had slept the dull heavy sleep of sheer worn-out misery. But she had one dream, not of the trouble of the past day, only a dream of her own sensation—her own aching head and burning limbs—and that her mother came to her and kissed her, not the young mother, that the old portrait always presented to her fancy ; but somebody tall and spare and elderly that still she knew was her mother. She awoke under the kiss and waking seemed to feel it still on her cheek. The red light of a dull Autumn morning was strong in the room, and there stood Mrs. Edwardes, come to rouse her and to offer a refreshing cup of tea.

CHAPTER XXIII.

A PATENT AND A FLUTE.

IT is an old adage that 'troubles never come alone.' Perhaps we ought to thank God that they very seldom do. When many bitter ingredients are mingled in a cup, we do not take the full loathsomeness of each. Poverty will not leave us to brood over bereavement and bereavement throws poverty into the back-ground, disarmed. Domestic trouble makes us to rejoice over changes that we could once scarcely think of calmly. And change with its wonderful essence of Lethe, takes the edge from domestic trouble.

The Capels left the Queen's Road. It had now too bitter associations to permit any sentiment at their departure. They removed to such rooms as Anthony Fiske had advised. Three rooms at the very top of a quiet house in a humble street, where everybody got their living by labor of their hands. Wide low rooms, quaint with cross beams, and out-of-the-way shelves, and long old-fashioned windows spreading along the wall, and cut off at the end to light the stair-case.　Rooms that did not, like the old home in Queen's Road, strike a painful contrast by suggestions of leisure and luxury.　These seemed made simply to work in, and to pray in, and to rest in, with the few dear ones who are really all one's world.　They were congenial to the Capels' future, with its humble industries and small economies. Hester drew her breath freely.　The sense of suffocation was gone.　There was harmony now in the very atmosphere.　For to dwell poor, under the formula of competence, is to endure the evils of two zones—to be frozen and scorched at the same time.

It was wonderful how quickly things adjusted themselves.　Reality seldom becomes dramatic in a day, it has the leisure of so many years to work in. Nobody left them an unexpected fortune.　Nobody resolved to adopt them.　Nobody in any way interfered with their plain work-day prospects.　But the surplus furniture sold for rather more than they had dared to hope, and the unlooked-for payment of a bad debt, brought in another welcome trifle.　Scraps of Dora's writing, too, were regularly finding their way into print, bringing in little payments that would at least serve to eke out their resources while they sought for something more reliable.

Popps was with them for the present—scarcely as servant, but thoroughly serviceable.　Her marriage with Tom was now drawing very near—nearer than January, for he was now resolved that she should have "a home of her own" before Christmas.　The poor girl was strangely unhinged by a piece of good fortune that had befallen her lover. Tom Moxon had not attended Mechanics' Institutes and scientific lectures for nothing. His skilful hand, trained by experience, had found a point in his trade, where force was wasted. His shrewd eye, educated, had gradually puzzled out the mechanism whereby this same force might be saved. It was not done in a day. He had talked of the flaw to older men when he was a boy, and they had said, " it could not be helped." Later on he had prophesied that it would be helped, and had been roundly laughed at. His mother had made a grievance of his " rather sittin' in his cold bedroom, a-wasting a second candle into the bargain, than comin' to her comfortable fireside, and making himself sociable-like." He had told Popps of his vision of invention, and she had been pleased at first, and curious, but presently grew doubtful, and let the subject drop from their conversations, and did not even mention it to her young ladies, for fear they'd think he was a-turning out unsteady. He had been so quiet and absent for some weeks lately, that poor Popps had been secretly haunted with a dread that he knew he was going to lose his situation. When suddenly, he came one evening to the new home, and standing in the passage, gravely elate, told Popps that he was a Patented Inventor, and had just been hired by the greatest Engineer in London, at a salary of two hundred a year, beside what his discovery would sure to bring in.

Anthony Fiske chanced to be visiting the Capels that evening, and so Tom was invited into their garret-sitting room, to show the sketches of his models, and to tell the details of his good news.

There was somebody else there, too. Only Philip Lewis, the very thought of whom often made Hester's heart to ache with sorrow and shame. The whole truth had come home to him at last; and that once accepted, the poor fellow had a dogged belief in the grandeur of stoical endurance. Too sensible, wilfully to upset his whole future for sake of false woman, he was too stubbornly proud to accept even the palliative of a temporary change of scene and society. He would at once be what he had been. The very effort defeated itself. And now Hester saw and pitifully deplored the peculiar misery of the very temperament which she had often envied. "Comfortable commonplace," she had once said, bitterly, of him. But no soul is commonplace itself, and the more it is swathed in platitude and dogma, the lonelier it dwells within—so bound and stiffened that it cannot even raise a hand to seek the grasp of sympathy and succor. He had not understood her. Now he could not understand himself. If he had formerly heightened her anguish by comfortless nostrums of truism and theory, at least he had no better recipe for his own pain. She had always had consciousness of a higher sphere than her sphere of antagonism and resistance, and if this had made her restless it had been with the restlessness of endeavor, which is Hope in action. Philip had mistaken the limits of a narrow experience for the boundaries of creation, till a rude concussion had shattered them to the ground and left him standing in a wilderness of which he had never dreamed. And now Hester pondered that the earthquake in which the sham spiritual edifice falls, may so shock the true soil beneath, that perhaps no more fresh good life even of the old coarse sort will grow out of it! Oh, false light-souled Sibyl, asking hardly what harm you have done him in robbing him of your worthiest self? the answer would be truly, none at all, if you could restore him his old honest faith in God and man, even with all its ignorance, and his own buoyant energies, even with their innocent egotism. And is it such as you, Oh, false Sibyl, who care what harm you do, are not such as you ready to count the damnation of a man's soul as an even prouder trophy of your prowess than the wreck of his happiness?

Philip's mother in the country, having been duly informed of her son's engagement, of course had to hear of its miserable end. She wrote back that she thanked God that he had made such a lucky escape and she trusted this would teach him to be more careful next time. And she never again alluded to the matter. An evil sorrow, like an evil disease, must be covered up. It is etiquette, rather to let us die of it, than to annoy us about it. And in the main, this is a wise and merciful etiquette, for Job's comforters like quack-doctors, are worse than none at all.

But Philip constantly visited the women who should have become his sisters. They knew all about everything. They had this sorrow and shame in common, and in silence. Hester was very kind to him now, she would have given a great deal to hear him once more dogmatizing the old narrow way, unless indeed, he rose out of it into a higher and wider wisdom. But he and Hester did not say much to each other. He knew what her judgment had always been and he could not refrain from resenting its correctness. There was no such pang between him and Dora. Dora had once herself adored Sibyl, and Dora believed in a poetic world, which was intellectual change of air to Philip, even while it left his pride free to comfort itself that it doggedly remained immoveable.

Tom Moxon entered the sitting-room, with that unostentatious bashfulness, which bears evidence of respect and self-respect. He had talked with a great many gentlemen lately. But these people were different. Those were strangers, never known till he had gone to them with his patent in his hand.

He had never worked in their kitchen. He had never courted their servant. These were at once nearer and farther.

"And so you have invented something that nobody's ever invented before, eh," said the fluent Anthony. "That's the wonderful part of it. I've invented things over and over again—things I'd never seen or heard of, I solemnly assure you. But they had always been invented before that."

Philip turned over the drawings with appreciative eye.

"And you've got a patent, and a good situation besides!" Anthony went on, "Dear me! You'll be a Sir Joseph Paxton, someday, I suppose, and be sending us invitations to dinner at corporation banquets."

"Not much fear of that, sir," said the half-smiling—half embarrassed Tom. "If I can only afford to keep to the work that I like best, and to make things comfortable for them that belong to me,.I'll be thankful and content."

"I should rather think so. That is a very fair share of life!" observed Dora, who was growing more sociable, and more ready to join in conversation than merely to listen.

"But it all depends upon one's ideas of comfort," said Anthony, shaking his head; "my general experience has been that it is something just beyond our means whether they be twenty pounds or half a million."

"We must just take what comes to us in this world, and between one thing and another, I think it all comes to the same." Thus spoke Philip Lewis, bending over the plans. And Hester felt the bitter change from his old hopeful energy.

"Why can't we all invent something?"—asked Anthony Fiske. "Why didn't I invent the perforation of postage stamps? There's some improvement to be invented for every article in this room—why can't we find out their deficiencies as well as other people? Miss Hetty, tell me what is wrong about that candlestick, and I will set my brains to work to rectify it. The fact is it takes a sort of second sight to find out flaws—let alone how to mend them. In politics now, it's enough to do the first, and go speechifying about the wrong, without indicating the right. In fact, in politics, a wrong that can be righted is never an inter‑esting wrong or a popular wrong. I once undertook to get up—I mean I was engaged—at least I made it my duty to occupy myself in a scheme for procuring better dwellings for the working classes. Part of my duty called me to be present at lectures and discus‑sions on the subject (poor Anthony had really been chair-arranger, prospectus-distributor, inquirer-answer‑er and generally-useful factotum), but our rooms were as empty as a drum, because there was a stump‑orator speaking in the town that night, flaring away about 'Down with the bloated aristocracy,' and 'Down with Priestcraft and Capitalists,' and 'Up with Liberty, Equality and Fraternity in Blackguardism,' and 'Why should you be working so hard while others have nothing to do but pay you?' The working-men did not come near us. They went to hear him. They'd rather keep their grievances at their blackest, since they could not turn them at once into a coach-and-four and a mansion in Grosvenor square."

"Not all of them, if you please, sir," said Tom, stiffly.

"I beg your pardon, heartily, Mr. Moxon. You cannot suppose I mean the working-men who take out patents. No, no."

"That's the worst of you, gentlemen," Tom went
on, with a simple earnestness. "You put off all the
discontent on our heads. There's discontented in all
classes—those that can't get on are discontented whoever they be. I've read in history that even royal
princes who yet ain't heirs to the throne, especially if
they've been so once, and been cut out by a baby, are
always ready to take a kick at the throne. It's always
a lawyer who can't get fees, or a newspaper-gentleman
out of work that leads away the working-men at first."

"But you don't mean that people are right to rest
satisfied in their own prosperity?" said Hetty.

"No, miss, that's just what I don't mean," answered Tom ; "but there's few of us can help other
people better than by helping ourselves in the right
way. No meetings will lighten the burden of poor-
rates, as it would if each working-man wouldn't grudge
a little overtime to support his father and mother, or
to lay by a few pounds to help his own wife to help
herself when she's left a widow. The nation's made
up of individuals, Miss—and if each of them is doing
well, and if any of them aren't, it's more likely to be
through their own faults than any other body's."

"But there is affliction," said Dora ; "sickness—
failure."

"Of course there is, Miss," asserted Tom ; "but
it isn't the man who can't help himself, who has help
to spare for others. A man's first business is to work
hard that nobody need to help him, and then to

work a little harder that he may help others. That's being just first and finishing up with generosity."

" But things are so unfair," Hester mused aloud. " See what cruel wages are given. If it is wrong, men agitate and combine in strikes and trades-unions. How else are they to protect themselves from wrong ? "

Tom looked at her, fascinated. All these problems had vexed his own soul once upon a time, though he had long since worked them out to his own satisfaction, by the simple process of doing diligently whatsoever his hand found to do, and keeping his eyes open in the meantime. But he remembered his hours of self-conflict, and how his mother and Popps had thrown freezing water on all his hints of the questions that perplexed him. He had come at last to agree with their roughly-stated propositions, " that folks had better mind their own business." But he knew that they had argued it at second-hand, and not as the best, but as the safest course. He had ascribed it less to their natures in particular than to woman's general docility to authority and dogma, and had so made up his mind that one-half of his life must be lived out alone. But here was a lady actually stumbling over the very difficulties that had tripped him up. Here was somebody who would not have snubbed and silenced him.

" You may guess that I've often thought that over, Miss," he said. And I've come to the conclusion that there are wrongs to be righted. But if you've got to batter down a wall, its not wise for you to break your own head, thumping it against it. Better wait awhile, and let it stand, till you've got a good battering-ram that'll do the work in no time and like play to yourself. Strikes are like using heads and fists against granite. They may hurt the masters a bit, but they hurt the workman a deal more.

" When a trade's going down, cheapening, and so on—there's some reason for it, be sure, and instead of making up meetings and spending all their savings on strikes, the men had better turn over in their minds what else they can do—and go and do it— and if not at home go out in the Colonies. The man's as free as his master. If he's not compelled as to what he offers, they're not compelled as to taking it. Wages go down chiefly because times change, and demands with 'em, and the time men waste making speeches and hanging about, they had better spend in qualifying themselves for the new demands that are coming up. There's a deal of talk, as this gentleman says about the unfair advantage of capital over labor—but there's sides to that question that working-men forget. If a capitalist wouldn't take his money in time out of a concern that was failing, but watched his dividend growing less, and did nothing but grumble that the affair was not *made* to be prosperous, whether or no, would you pity him when he was ruined? Not you, Miss—except maybe thinking he was a little wrong in his head. That's like the working-men. If they will keep their labor in work that isn't wanted, who's to help em? and the same if they will keep their labor *where* it is not wanted. They say it is hard to be turned away from their native land. So it is. But it's hard to starve, only if they choose that last out o' the two chances, who's to help it? All they've got to do is to find out what *must* be done, and do it and hold their tongues about it, and they'd soon discover it's the best hardship in the end. I don't go with my class holding up its drawbacks. There's people, chiefly gentlemen who can't make a genteel living in their own proper ways (Tom was quite innocent of personality to any member of the party), who take to interesting themselves in other people's livings. They find out the case of some poor half-skilled, sottish workman, who is glad to hire himself for half-a-crown a-day, and may be that's more than he's worth. Then it gets into the papers, and draws a lot of sympathy, which means that it makes people think folks of that trade are a poor beggarly lot; that ought to go down on their knees with thankfulness for three shillings a day, and every now and then, in hard times, to be glad of eighteen-pence. But I'm talking a deal too much, Miss. For I want to give a look in at the little place I'm fitting up to live in."

Mr. Fiske left with Tom, and Elizabeth, and Hester retired to another room about some household business. Dora and Philip were left alone.

" Is it not p'easant to find that there is still poetry and heroism in life ? " asked the girl, who was reflecting humbly that she herself had hitherto had no better insight than to prefer a streak of bright tinsel to a mine of richest ore. " Why, I see now that there is a spirit in which emigration is as grand as the crusades ! I see now it does not matter what one's circumstances are, but if one stands behind and rules them, one is a hero, but those who go before and are slavishly pressed by them, are only " dull driven cattle."

" How easily you express yourself ! " said Philip. There was something of the sort in my mind, but I could not have said it, till you had said it for me."

" I have always tried 'to say,'" sighed Dora, " rather than ' to do ; ' I'm afraid. One can soon find words, if one gives one's mind to search for them."

" But what made you give your mind to the search, and what made me not do so ? " asked Philip. " The difference lies there, I suspect. I don't think I could ever speak myself out—if I could play, I think I could play myself out."

" Then you are very wicked not to try that," said Dora.

Poor Philip looked rather shamefaced. " I have tried," he admitted. But I can only play—horridly ! "

" You cannot judge yourself fairly." Dora pleaded.

Philip turned towards his bag.

" My flute is there," he said ; " I will shut the door and play softly, and you will tell me what my music says ; I can only play my own music. I cannot follow notes anywhere, but in my own head. I never play the same thing twice."

13

He began.   And Dora, very calmly attentive at first, presently moved nearer to him and looked up raptly in his face.   Twice she drew a long breath like one struggling : once she sighed : just once she gave a little laugh.

"You must not go on," she burst out when he paused.   "You have told me more already than I can remember to repeat."

"What was it ?" he asked, eagerly.

"First, it was somebody who had lost himself and he did not know it, and he sang as he went along and then it grew dark, and a storm came on.   And the traveller wandered and wandered on.   And then the storm was over, and it was very dark and still and dreary.   And the traveller was so tired that he could go no further, and he lay down to die.   And he fell asleep.   And while he slept, angels came and carried him far back into the right path.   And he awoke and the sun was shining, and his own home was in sight."

"Did it really mean all that ?" said the delighted Philip.

"Yes, it really did," Dora answered ; "a great deal more besides."

"I have not been playing lately, and I really seem to have improved without practice," observed Philip.

"Angels come in the night season," said Dora ; " and all things grow out of sight."

"I shall like to play to you again," was Philip's happy answer.

CHAPTER XXIV.

THE DAY OF THANKSGIVING.

HESTER felt all the brighter for Tom Moxon's homely talk. It was another bit of harmony in the new atmosphere around her. She was inclined to congratulate Popps warmly, both on her lover himself and his good fortune. Popps seemed rather grave and doubtful.

The more that Hester praised, the more she remembered that unlucky bonnet of last spring and asked herself the stinging question: " If Tom was fit to talk to the likes of Miss Hester, was such as herself fit to be company for him ? The little house at Islington which Tom was furnishing so sprucely, was very pleasant, and she was proud of it. But its image was not yet at home in her mind, it was not her old dream of two attics. She was also to have a little maid hired to keep her in her housework. Poor Popps ! She was losing herself—her own rough hard-working shrewd identity. There is a great deal of sympathy felt for those who fall; do any pity those who rise ? not of their own force, but drawn upwards

by dear hands, which seem perhaps to grow cold in
the effort !

Hester walked out alone one afternoon two or
three days after Moxon's visit. She had her name
down on one or two registries, " for nursery teaching,"
and had inserted two or three advertisements in different newspapers. But nothing had come her way
as yet.

But this afternoon she felt hopeful. She went towards the West End. The shops were bright with the
approach of Christmas. And the streets were
crowded with carriages and richly-dressed ladies, the
value of one of whose toilets would ransom a fellow-
creature from starvation for a year ! But Hester did
not think of that to-day. Rather she noted many a
worn thin face, looking wishfully out from lace and
scalskin, as if there was something very good in the
world, which its poor wealthy owner had missed.
Hester felt bright and brave and so healthily free
from all shadow of the past, that she was sure, had
she seen an announcement of " Bot makers or book-
folders wanted," she might have gone in and sought
to make terms for her instruction and subsequent employment in these humble arts, with as little embar-
rassment as ever she had found in the purchase of a
pair of gloves.

But there seemed to be no such notices to-day.
And after awhile Hester grew weary of walking.
She was in the neighborhood of Oxford street and re-

membered that she could find a resting-place in one of the two or three bazars which enliven that region.

Hester entered the nearest. The atmosphere was rather stifling and heavy with the scent that was trickling from the fountain in a perfumer's stand. The first rooms were very crowded, being set out with the trumpery in vogue at the season. Hester pushed her way on to some less popular department.

She found it presently; a long low gallery-like room, little more than the top landing of a less frequented stair-case. It had a great window at one end, whose swinging ventilator kept the atmosphere light and pure while the cheerful fire of an open grate gave out a more genial warmth than the stoves in the other part of the building. A great evergreen in a bright red pot stood on the window-sill. And the only occupant of this peaceful retreat was a middle-aged woman sitting sewing, behind a wide counter, well-stocked with every conceivable article of household napery and body-linen.

She looked up as Hester entered and took a seat on an empty bench near the fire. But even in that second's pause her needle went on.

She was a wholesome-looking woman with young brown eyes, and thick silver hair, scarcely shaded by a small frilled net-cap, with open lappets that drooped upon her shoulders. Her black dress made scrupulously plain, was of some fine serviceable material, and on her left hand she wore a ring; Hester did not think it was a wedding-ring.

Hester could not help watching her—with some vague thought of the good godmothers of fairy-fiction —she seemed to work to music. There was something rhythmic in her movements. And over her face the while, there flickered such an expression as might have been looked for had she been carrying on a pleasant talk with somebody out of sight.

Should she speak to her? should she ask counsel of this working-woman, an utter stranger? Perhaps she could understand and advise. Hester looked at her again ; and it seemed to her as if among the many lights which passed over that happy face, the moonlight of sorrow had been there, and the starlight of patience was there always, although unseen when the sunshine of peace broke out in smiles—Hester's mind was made up.

She rose and crossed to the counter.

" Will you kindly tell me if you have any work to give, or if you know any body who has; I want work very much."

The other stopped in her sewing and looked at Hester—a look which could not have been so kindly had it been less shrewd and searching.

" You want it for yourself? "

" Yes, I have wanted some for a long time."

" And do you want it earnestly as men want work ; to earn money, to live, or do you want it for an excitement and a few spare shillings to buy a new bonnet when you like ? "

These questions came with a smile.

"To earn money to live," said Hester ; and tears would crowd into her eyes.

" Well, my dear, as I dare say you are tired and it is awkward to speak across this table, will you just lift up that bar by your right hand, and step inside. There is a chair beside me and then we shall talk comfortably."

" Now, my child," she said, as Hester took the place indicated ; " I shall perhaps be able to serve you. I cannot tell yet, that will rest as much with you as with me. But you must not mind telling me about yourself and what you want to do, and what you can do ; your name is ? "—

" Hester Capel ; I am an orphan. What I want to do is to keep myself and to help my eldest sister. Not that she could not keep herself," said Hester, looking confidingly into those young brown eyes. " Only we have been always together, and she likes housekeeping and dressmaking and doing all sorts of little things among oneselves. She would help out anything I could earn, she added, " so my help in return would be only fair."

Hester wondered at herself she felt so childlike. She could not have been so simple, frank even yesterday.

" You are right. That is the happiest plan for working-women. When men say that women's work should be cheaper than men's, because they have nobody to keep, they are very silly ; women who work should have somebody to keep, women who work generally do. And have you any more family besides this dear sister ; other sisters or brothers ? ”

“ One sister.”

“ Living with you ? ”

“ No,” said poor Hester.

“ Married ? ”

“ Lost,” said Hester, quietly.

“ Lost,” echoed the kind voice ; “ poor, poor thing : Then she was not like you. What sad differences there are in families, to be sure ! Now to business. Plain work is not well paid. You could not make such a living as you require from that. I am doing some, you see, only because I am fond of plain work. It makes me feel happy. But do you understand French ? ”

I can read and write it,” said Hester ; “ I could not converse in it.”

“ For what I now have in my mind that would not be required. Are you a good correspondent ? ”

Hester said she believed she was, and a tolerably fair accountant, though no bookkeeper.

“ Would you be willing to go to King’s Road, Chelsea, for three hours every day, for forty pounds a year, to make yourself generally useful in such ways as my last questions have suggested ? ”

“ I should be ever so willing,” said poor Hester.

“ You would also be able to take home as much needle-work as you would like for yourself—and your sister—chiefly in fulfilment of special orders and therefore well paid. So that between you, without killing yourselves, I think you might easily raise the forty pounds to eighty or ninety. The counting-house salary may rise in proportion to the business and the value of your services. So that it may ultimately require your whole time; would you be inclined to consider such an offer?"

" It does not need any consideration," said Hester, trembling with delight.

The young brown eyes, and the firm sensible mouth smiled in union; "perhaps not," said their owner. "Well, I am an agent for Melville and Co, of the King's Road, ladies outfitters (Hester had never noticed the name of the establishment, where she had so sadly applied in vain for work), young Mr. Melville has been very naturally struck with some of the injustices of female employment. His business has thrown him very much in the way of women wanting work. He cannot see why women should be allowed to serve behind the counter, but not behind the desk, why they should always do the underpaid and harder work. He spoke to me about it. I knew him when he was a child, and he has confidence in me. And the result was, that we arranged that I should look out for a young lady fitted for the post I have named to you, and engage her in his name. You will only have to send in your references, and he will write and tell you when you are to commence work.

"My own name is Helen Oakshaw," and as she looked at the card on which Hester had been writing out her own name and address, she added; " So you live

. 13*

in Clerkenwell; I lived there once—long, long, ago." And for a moment the starlight in her face was very soft and tender, and then the sun shone out, almost brighter than before, as she went on. "You are just beginning. You cannot think what peace and blessing there are in a quiet life of labor."

"Did you once attend a stall in the Pantheon?" asked Hester, eagerly.

"Yes, why do you ask?" said Miss Oakshew, looking up, surprised.

Hester was half sorry for her inadvertent inquiry and faltered out: "I fancied I had heard of you—although I did not know your name. Do you know, the name of Fiske?"

"Fiske! Yes, (very softly.) It was the name of a young gentleman in the office with—somebody I was going to marry!"

"Mr. Richard Wriksworth," said Hester, gently.

There came no tear to Helen Oakshew's eye. Only a smile, with pathos beyond tears. "That was his name," she answered. "I wonder what they call him now—"

"How sad it was for you who loved so much," Hester murmured, tenderly; "and are you all alone now?"

"Never alone!" she said, brightly. "His love is always around me, safe under God's own love. Why, he gave me that on my last birthday," and she pointed to a tiny coral brooch which clasped her collar; "with a little of the interest from the money my darling left me, I always buy something such as he would have given me himself. They are his gifts still, you know; I don't talk about this to many people, my dear, for they would think me crazy. But—I feel that you will understand, and with the rest of the interest—I help people who want help. That makes them to be Richard's friends, you know, and I love them better for his sake, and have more patience with them.

So they parted. Hester almost flew along the streets of her homeward way. More than one passer-by turned and looked after her. Just as she came within sight of home, Popps overtook her, breathless and delighted. She and Tom had just been looking over their new habitation.

"It's real pretty!" Popps panted; "and while I was just a' thinking whether it wasn't a deal too good for me, says Tom, says he 'Oh Bess, what a blessing it is to be with somebody like you that knows all about everything, and isn't watching to hear if you stick in an extra h, or make a hole in your grammar,' an' I think I'll never fret again that Tom ain't satisfied with me, for if he liked me a fine lady one while, may be he'd wish old Popps back again another, and you'll always tell me about the right colors and like won't you, Miss, though why blue and green together isn't reckoned pretty I never can tell, since God puts 'em together in His blessed flowers, and in the trees and skies. Also Tom and me have been a huntin' after Mrs. Edwardes; we wanted her too in our house till—the day, Miss." But we can't find her—what a hole she did live in, to be sure! Nobody could tell us where she'd gone, she just took off her bundle and went, they said. There was more than seemed in that Mrs. Edwardes. I'll be bound, I always thought she had something on her mind, though she was a decent woman in her way, too. She always seemed to have such respect for all of you, that I wonder she did not let us know where she was. Like her in-prudence; giving up chance o' good work so easy!"

Not many days afterwards as Hester was return-ing from the final ratification of her engagement as clerk and correspondent to Mr. Andrew Melville of King's Road, she went a little out of her way to stand once more under the trees of Cheyne walk.

Bare and leafless were those trees now under a dull wintry sky! But there was sunshine in Hester's heart; God had sent his little human sparrow to be her crumb of joy and comfort; would she ever again so faithlessly pay for sorrow in advance? Oh, into what hard and unworthy doubts had her weak fears betray-ed her! She had trembled more than she had trusted, because she had thought less of God than of herself. Down in the very heart of her despair, her enlightened sense now saw the idol that had seemed most hateful to her; even the ugly image of self—with a burst of thankful tears she owned the guiding Hand that had led her safely on, though, like a wilful child, she had made the way very hard for herself, and as one beau-tiful blighted figure rose upon her memory, it was with the sorrowfully sincere ejaculation. There, but or the grace of God, is Hester Capel!"

CHAPTER XXV.

CONCLUSION.

"Be quiet, take things as they come,
    Each hour will draw out some surprise.
With blessing let the days go home,
    Thou shalt have thanks from evening skies."
                                        R. LYTTON.

HAT is there to tell about quiet years of happy and prosperous labor, undisturbed by any undisciplined heart's impatient question, "what next?"

The world went on. People got married. Tom Moxon and his wife had children and flourished and rose in the world. Lizzie and Hester who went into no society, were presently obliged to keep black-silk dresses of suitable fashion, not to disgrace the little parties where celebrated authors and artists, and now and then a stray noble, came to do honor to a great Inventor who had once been a working-man. At first these people pronounced Mrs. Moxon to be very shy and and nervous (what a kind word "nervous" is?) But that presently wore off and then they found her charmingly " original," and "quite a character." She learned something like good English—as she had once learned bad—by constantly hearing it spoken—and if a homely domestic metaphor would sometimes start into her conversation, why it only imparted a piquant salt. And if any of her grand visitors were ill-bred enough to patronize and laugh at her behind her back, it might be well for them to know that she could too well make observations, and ask very difficult questions, though her good feeling kept her from doing so, to anybody except her " Mr. Moxon" or her dear "ladies" the Misses Capel.

And Philip Lewis was also married and prosperous. Hester was soon relieved from her fears and regrets for him ; who did he marry? He married Dora. He plays on the flute every night, when they have no visitors, also, he will sometimes play for other people besides Dora. Competent judges say that his music is very sweet and wonderful, and he delights to tell them how he had longed for this power, and how it came to him when he had lost all hope of it, and had given up practicing. There is a shadow on his face sometimes as he recounts this ; but it is always gone before he has finished. And this is the only sign of his great sorrow, for as a faithful historian, we regret to relate he soon grew as dogmatic and self-satisfied as ever, and neither better nor worse for the storms that had passed over him.

Years and years passed by. Philip and Dora, and Tom and Bessie were old in married life.

Anthony Fiske grew a gray-headed and spectacled man ; who got his living as a law-writer and taught an infant-class in a Sabbath-school. Lizzie and Hester had long since gone to reside with their dear friend Helen Oakshew. Anthony Fiske regularly supplied them with a newspaper to beguile their evening leisure. But one day he failed to do so. He made some excuse next evening, and they never saw the missed journal, or they would have read, how, one stormy autumn night a policeman stumbled over something on the dark pavement of the wild East-End of London. Only a woman ; she could not move ; she could not answer him. Only when he tried to lift her, he heard her murmur :

"Oh, Syb—don't you wish you were safe at home again !"

And fell back dead !

They would have read of the sad sisterhood who crept from their foul dens to tell the history of the dead.

"She was one of us too. She had been a lady brought up, but she was an awful violent woman, and a dreadful drunkard. She was better off when we first knew her, and had good clothes and furniture, and used to be called "my Lady," and the Countess, because of her finery. She used so many names, we don't know whether we ever heard the real one—Never heard speak of her family—Never knew of any friends of her's—except —perhaps, one elderly woman. She was always after the Countess, wanting her to leave her ways of life. Sometimes she did for a little while, and then this woman used to take her into her room, and find work for her, but the Countess always soon tired of that, and came back to us. This woman always managed to live near the Countess. We used to think she was wrong in her head. Some people said she was the Countess' mother. She was an awful ghostly figure—I've seen the Countess look like her when in a faint. The woman's name was Edwardes. Do we know where to find her, Sir? Lor, Sir; she died months ago, and was buried by the parish."

When God preaches his sermons and points his morals in hard fact ; people say the language, and especially the illustration is too coarse for their perusal. And so those good women in their quiet suburban home, never dream of the evil shadow, that a friendly hand averted from their path that day! And Lizzie still ponders on a possible journey to a lonely grave in the Protestant Churchyard of Ligney, but begins to shrink from the railway travelling, and to feel that Heaven is nearer than that far-off shore. And Hester still prays for Sibyl, and sometimes goes out in the darkness, and looks, and looks, for the face she will never see again.

No marriage—No love? Who shall say that? Some people can keep secrets almost from themselves. But anyhow Hester is a happy woman. People say, with a playfulness that only half disguises truth, " that they fall in love with her—why did not somebody marry her? or why didn't she marry somebody? "

Dora (who writes a very pathetic song now and then, but who has grown a very merry little woman), declares that she thinks Mr. Andrew Melville calls upon her cousins a great deal too often. Dora is too wise now to despise the college-student who became a tradesman, because he was a dutiful son and a just brother. Dora knows that her cousin Hester honors and admires him heartily ; and to love and obey, follow easily after that, says the contented young matron to her spouse ; and presently asks Philip if he cannot strike out a new idea in the way of a " rational and original wedding-present ? "

THE END.